KILLER INSTINCTS

ASSASSINS IN LOVE BOOK #1

TAWNA FENSKE

This is a work of fiction. Names, characters, organizations, places, events, and incidents are either products of the author's imagination or are used fictitiously.

Text copyright © 2022 Tawna Fenske

All rights reserved.

No part of this book may be reproduced, or stored in a retrieval system, or transmitted in any form or by any means, electronic, mechanical, photocopying, recording, or otherwise, without express written permission of the author.

www.tawnafenske.com

Cover design by Amy Pinkston at wellcoveredbooks.com

❀ Created with Vellum

THE ASSASSINS IN LOVE SERIES

- Killer Looks (free prequel novella)
- Killer Instincts (Dante and Jen)
- Killer Moves (Matteo and Renee)
- Killer Smile (Sebastian and Nicole)

DEDICATON

For Hot Lips and Lucy.
I miss you madly and will remember you always as two of the
cleverest, kindest, funniest, most badass ladies to ever grandma.

DEDICATION

CHAPTER 1

*D*ante stares at the gun on the seat beside him. A Ruger Mark IV Hunter, barrel threaded with a silencer. It's next to a bag of Cheez-Its. His favorite.

The gun, not the Cheez-Its, though the Cheez-Its have grown on him. One of eight dozen things he likes about America. Others, in no set order, include soft drink refills, treating pets as family, a cultural tolerance for pajamas in grocery stores, and those bizarre drug commercials listing every side effect for prescriptions he hopes never to need.

But back to the gun.

The job went smoother than expected. A last favor to the Duke of Dovlano, and a chance to rid the world of an exiled prince with a penchant for young boys. Dante might've refused, but there was the dog fighting ring. Once Dante neutralized the target, he waited to make sure his anonymous tip to a Seattle shelter got the animals to safety.

So. That's that. He grabs some Cheez-Its and shoves them in his mouth, chewing as he studies a map of Oregon. Matteo gives him grief for using printed maps instead of GPS or a phone app like a normal guy.

But Matteo's behind bars, and Dante's hardly a normal guy, so printed map it is. Setting it aside, he grabs a last handful of crackers and cranks the engine on the battered Ford pickup. Beige and unremarkable, it gets lousy gas mileage but has a canopy to conceal anything he might wish to hide.

Hypothetically speaking.

Also, there's a bumper sticker that says "mean people suck." It came with the truck and makes him smile.

Easing onto I-5, he aims the rig in a southerly direction and loses a few hours to the soothing swish of wet tires on asphalt. It rains more on this side of the mountains than in Central Oregon, but that's fine by him. Gray skies with sunlight squiggling through like determined, golden worms. Fields of green with lots of bored-looking cows, and tidy rows of grapevines dripping rainbow dew. It reminds him of home.

He's a long fucking way from home.

Checking the map again, he takes a hard right on a chunky gravel road. It's like Matteo described it. Red gate. Tree-lined ridge to the south. Rustic wood sign with curlicue letters declaring it the home of Bello-Devon Vineyards.

He parks beside the barn and looks around. It'll be a quick visit. If he read Teo's code right, there'll be a shed behind the east barn. A shed containing *something* to help spring his pal from prison. Evidence of some sort?

He's not sure, but today's about reconnaissance. A chance to check things out, be sure his buddy's kid sister is getting along okay. He scoped out the older sister last week. She's faring fine, running a daycare across town, but the younger one...well, Matteo has concerns.

And Dante's glad to help. That's part of the code, honor among men and all that. Glancing at his reflection in the rearview mirror, he touches the four-inch scar near his temple. Considers a ball cap. No telling if Jen's a lady who's scared of scowling bald men.

He should do something about the scowl.

Tucking the Ruger in his chest holster, Dante settles a blue trucker cap on his hairless scalp. If Matteo's right, the sister's either in the tasting room or tending things in the barn. Either way, Dante knows to keep it light. Ask a few questions about wine, maybe buy a bottle while checking her over to be sure she's safe. He knows the drill.

Popping the door open, he eases out of the cab. His boots are black and plain, but sturdy. A little leak of sun seeps through the clouds and pools on the shoulders of his black fleece jacket. It leaves him warm and oddly cheerful. His feet make no sound on the gravel. Years of training at work.

He's halfway to the tasting room when he hears the shout.

"Hey! Are you Guy?"

He isn't Guy, but he turns.

Turns and feels his heart stumble like a drunk toddler because *good God*, the most stunning woman he's seen stands in the barn's doorway. An angel, he's positive, even if this angel grips a pitchfork.

"Jen?" He prays he's kept his eyes from bugging out of his skull. "That is—Jennifer Bello?"

She frowns and glances at her watch. "You're twenty minutes late. Not a great start to a job interview."

Job interview? Dante stares, trying to find his voice. His voice and maybe some common sense. For God's sake, she's his best friend's sister.

Stop fucking staring.

Dante clears his throat. "The name's D—Dan, actually." He starts to explain he's not here for a job, then stops. This could be useful. "I apologize for the delay. Road construction."

"That mess over on Amity-Dayton Highway?"

"That's it."

Her scowl softens. There's still a steely edge to those pale green eyes, and she stands with shoulders squared and a gloved

TAWNA FENSKE

fist around the pitchfork handle. She's small, but fierce. Hair the
color of warm molasses twists into a braid she wears looped over
one shoulder. Matteo called her smart and scrappy and sweet,
but did he ever mention his younger sister was so—so—

"Your accent," she says, jarring him back on track. "It's
familiar."

Crap. He's normally better at hiding it. Better at blending in,
since he's worked all over the globe and can pass for American if
he needs to.

Right now, he needs damage control. "My mother's from
Europe." True fact, and he hopes it's enough as he nods at a
shovel propped against the barn. "May I help?"

Jen frowns. "Like an audition for the job, or are you implying
I don't look like I'm managing on my own?"

A trick question, he's pretty sure. Dante holds her gaze.
"Thought you might want to talk. Interview me. A man thinks
best when he's working, so—"

"Right, yeah, sorry." The softness slips back in her eyes as she
tugs the end of her braid. "Sorry I'm being bitchy. Rough
morning."

The back of his neck prickles. "Something's wrong?"

"It's fine, it's just—" She sighs. "A crisis with weed killer.
Slaughtered a row of my best Pinot grapes, so I'm regrouping this
morning. I didn't mean to take it out on you."

"Not a problem." Dante files away the information. He's not
sure what job he's here to interview for or if Guy—whoever he is
—will show up and blow this.

But something tells him this is a rare opportunity, so he
thinks fast. "I've got experience with weed killer, if you want me
to take a look."

Jen stares at him. Dante declines to add that his experience is
limited to building explosives. He's happy to look at her grapes,
or anything else she wants to show him.

She seems to decide something. "I've got it handled." Hesitat-

4

ing, she grabs the shovel and offers it to him. "But dealing with that set me back on chores, so I could use a hand this morning."

"I can do that." Dante takes the tool, fingers buzzing as they brush hers. Even with them both wearing gloves, the contact disarms him.

He nods toward the barn. "Lead the way." He clears his throat, adding as an afterthought, "Ma'am."

Jen makes a face. "Please. Just Jen is fine. You said your name's Dan?"

"I did."

"Huh. I could've sworn your Craigslist reply said Guy. Is that your middle name or something?"

He considers the best way to answer. Is still considering when he's saved by a blow to the testicles.

Make it an *almost* blow. Reflexes trigger, and he turns at the last second to face his attacker. His attacker stares with odd, slanted eyes. Bleats once and drags a hoof through the dirt.

"Scape!" Jen grabs the goat by its red harness with apology in her eyes. "I'm so sorry. He's supposed to be tethered outside Maple's stall. He must've chewed through again."

Dante darts a glance to where half a frayed tether lies limp beside a horse stall. A lean, cocoa-colored thoroughbred sticks its head out and whinnies.

He looks back at Jen. "You have a goat named Scape and a horse named Maple?"

Like he wasn't already half in love with her.

Jen's cheeks pinken like he's spoken out loud. "Scape Goat and Maple Stirrup, yes." Her chin tips up. "Pony Soprano's on loan to a kids' petting zoo this week."

It's official. She's his dream girl.

But that's not a thing, so Dante kicks himself in the crotch— figuratively speaking—and nods. "You've got a lot of animals."

"This is barely the tip of the iceberg." She lets go of the goat's harness. "Be good," she chides as Scape trots toward him.

Dante's not sure who she's addressing.

But he holds out a hand, and this time, Scape lowers his ears for scratching. "Nice goat," he murmurs as he rubs the spot behind the animal's nubby horns. "American Lamancha, right?"

Surprise brightens Jen's eyes. "That's right. I—you mentioned you didn't have tons of experience with goats?"

He did? Or rather, Guy did. He may need to tap Matteo to hack his sister's email and find out what's been said. Not that he's considering a job here. Even the word *job* means something different in his world.

"Had dairy goats growing up," he says, since he still hasn't answered her question. "It's been a while, but I know which end to feed hay to."

She laughs, and Dante finds himself smiling. *Smiling*, for God's sake.

"Oh, good." Jen shoves a lock of hair off her forehead. "What about castration? You have experience there, I assume?"

More than he liked to admit. "Some."

"Because we follow strictly humane practices here. Banding— no scalpels—and my vet helps with pain management."

Dante nods, because how else should he respond? "I can do that."

"Good." She eyes him like she's waiting for more information, but this is a place he'd prefer not to dwell. "I'll need help with the spring lambs."

"Of course." He'll happily castrate anyone or anything she asks him to. Glancing at Scape, he scratches the goat's ear some more. "I can be gentle."

Not something he includes on his resumé, but it's true. When he looks up, Jen's watching him with an expression he can't read. Watching his *hand*, which seems odd.

Her mouth opens, then closes. "You have—really large hands."

"Yes." He draws back in case he's scaring her. "I have gloves custom made."

It's a silly thing to say but makes her smile for some reason. "Oh. Good." She licks her lips. "That's—great."

He hefts his shovel. "How deep do you want the hole?"

Jen blinks. "What?"

He said *hole* and not *grave*, right? English isn't his first language, but he thought he'd mastered it well enough.

"Oh, you mean the chores?" She hoists her pitchfork, making his heart pound with the dainty dusting of freckles across her nose. "We're mucking stalls. Come on, we'll start in the east barn."

He'll follow her anywhere, even if it involves manure. He'd shovel it with bare hands to spend an hour with her.

As he trails her to the next barn, he catches sight of a charred heap. Burnt wood, twisted metal. Concrete footing the size of a small shed. "What happened there?"

Jen looks where he's pointing. "Electrical fire." Her chin tips up again. "I hired an electrician to rewire the overhead light and something went wrong. Don't worry—I used a different guy to wire the bunkhouse."

That's not why he's worried. "Was anyone hurt?"

"No, but the shed's a total loss." She shrugs. "Luckily, there wasn't much in there."

Just Matteo's chance at freedom. He'll have to find another way to help his pal. As Jen leads him to the east barn, he hears Teo's voice in his head.

"My youngest sister, she's had a hard time." A pause. "She's... fragile. I need you to watch out for her."

Watching out for her does not involve watching the sway of her hips as she moves, so Dante doesn't do that. Much. Also doesn't notice there's another sweet spray of freckles on the back of her neck. Would they taste like cinnamon if he kissed her there?

He's not thinking that, of course. He's here to help a friend, nothing more.

They set to work in companionable silence. Jen's raking, Dante's shoveling heaps of dung into a battered black trailer. He tries to think of something to say. Something besides, *I should probably tell you that I know your brother—*

"So where are you from, Dan?"

He swallows back his earlier thought. "I've lived all over the place."

She waits for him to offer more, which he should probably do if this is a job interview. "Spent some time in Central Oregon."

"Yeah?" She stops moving and looks at him. "At a ranch or something?"

He needs to tread carefully. "Most recently, at Ponderosa Luxury Ranch Resort."

There, that's good. The truth, more or less. No need to say he went on official palace business, keeping watch over a reluctant duchess and the thug sent to eliminate her. Lady Isabella wound up marrying an American doctor, while the thug takes a long nap at the bottom of a mountain lake.

Jen's still stuck on Ponderosa Resort. "That's right, they have stables there." She uses her pitchfork to drag a fragrant heap closer, and Dante scoops it with his shovel. "I mean, I've never been," she says. "A little too rich for my blood."

He flings another heap of dung into the trailer, choosing his words with caution. "Money's tight, I take it?"

She snorts in response. "I can pay your salary, if that's what you're asking." Frowning, she shakes her head. "Sorry, that's not what you asked. I'm touchy today."

"About money?" An American thing, he's learned. Probably rude to bring it up, but she did first.

Jen stops raking and looks at him. After a pause, she sighs. "I suppose, you'll hear it anyway if I hire you."

"Hear what?"

He watches her gloved hand grip the pitchfork tighter and

gauges how fast she could swing it. To be safe, he takes a step back.

"Johnny Devon—as in Bello-Devon Vineyards?" She frowns. "We broke up a while ago. It's awkward and weird and I feel really stupid having his name on the sign, but I own this place fair and square. The land belonged to my grandmother, and it's mine, okay?"

"Okay." He's not sure he follows, but hair prickles on his arms. "He's causing you problems?"

"Johnny? No, not really." She rolls her eyes. "It's complicated, financially, since we were never married. I handled farming, he handled wine. I had to hire a new winemaker and I'm working on a plan to pay Johnny off for some equipment. For his portion of the business. But I'm looking at loans and I've got plans for expanding growing operations and livestock and all of that is why you're here, right?"

"Right." He answers automatically, even though none of that's why he's here.

Why is he here again?

"Tell me about the weed killer."

Jen blinks in surprise. "What do you want to know?"

"How did it happen?"

She shrugs. "Over-zealous neighbor, I'm guessing. Happens sometimes. Our properties are close."

He studies her face. "I could talk to him."

"The neighbor?" She laughs. "Thanks, but no. I'm good."

She looks good. Wait, no. She looks...concerned. Her mask is a brave one, but it wouldn't take much to peel it back.

"So, you're hiring a farmhand."

"That's the plan." She shifts the pitchfork from one hand to the other. "I've been handling things on my own for a while but expanding requires more manpower." A pause. "Or woman power. I don't discriminate."

"You've got family here to help?"

9

It's the wrong question. He sees it in her eyes, and orders himself not to react. To stand here and catalogue what he's learned.

"No." She presses her lips together. "My grandma's gone. She passed last year."

"I'm sorry." He sees in the slump of her shoulders what this grandmother meant to her. Knows a bit more from Matteo. "My condolences."

"Thank you." Jen takes a breath. "I've got a sister, but she's not the farming type." Her lips move like she's got more to say, but she clamps them closed instead.

"So it's just you." He watches her face, not pushing. Just needing to see what she looks like when she doesn't quite tell the truth.

"Just me."

"I see."

He sees more than she realizes. The tiniest twitch beside her right eye. How she blinks fast when skirting the real story. A tightening of her grip on the pitchfork handle. The swell of small but perfect breasts beneath the red flannel shirt.

That last one's not a tell. It's a clinical observation, nothing more.

Jen stares at him a long time. "I need to check your references."

"Of course."

He makes a mental note to fabricate some. Also, to punch himself in the throat, because what is he thinking?

"Let me send you an updated resumé tonight." He blurts this against his better judgment. "One with a reference list."

"Thank you." Her green eyes search his, like she's looking for something she hasn't quite found.

He's probably imagining that.

But he's not imagining the faint softening in her eyes, the way her tongue darts out to lick her lips. "How soon could you start?"

CHAPTER 2

*J*en watches Dan's taillights move down the gravel drive. At the bottom, he pauses by a camo-painted truck stopped at the highway's edge. Dan gets out and speaks with the driver while Jen tries to watch with professional detachment instead of an eye for the fine shape of his rear.

That's the last thing she needs. Attractive men are a distraction. She's been sidetracked like that before and look where it got her.

The other motorist drives away, and Dan gets back in his truck. Jen makes a note that he's the kind of guy who gives directions to lost strangers. A good sign. A sign she's not acting rashly or making a poor snap judgment in hiring Dan...Dan...

Hell.

Not catching his last name is a strike against her. She should read his email again, jog her memory on his background.

First, it's time to deal with the poisoned vines. Not poisoned —that word reeks of accusation, and surely Harry and Gail didn't do it on purpose. Her neighbors aren't perfect, but they're not malicious.

Then again, Jen never thought Johnny would bang the wine distributor. Maybe she's not the best judge of character.

With a sigh, she trudges into her kitchen and peels off her work gloves. Scrubbing her hands at the sink, she spots the tray of brownies she baked last night. She used her grandma's recipe and that makes her heart squeeze so hard she has to stop and catch her breath.

I miss you so much, Nondi.

Drawing a breath, she dries her hands and piles six treats on a paper plate declaring, "happy bar mitzvah." No one in her family is Jewish, so she must've picked them up on a clearance rack somewhere. Securing the offering with cling wrap, she shrugs into her jacket and steps out into lukewarm sunshine.

The walk to the Gibson farmhouse takes ten minutes. She could drive it in two, but the early evening skies feel warm without a trace of rain trickling from fluffy clouds hunched on the horizon. Most of her twenty-six years have been here in Oregon's Willamette Valley, and she never tires of the weather's mood swings. Gray skies shift like tides bringing oceans of blue, followed by fierce showers easing into bright waves of blooms. Beautiful, just like Matteo and Nicole describe the Dovlano countryside of their childhood. She doesn't remember it, but they've told her enough so she pictures it in her mind.

She's barely winded when she hits the hilltop where the Gibson farmhouse sits. Credit long hours spent bucking hay and hiking fields to check grapes. She's sometimes wondered if running a farm has killed her bottom line, but it's great for her bottom. Such as it is.

Lots of supermodels have boyish figures like you. I think it's great! But maybe you could wear skirts sometimes?

Johnny's words bubble like acid in her brain, snuffing her good mood. He'd phrased it gently enough, but the question still stung. The implication that farm life, and its not-so-glamorous uniform, made her less feminine. The suggestion that her compact, muscular frame and nonexistent boobs and booty didn't measure up.

Pushing that aside, she rings the doorbell with the brownie plate tucked against her ribs. Gail Gibson comes to the door wiping her hands on a polka-dotted apron, her silver-streaked hair loose around her shoulders.

"Jennifer, hello." She glances at the brownies. "What's the occasion?"

She considers the best way to phrase it. "A peace offering." She holds out the plate, and Gail takes it with a frown. "And a request for extra caution with weed killer on the property line."

"Oh." Gail pauses, then looks at the brownies. "I don't think Harry's been spreading weed killer."

Thundering footsteps announce the arrival of Harry Gibson. He lumbers to the doorframe with a scowl. "Haven't sprayed a damn thing for weeks."

Jen takes a breath and forces a smile. "You're sure? Because a whole row of pinot grapes along my northern property line are showing symptoms of herbicide drift. That could be MCPA or clopyralid or triclopyr or any number of growth-regulator chemicals that—"

"Nope." Harry folds his arms over his chest. "You must be mistaken."

She tries to read his expression. Sinister asshole, or regular asshole? If only it were easy to tell.

"Whatever you say." She's trying for glib and casual, but her tone lands closer to dismissive. Johnny used to point that out, along with her habit of not smiling enough. She forces up the edges of her mouth and tries again. "Could I just ask you to be mindful of wind direction? Herbicides can drift a half-mile or more, and I'm trying to run an organic vineyard."

"Whatever." Harry turns and stomps away, done with the conversation.

Gail glances at the brownies, not sure she's allowed to keep them. "I'll have a word with him," she offers in a conspiratorial whisper.

"Thank you." Jen glances over Gail's shoulder to see Harry in the living room cleaning his shotgun. A warning, or basic task of country life?

She looks back at Gail. "Just so you know, I hired a farmhand today."

"Oh?"

"Assuming his references check out. He'll be living in the bunkhouse above the barn."

Gail's brow furrows. "It's livable?"

"I did all the work myself. Framing, drywall, tile-setting—everything but plumbing and electric." Pride brightens her voice, and she *is* proud. And a little surprised she mastered all that stuff alone. "He's moving in this week."

"Wonderful." Gail smiles. "I've worried about you over there without a man to look after things. And with your grandma gone…"

Jen straightens. "I'm doing fine. Just need an extra set of hands for chores."

"And he's okay taking orders from a woman?" Clearly, this concept is foreign to Gail.

"No problem at all." She assumes not, anyway, or he wouldn't take the job. "You might see Dan around. Tall guy, broad shoulders. Bald. *Big*. Really strong and ruggedly handsom—*handy* with a shovel."

"I see." Gail studies her face. "Have the hotel people been by your place?"

A sour ooze swishes in her belly. "Last week. They want you to sell, too?"

"No." Gail frowns. "Our property's too hilly. But they thought we might have some pull with you."

"Did they?" Jen's not sure what to make of this. "Well. If they

14

come by again, you can tell them my answer hasn't changed. I'm not selling."

Gail's eyes go wistful. "They said there'd be a spa. If they put a hotel here, I mean. They have a good neighbor discount."

Jen adds this to her mental file and considers whether Gail and Harry might throw her under the bus for a hot stone massage.

"Still not interested." She steps back and shoves her hands in her pockets. "Better get back. Have a good night."

"You, too."

The door shuts behind her as she trudges back toward her place. Her belly rumbles, reminding her it's dinnertime. She's got leftover drumsticks in the fridge, which she'll pair with whatever greens the deer didn't get in last night's garden raid. Plucking fistfuls of arugula into her grandma's copper colander, she makes a mental note to ask Dan what he knows about humane forms of deer abatement. She's tried windchimes and motion-sensor lights and a product from the feedstore that says it's made with pigs' blood.

With a shudder, she opens the door, conscious of her phone ringing in the kitchen. Must've left it behind, and she's winded by the time she gets to it.

"Hello?"

This is a call from an inmate at an Oregon correctional facility...

She knows the automated monologue by heart and accepts the call before she's asked to. Moments later, her brother's voice fills her ear.

"How are you?" No hello, no casual air to the question. It's a demand for information, sprinkled with certainty she's answering from a pit of quicksand with a viper latched on her left ear.

"I'm great!" She knows he'll hear through her perky veneer. "Got a lot of work done in the barn today. And I'm talking with a new winemaker from—"

"Did that asshole sign the paperwork yet?"

Jen doesn't need to ask which asshole. There aren't many in her life. "Johnny's lawyer is looking things over."

"Do you have a lawyer?"

"I don't think—"

"I'm sending you a lawyer."

Jen sighs. There's no sense arguing with her brother when he's like this.

Also, no end to his ability to shield her, even from a cell at the Oregon State Penitentiary.

"He's getting married soon." She closes her eyes, not sure why she's sharing this. "That's why he's got a lawyer."

Her brother grunts. "Son of a bitch isn't making the same mistake twice."

Jen winces, though Teo's talking about money. About her poor choice to start a business with a man minus a prenup. On the movie screen in her mind, she can't stop seeing the wine rep's lithe, curvy body. Her manicured hands clutching Johnny's back. Her filmy pastel skirt tossed over an armchair.

Jen's not the skirt tossing type. She may not even own a skirt.

"She's British." Jen opens her eyes so she can stop seeing Penelope's face. "An International Master Sommelier. She looks like a runway model, but with boobs."

There's no reason to share this with her brother, and she doesn't expect a response.

"His loss." Matteo clears his throat. "I knew the second you said he doesn't own a laptop what kind of guy Johnny was."

Only in Matteo's world would a lack of tech savvy be an unforgivable character flaw. Of course, he's not wrong.

"Are you still teaching GED classes at the—in the—"

"Prison." Matteo coughs. "Saying the word doesn't make me stuck here any longer."

"I know." She presses her lips together. "I just don't like to think of you alone in there."

"And I don't like thinking of you alone out there. Especially with Nondi gone." His voice goes gruff on their grandmother's nickname. They lost her not long after Teo went to prison, and if that's not proof life isn't fair, Jen's not sure what it is.

She tugs a string on the frayed knee of her jeans. "I'm not alone, actually."

"Nicole is not your keeper. Besides, she's got a daycare to run."

She sighs because it's easier than arguing she'd never ask her sister to look out for her. Nic would do it—gladly—but that's not what Jen needs. "I wasn't talking about Nicole."

"Do not say you're dating some new idiot."

"I hired a farmhand." She ignores that jab, too. "A guy who answered my Craigslist ad."

"Who?"

Since he can't see, she goes ahead and rolls her eyes. "Just a guy. Big. Burly. Bald. Intimidating." That may not be a point in his favor. "Seems very protective."

There's a long silence. Jen braces for a lecture, for Matteo to send the National Guard.

"Good."

Jen blinks. "What?"

"You did a reference check, right? What's the guy's name?"

"D—Dan." She blinks again. "You're okay with this?"

"I like the idea of someone looking out for you. I'll have him checked out, of course."

"Of course." She's too stunned to argue. "Thank you."

"Not a problem. I just want you safe and happy."

"I am safe." Maybe not happy. Not yet, anyway. A broken engagement will do that. "And I'm on my way to happy."

"Good." Another pause. "Proud of you, *Lentiggini*."

The childhood nickname sucks the breath from her lungs as her memory floods with visions of their Italian grandma pressing thumbs into plump bits of pasta dough. *Lentiggini*, she'd tease. *Freckles*, as Jen danced around her ankles in this same kitchen.

Jen closes her eyes again as a fierce wave of sadness grabs her ankle and pulls her underwater. She fights her way back up, breathing deeply as she answers.

"I love you, Matteo."

"Love you, too, kid."

* * *

BY THE TIME Jen checks email, it's nearly 9 p.m. She's not expecting much, so it's a pleasant surprise to have a message from Dan. Peering closer, she sees how she made her mistake.

guynameddan@gmail.com

Huh. She must've glanced too quickly the first time, thinking "Nameddan" was some sort of foreign surname. She's seen plenty of those from distant family in Dovlano and Italy, so she knows better than to make assumptions.

Scanning their earlier string of emails, she confirms he's been "guynameddan" all along. Clicking the newest message, she skims his words.

JEN,

It was nice meeting you this morning. Thank you for the opportunity to assist you at Bello Vineyards.

SHE SMILES, appreciating how he's left off Johnny's part of the vineyard name. *Guynameddan* pays attention. Sipping her wine, she keeps reading.

ATTACHED IS a recent background check through the Oregon State Police, and an updated resumé containing several references. Please call if you need additional information.

. . .

SHE SQUINTS at a name on the list, unsure why a Dr. Bradley Parker is a reference for a farmhand. He's listed alongside an Isabella Blankenship-Parker, which sounds oddly familiar. Jen picks up the phone to call them but ends up dialing Dan instead.

He answers on the first ring. "Hello."

Her stomach flips as she grips the phone tighter. "Dan. Hello, it's Jennifer. Jen Bello. I got your email."

"You have questions?"

She skims the page, wishing she'd thought of some. Wishing she could pretend she called for reasons besides loneliness and an urge to hear his voice.

"Tell me about your references," she says. "You've got a Dr. Bradley Parker on here—"

"Doc Parker. Yep." He clears his throat. "His family has a ranch in Central Oregon."

Ah. That makes sense. "And you've done work for him?"

"Yep." A pause. "Good man. Ex-military."

An odd answer, but she's realizing Dan's an odd guy. In an endearing way. A charming way. An appealing, attractive—

"Tell me about the things you've listed here under hobbies." She scans the list, intrigued by a few items. "You enjoy cooking, martial arts, animals, magic tricks, and collecting."

She's hoping he'll fill in the blank on what, exactly, he collects.

"I make an excellent elk chili," he says after a long pause. "Secret ingredient is cocoa powder."

"Cocoa powder?" Her shoulders relax as she realizes he's revealed a secret. A psychopath wouldn't do that, right? "You put cocoa in chili?"

"Adds an extra dimension to the flavor," he says. "A richness."

"Chocolate?"

"You don't taste chocolate." His voice, low and oddly soothing. "This is unsweetened cocoa. Baking cocoa, I think it's called."

"Huh." The idea of a hulking bald stranger cooking for her has Jen's mouth watering. She blames her meager dinner. "Tell me about the magic. You do tricks?"

"I make things disappear."

Jen frowns. "Things like coins or pens or...or..." What else do magicians make disappear?

"Sure." He clears his throat again. "Sleight of hand."

Huh. She's tempted to pursue that line of questioning. To probe Dan's innermost thoughts and learn about his history, his future, what makes him tick.

But she's just being needy. Her urge to talk to him has less to do with best hiring practices and everything to do with how his voice makes her feel like she's sitting in a warm bath. Naked. With a glass of wine and water sluicing over her bare breasts as she slips a hand under the water and—

"This all looks good." She speaks too quickly, picking up her wineglass. "Let's move forward with having you come in tomorrow."

"Okay." A pause. "You lock your door, right?"

Jen's pulse quickens. "What?"

"The doors to your house. You lock them at night?"

A pause as she sets down her wineglass. "I live in the country. No one locks their doors out here. Besides, I have a hunting rifle."

"That so?" His voice holds the hint of a smile. "Which you keep locked in a gun safe, I presume?"

"I—" She stops, knowing he's right. Not that there's an urgent need to reach a firearm, but she could get to it fast if she had to. The safe has a touchpad, and she's practiced using it. She'll have her classic Winchester in hand in under five seconds.

For some reason, she says none of this. "I believe in gun safety."

"And I believe in taking extra steps to keep important things safe. So do me a favor and lock your door."

Jen fights the threat of a smile. He's being creepy. He's being controlling. He's being like her goddamn brother. He's—

"Okay," she says softly. "I will."

"Good." Another pause. "Was there anything else?"

"No." Nothing besides the urge to keep talking with him all night.

But Jen's a smarter woman than that, so instead she says good night. "I'll see you tomorrow."

"See you tomorrow."

It's not until they hang up that she realizes she's smiling.

CHAPTER 3

*D*ante arrives thirty minutes early the next morning. It's a chance to scope out the property, and also to remind himself he's *Dan*, not Dante.

That'll take practice.

Standing on the hillside by the barn, he looks to the bottom of the driveway where he met the real Guy. His guilt over stealing the man's job lasted six seconds. That's how long it took to read Guy's bumper stickers.

Lost your cat? Look under my tires.

I nailed your honor student.

Dante got out of his truck before he'd come to a full stop.

"Afternoon." He'd started to tip his baseball cap, then removed it entirely. Watched Guy's eyes dart to the scary scar. "Looking for something?"

The man gripped his steering wheel with one hand, using the other to auger a toothpick into his molar. "Job interview. Got caught in road construction."

He smelled beer on Guy's breath and glanced at his watch. "For three hours?"

"I got lost, okay?"

Dante did a quick appraisal of the man, not missing the swastika tattoo on his right thumb. "Job's been filled."

"That so?" The man eyed him. "By who?"

"Whom." He leaned against the side of the truck. "By someone who doesn't currently have a warrant out for his arrest."

A wild guess, but he watched it hit the mark. The prison tat on Guy's forearm was a giveaway, along with how he tensed as a cop car cruised past.

For good measure, Dante rolled his shoulders, stretching to reveal the firearm in his chest holster. "Better move along." He made sure his tone implied there was no other option.

Guy grunted. "Didn't want the fucking job, anyway."

The man gunned the engine, then thought better of speeding off in a spray of gravel. Knuckles white on the wheel, Guy eased back onto the highway and vanished.

So. That's that. One less asshole to worry about. There are always more.

When Dante reached Matteo for help accessing Jen's email, they did a background check on her ex-boyfriend. Ex-*fiancé*.

Clean.

Pondering this, he moves around the barn. A clean record doesn't mean much since he produced one himself. He'd like to check out the neighbor. Maybe Jen can introduce him.

He's almost to the barn when motion snags his eye. He pivots, fingers flexing as he finds his weapon. Drops his hand as he identifies the threat.

"Hey, Scape." He bends down, partly to pet the goat, mostly to dodge testicular assault. "You got loose again?"

"I let him out this time." Jen steps out of the barn, shielding her eyes from morning sun. "He hasn't shown much interest in going far. I'll ease up as long as he keeps Maple company."

"Because goats calm racehorses." He read this on the internet, along with countless other farm facts he didn't know. "Does Maple race?"

"Retired." Jen shrugs. "Johnny used to race her. She's getting old, and he wanted to get rid of her. Slaughterhouse, probably. I paid him off to keep her here."

He might actually love Jen if he was capable of that kind of thing. "I'm happy to help exercise her."

"Thanks. I might take you up on that." She shoves her hands in her back pockets and rocks back on her heels. "There's something I wanted to ask before we get started."

"What's that?"

"Do you have any issues taking orders from a woman?"

"Nope."

She stares at him, so Dante elaborates. "Someone signs my paycheck, I'm up for anything."

"Anything?"

He must be imagining the salacious glint in her eye.

Dante clears his throat. "Pretty much."

Her smile spreads wider as green eyes sweep the property. "What if I asked you to swim across the irrigation pond?"

With a glance that direction, he sees it's shaped like a lopsided heart. "There leeches in it?"

"Is that a deciding factor?"

"Only in whether I request a wetsuit."

Jen looks thoughtful. "Singing karaoke in a dive bar?"

"Song?"

"Dolly Parton's 'Jolene.'" An answer without hesitation, like she's given this thought.

He scratches Scape's ears and tries to recall the last time he sang anyplace but the shower. "Sure."

"Really?" She sounds impressed.

"You didn't say I had to sing *well*."

"True, but—" She stops herself, shaking her head. "Okay, how about wearing fishnets and a feather boa to the feedstore?"

"Color?"

"Does it matter?"

"I like to know what I'm working with." He shrugs. "Not really, though."

He doesn't tell her he's been asked to do much worse. That he's done it without question, without blinking.

She's watching him like she's trying to read his mind, so he looks away.

"Okay," she says, "what about killing f—"

"Yes." It dawns on him she hasn't finished the question.

He watches it dawn on her, too. Her forehead scrunches like her freckle-dusted nose. "How'd you know what I was going to say?"

Dante scans the pond. "Flies?"

"So you're a mind reader?" Her tone is teasing, but there's an undercurrent of something else. Something that makes him twitchy. "Didn't see that on your resumé."

He looks back at her and his heart heaves against his ribcage like a bird hitting a window. God, she's beautiful. "Should we get to work?"

Her eyes hold his for a few beats. He orders himself not to glance away. Not to let his attraction show. A lifetime of keeping a flat, emotionless expression, and he's suddenly undone by a woman in rubber boots and ragged blue jeans.

What would it feel like to stretch out a hand? To cup her cheek. To thread fingers through her hair. To pull her close, feeling her gasp with surprise, then melt against him as she tips her face up to let him kiss her softly, so softly—

"Right." Jen licks her lips and takes a step back. "I suppose you'll want to unpack first."

He shrugs, heart still hammering in his ears. "Not much to unpack." He'd rather do it later, when she's not watching him drag a gun safe the size of an outhouse.

"Suit yourself." She starts toward the barn and Dante follows, taking care to keep his eyes on their surroundings and not on her. It's no simple feat, since her shirt is bright red flannel and keeps catching his eye. Or maybe it's the shape of her beneath the shirt, strong shoulders and narrow hips and the sweet, delicate—

"Shit." She stops and Dante nearly runs into her.

He halts by catching her arms. She turns to face him, and like an idiot, he doesn't let go. "Are you okay?"

Her cheeks flush with color. "I—what?"

They stare at each other, Dante swallowing his own heartbeat. Her skin feels hot through the flannel. Her eyes, they're different colors. The left is the color of forest moss. The right looks more like damp grass in the dark.

What were they doing again?

Jen makes a soft sound in the back of her throat. "Visitor," she whispers, and Dante drops his hands.

They turn to watch a black sedan gliding the last hundred feet up the gravel drive. Dante frowns at the tinted windows.

"Do you know who that is?" His pulse jumps to overdrive. His fingers twitch.

"No." Jen bites her lip as the car draws closer. "The tasting room's closed today. Anyone in a car like that wants money or my brother."

He tries not to flinch. It's the first time she's mentioned Matteo, and he wonders if she meant to. He's about to probe when the car halts and the driver's door swings open.

A dark-haired man in a suit steps out, adjusting his necktie. He starts forward with a briefcase in one hand. It's overcast, but the man's wearing sunglasses.

Dante's hand drifts to his chest. He can have the Ruger unholstered in 3, 2, 1…

"Ms. Bello?" The man stops, lifting the briefcase. "Ms. Jennifer Bello?"

Dante moves to shield her with his body, but she steps forward with shoulders squared.

"Who's asking?" Her voice is strong and clear, no trace of a tremble.

She's braver than he is.

Dante stays alert, watching every movement. The stranger lifts a hand, sliding the sunglasses to the top of his head. His eyes are eerie gold, and Dante braces as the man drops a hand to his coat pocket.

Widening his stance, Dante slips his fingers to his holster. He grabs the pistol's grip as the visitor draws out...

A business card?

"Rhett Strijker, attorney at law." He holds out the card, and Jen hesitates before taking it. "I understand you're dealing with some legal and financial matters."

Dante drops his hand. He doesn't drop his gaze from Rhett's though, or from Jen's response. She's coiled tight with an energy he can't read.

"There's been a mistake." She tries to hand the card back, but the man doesn't take it. "I can't afford a lawyer."

Rhett doesn't blink. "My fees have been handled."

Hair prickles on Dante's neck. It's not his place to demand answers, so he's glad when Jen does.

"By whom?"

He's so charmed by her grammar he almost misses the answer.

"By a mutual acquaintance." His gaze flicks to Dante for a split second. Long enough that Dante knows who sent him.

Jen sighs and stuffs the card in her pocket. "Do I even want to know how my brother paid a lawyer from prison?"

She pivots fast to face Dante. Folds her arms and stares him down. "That's right. I have a jailbird brother. You may as well know before you move in."

Dante senses he should look surprised. Moves his face in a shape he hopes resembles mild shock. "Is he dangerous?"

"Matteo?" She laughs. "No. Well, not unless you're a bad guy. Are you a bad guy?"

The question gives him pause. He's not a good guy, but a

bad one?

He's still pondering as Jen turns back to Rhett. "Look, I don't know what my brother told you, but—"

"Ma'am, if you'll allow me?" He flips the clasp on his briefcase and Dante tenses again.

But the case opens to show only documents. Since Dante's not leery of paper cuts, he lets his hands drop.

Rhett hands a crisp stack to Jen. "I've taken the liberty of looking into financial matters concerning the vineyard—"

"Great," Jen mutters as the man keeps talking.

"—and I understand the goal is to free yourself financially from a Mr. Jonathan Devon. Is this correct?"

Her response grits through clenched teeth as she skims the pages. "Correct."

"If you'll turn to page three, you'll see the estimated cost to buy out his share of any business interests and leave yourself free and clear of—"

"You've got to be kidding me." She chokes and Dante prepares to offer the Heimlich. "There's no way." She looks at Rhett and shakes her head. "Not even if I sold the property. Or became a high dollar hooker, which I can tell you right now, I'd do before I sold even a square foot of my grandmother's land."

Distracted by thoughts of Jen in heels and fishnets—holding her pitchfork, of course—Dante forgets his Americanized monetary tact. "How much?"

Her eyes flash.

"Not for sex," he clarifies, and she bursts out laughing.

He's not sure what's funny, but he wants to be clear. "I have money." He can't see what's printed on the forms, but his years in Dovlano palace security paid handsomely. And Dante saved, saved most of it, in fact—

"We just met." Jen stares like he's gone mad. "And call me crazy, but I doubt you'd take a job as a ranch hand if you had this kind of cash."

He catches sight of the figure and—okay, yeah. That's a lot.

But he has it. And he owes Matteo, owes him his life, actually. And if it weren't for Dante, Matteo might not even be behind bars, so—

"Besides," Jen continues like he's not doing complex hitman math in his head. "I got into this mess by tying myself financially to a man. I don't think that's how I'll get out of it."

He starts to argue it wouldn't be a loan. He'd give her the cash free and clear.

But he shuts his mouth instead. He knows what it's like to feel indebted. He wouldn't wish that on anyone, especially not her.

So he turns to Rhett instead. "You're saying if she came up with that money, you could get rid of her ex once and for all."

Wrong word choice. The lawyer doesn't flinch though, which confirms he's working for Matteo. It's not the attorney's first brush with a criminal element.

Rhett clips his briefcase closed. "Take a look at the paperwork. Check into loans or grants or other forms of fresh revenue." He regards Jen. "But yes, if you found a way to raise these funds, you'd be free from any further connection to Mr. Devon."

Jen's shaking her head, her expression between bemusement and anger. "It'll never happen. Not in this lifetime. But thank you for trying."

Still, she doesn't let go of the papers. He sees longing in her eyes as she takes a last glance at the numbers.

Rhett steps back. "I won't take any more of your time. Ms. Bello, Mr. Goodman—good day."

The attorney turns and strides back to his car. They watch in silence as he starts the engine, then executes a perfect three-point turn to aim the sedan back down the driveway.

As soon as he's out of sight, Jen turns to him.

"So." She folds her arms and locks green eyes with his. "Care to explain how he knew your last name?"

CHAPTER 4

*J*en watches Dan's face. Sees his throat move as he swallows her question.

Care to explain how he knew your last name?

She sounds like a suspicious bitch, but who cares. How many times did she ignore signs with Johnny, trusting him when he swore his overnight trip with the wine rep was purely professional?

Dan looks her in the eye long enough she forgets the question.

"Guess he saw this?" He draws back the edge of his jacket.

Jen's eyes drop to his chest and lock. That's a nice chest. Intent on admiring it, she nearly misses the detail.

"Oh." There's lettering stitched on the front of his coveralls.

D. Goodman.

She drags her gaze back to his. "I see."

She's seeing a lot more. What kind of man offers absurd sums of money to a woman he's just met?

Jen licks her lips. "We should get to work."

He nods and lets go of his jacket. "Do you want to talk about it?"

Still picturing his chest, she blinks. "About what?"

A nod at the papers in her hand. "About what it would take to raise that kind of money."

Smothering a laugh, she takes a step back to gain distance from his magnetic pectorals. "Unless you're a criminal mastermind with a scheme for making insane piles of cash overnight, there's nothing to talk about."

He doesn't laugh. Jen gets the sense he seldom does. In a way, it's a welcome break from Johnny's smarmy charm and booming laugh.

"What about a fundraiser?" Dan asks.

"A fundraiser."

"Sure." He scrubs a hand over his chin. "Hunting down missing people or something."

"That's your idea of a fundraiser?"

He frowns. "What's yours?"

"I don't know—a dunk tank or a cakewalk or a kissing booth or something?"

There's a shift in his emotionless expression. A flash in his eyes has her replaying those words. Kissing? Really?

"Or pony rides," she spits as heat floods her face.

Dan lifts an eyebrow. "You have a lot of ponies?"

"No." Jen takes another step back, pretty sure his proximity has pickled her brain. "Maybe a bake sale."

A silly idea, unless she prices cupcakes at six thousand dollars each. "Ugh, this isn't helping."

"You're doing great," he says with surprising confidence. "We're brainstorming."

She shoves her hands in her pockets so he can't see she's shaking with unspent energy. Maybe she should go for a jog, though she hasn't jogged since middle school PE. "Do you have more ideas?"

He looks thoughtful. "Axe throwing's popular."

"Axe throwing?"

"Sure. Aren't there tons of axe throwing bars around Oregon?"

She's never heard of such a thing, but it sounds Oregon-esque. "If there are tons of them already, why would people spend money to come to ours?"

"Good point." He rubs his chin again. "What about a shooting gallery?"

"Shooting? Like—guns?"

No, dumbass. Shooting photos of floral arrangements.

Dan's lips twitch like he's read her thoughts. "Like at a carnival—people shoot air guns at plastic ducks or playing cards."

Her brow furrows. "Do you have any ideas that don't involve weapons?" She winces. "Sorry, I know you're trying. I just—I'm frustrated and I don't think there's any way—"

"Wine," he says, halting her runaway mouth.

"What?"

"This is a vineyard. What about something to do with wine?"

She flicks a glance at the tasting room behind him. "Huh."

"People pay a lot of money for wine, don't they?"

"Sure, but we're missing a winemaker right now. The new gal I hired doesn't start for another couple weeks." He might be onto something, though. "It does make sense to do something tied to the business."

Her thoughts are whirling now. She can't believe she's actually thinking like this, but what if...*maybe*...

"We've got four barrels of Cabernet Sauvignon in oak that'll need to be bottled soon." She does mental math, recalling how much bold reds go for these days. "Johnny left that behind, since it's a blend made by a guest winemaker. What if we auctioned off the right to name it? Then we could sell bottles for a steep price."

"Brilliant." His lips twitch again. "Now you're stewing."

"Stewing?"

"Sautéing?" He frowns. "Isn't that the expression?"

She laughs, recognizing that hint of an accent again. "Cooking," she says, threading a hand through her hair. "Now you're cooking. Speaking of which, I owe you a meal."

He looks perplexed. "Why?"

"Because you're new to town and a guest on my property and my grandma taught me to feed guests. How about dinner?"

Dan cocks his head. "You're inviting me to dinner?"

"Sure, it's no big deal." God, does he think she's propositioning him? Or worse, following through on her silly hooker joke? "It's nothing fancy. Probably meatloaf or roast chicken or grilled sausages or—" She clamps her mouth shut so she'll stop listing the contents of her freezer.

"Thank you," he says. "I accept the invitation."

"Tonight?"

Her voice sounds way too eager, but he nods. "I believe I'm free."

"Great! Let's say six! I've got wine!" Why is everything spewing from her mouth flecked with exclamation?

"I can bring bread." He folds his arms over a chest she is definitely not admiring. Again. "Is there an oven in the bunkhouse?"

"Yes." The fact that he's baking bread instead of buying it makes her knees all buttery. "I installed it myself."

Dan smiles for real this time. "Congratulations."

He sounds like he means it, so she smiles back. "Thank you. Shall we get to work?"

Nodding, he grabs the shovel leaned against the barn wall. "Lead the way."

* * *

JEN HATES herself for fussing over dinner. It's a meal, that's all. A simple dinner to welcome a new employee.

So why is she sticking wildflowers in a jelly jar and taking extra care to peel cute curls of parmesan instead of shaking canned stuff over the arugula salad?

The doorbell rings and she jumps. Glancing at her watch, she sees it's six on the dot. She races to the door, then stops to straighten the photo of her family posed beside the Dovlano Royal Palace. Not that a houseguest will care about a crooked frame, but she'll look eager if she opens the door too fast.

"Dan." She swings it open and does a double take. "Wow, you dressed up."

"It's not every day I'm invited for a home-cooked meal." He steps inside and runs a hand over a gray shirt that looks tailored. "I hope it's okay."

"It's wonderful. Truly, you look fabulous. Amazing!" God, make her shut up. "Wine?"

"A small glass. Thank you." He holds out bunch of sunflowers and a thick, golden sphere of bread. "It's still cooling, so I didn't wrap it."

"This smells wonderful." She wraps a palm around the loaf, grateful she washed her hands. Grateful for the sunflower stems filling her other hand so she doesn't send it roaming over his chest. "Thank you."

She leads him inside, wishing she'd thought to dress up. A silky top at least, or maybe a sundress. Her boots feel clunky and she's not sure when she last washed these jeans. "Have a seat while I get the flowers in water."

That keeps her busy, the hunt for a large vase. The task of tucking the loaf in her grandma's vintage bread warmer. At least she has nice wineglasses, and excellent wine to go in them. She pours the pinot carefully, not thinking until she hands him one that she should have asked if he'd like red or white.

"Thank you." His fingers graze hers on the Riedel stem and she shivers.

Retreating to the other side of the table, she sips her wine and tries not to watch his mouth and wonder what it's like to kiss a man that tall. Maybe it doesn't matter when sitting. Or lying on a bed with the sheets kicked off and—

"Very nice."

Jen blinks, then realizes he's talking about the wine. "Estate grown," she says. "These grapes are from up on the northwest ridge."

He sips again, holding her gaze. "The one hit with weed killer?"

"Right." She tries not to wince. "I asked my neighbor about it. About spraying chemicals close to the property line."

"And?"

"He says he didn't. That he hasn't sprayed for weeks."

Dan rubs his thumb over a spot on the table, and Jen gets jealous of a jelly splotch. "You believe him?"

She bites her lip. "Maybe."

"That doesn't sound certain."

She shrugs and sips her wine. "He's…grumpy." That's a polite way to put it. "I don't think he's mean-spirited or careless, but I do think he's not a fan of organic farming."

"I see." Dan's eyes sweep hers, like he's trying to see through her soul. "So he's a threat."

"Not exactly. I don't think he's anything, really. Just making conversation. I'll shut up now."

"Don't." He lifts his glass but doesn't drink. "I like hearing you talk."

The words spread through her like warm butter, and she licks her lips. "I have the habit of blurting things out."

"Like having a brother in prison?"

"Yes. That." Okay, they're going there. She takes a deep breath. "I'm sorry I didn't tell you sooner."

"Why would you owe me that information?"

"I don't know." She scratches another spot on the table, realizing she should wipe it down. She should also get the cheese and crackers she plated as an appetizer, but instead she stays glued to her seat. "It's the sort of thing you might want to know. Like maybe you think it's an indicator we're a bad family. Or that it's dangerous to be here."

"You're not," he says slowly. "And I don't."

"Okay."

He pauses. "You want to tell me about it?"

Does she? She seldom talks about Matteo, except with Nicole. They know what sort of man their brother is. They don't judge him by the orange jumpsuit.

To them, he's the boy who taught them to ride bikes and stayed home making soup when they caught colds. They know him as the man who dove into the irrigation pond wearing his best suit when someone tossed a litter of kittens in a rock-filled bag. He crawled to the muddy shore and sat heaving, coaxing the kittens to breathe again. Night after night, he bottle-fed those babies.

That man—the man she knows—couldn't have done the things that landed him behind bars. She's sure of it.

And she wants Dan to know it, too. "He raised us himself," she says softly. "Well, him and my grandma, but especially Matteo. Nondi was gone a lot—our grandma."

"Nondi?"

"I called her that when I was little." Her eyes sting, and she's not sure if it's the memory or how she's spilling her guts to this stranger. "A mashup of the Italian word for grandmother— Nonna—and the Dovlanese word, Disla." A pause as she scans his blank expression. "We weren't born in America. All three of us— our sister, Nicole—we were born in this tiny country in southern Europe. A place you've probably never heard of called—"

"Dovlano." He nods. "I know."

"You know?"

He hesitates. Holds her gaze for an exceptionally long time. When he speaks, his voice is hard to hear.

"I'm from Dovlano."

CHAPTER 5

*H*e watches Jen's face as he lays those words at her feet and backs away.

I'm from Dovlano.

As she stares, he questions his choice to share this.

But she shared with him about her lost love and money and family, so he owes her some shard of truth.

Jen licks her lips. "I—how—why—" She stops. "I'm sorry, I have questions."

"Thought you might."

She pauses to gather her thoughts. "Your accent—that's why it's familiar."

Nodding once, he sets his glass on the table. "I worked for the Duke of Dovlano. Palace security," he adds, praying she won't ask for details. "I also spent time in the Dovlanese military."

Her expression's unreadable. "Which branch?"

"Red Blades." He watches her face, wondering what she knows about Dovlanese Special Forces. "It was a while ago."

Another favorite American thing. That "a while" can mean *ten years* or *yesterday*. To his relief, she doesn't press. Not there, anyway.

"You didn't say so on your resumé."

"No." He's not surprised she focused there. "It wasn't to deceive you. I needed to tell you in person. I thought you might call Lady Isabella—"

"That's how I recognized the name." She slaps the table, making him jump. "It sounded familiar."

He nods, hesitant to go down that path. "Do you speak Dovlanese?"

With a glance at the table, she shakes her head. "My brother does. My sister, too. I was young when we came to America. Too young to have the memories they do."

"Understandable." Some of this he knew already. But hearing it from Jen, listening to her sweet, soft voice shaping these stories —it's different from Matteo's emotionless recitation of facts.

Besides, Teo's the most closed-off guy he knows. Getting details from Matteo Bello is like squeezing blood from a turnip. "You're close with your family?"

As she shrugs, he waits for her to call him out. To say he's diverting the conversation, dodging questions she hasn't thought to ask.

But with her jar of family memories uncapped, she's not ready to cram the lid back on. "Our parents died when we were little," she says softly. "Dad was Dovlanese. Mom was Italian." She looks down at the table. "Matteo needed to get us out of Dovlano for— reasons." She swallows, and Dante's glad he's not alone in hiding whole truths. "Our mom's mom came to America from Italy a few years earlier, so Matteo found a way to get us here to live with Nondi. To start over."

"That must have taken some doing."

"You have no idea." She laughs and studies her hands. "My brother's one of those tech geniuses. Recruited by MIT when he was twelve or thirteen, but he stuck around instead to raise us."

"MIT?" He whistles like he hadn't known this fact. "Impressive."

"He got to go later. Much later, once Nic and I were grown. He's a good man. A great man who stayed stuck behind bars when our grandma breathed her last breath and—"

As she breaks off, her pain socks him in the gut. He's heard broad strokes from Teo, but never this detail. Never this level of adoration. She loved her grandmother. Her brother, too, which makes Dante love her more.

No, not love. *Admire. Respect.* That's what he feels for this woman he hardly knows. He has a sudden urge to catch her hand. To hold her so she feels less alone. Would she slap him if he did?

He clears his throat. "Hey."

She looks up, eyes shimmering. "What?"

He shouldn't say these next words. "Want a hug?"

She laughs and swipes at her eyes. "You think I'm pathetic."

"I think you're brave."

A sobby hiccup as she studies his face. "I might actually believe you. Not that I'm brave, but that *you* think I might be." With a shaky laugh, she stands up. "Okay."

His brain takes three seconds to catch up. It's time he should spend getting to his feet, but he sits there like a dummy in her ladder-back chair, watching her walk around the table.

She halts in front of him and his heart stumbles to a stop. "I'll take you up on your offer."

"Oh." He starts to stand, but she's lowering herself onto his lap, and then...

Oh, God.

The weight of her on his knees, warm and solid as she wraps her arms around him and squeezes tight. His arms move on their own, enfolding her so she rests against his chest. He doesn't move. Doesn't breathe. He might not be alive, except yes, his heart hits his chest like a jackhammer.

Thank God he's only got an ankle holster, so there's nothing between them. Nothing but warm cotton and the thunder of his heartbeat. Hers, too. He feels it through the softness skimming his chest.

God, she's perfect. Solid and warm and *good Lord*, he'll pass out if he doesn't breathe. He fills his lungs and gets dizzy with the scent of honey and sweet hay and something he can't place. There's a burning in his chest he doesn't recognize either, but he doesn't want it to stop. Not ever. If he could just keep holding her like this—

"Dan," she murmurs, drawing back to look in his eyes.

He swallows hard. "Yeah?"

"Can I ask you something?"

Nodding, he swallows fear. There are things he can't tell her. Not ever. But in that moment, he swears he'd spill every secret if she asked.

"Are you married?" she asks. "Or have a girlfriend or—"

"No."

"Okay."

He hesitates. "Why?"

Jen bites her lip. "If you did, she might not like me sitting on your lap."

"True." He hesitates. "Or kissing you."

Her eyes flash, but she doesn't move. Neither does he. He shouldn't have said it, but he can't take it back. Doesn't want to.

Jen licks her lips. "Or kissing me." Her cheeks go pink. "For example."

He hesitates again, chest aching like he snapped the stem off his wineglass and slid it through his ribs. Her mouth is so close, *so close*. He'd give anything to taste those sweet, full lips. To know how she feels beneath him.

Your best friend's sister.

Your boss.

Warnings clang in his brain, but they're drowned by voices begging him to kiss her just once, only once, so he knows what it's like—

Crash!

He jumps, hauling her off his lap. Pushing her behind him, he spins to face the window. Curtains billow and glass spills icy on the floor. Outside, an engine revs.

"Get down." He shoves her under the table and grabs the gun at his ankle.

"Holy shit." Her eyes go wide as she clamps her mouth shut.

The spin of gravel sends him sprinting to the door. Whoever did this is getting away. Flinging open the door, he takes aim at the taillights. Drops his target to spinning tires. Finger on the trigger, he tabulates the odds.

He won't make the shot. The car's too fast, its plates wrapped in foil. He catalogues details—black or dark gray, late-model Dodge or Ford. He could give chase, but he won't make it in time.

The animals.

With a glance behind him, he spots her watching from the porch. Pictures the charred shed where Matteo's salvation once hid.

"Maple?" Her voice sounds high and scared. "Scape?"

"Stay there."

He doesn't wait for her nod. Sprinting to the barn, he finds it locked tight. No signs of foul play. When he peers through the slats, Scape lifts his head and bleats.

"You okay?"

The goat drags a hoof through the straw. Maple pops his head over the stall and whinnies.

"All right." He looks around, seeing no sign of trouble.

He should get back to Jen.

Sprinting across the gravel, he takes the front steps two at a time. The front door gapes open, and he's not sure if he left it like that. He shoulders it wider and steps inside.

"Jen?" He raises the pistol, sweeping the room like he's done a thousand times. "Honey?"

The word slips before he can stop it, but he'll think about that later. Right now, he needs to make sure she's safe. "Jen?"

"I'm okay."

He finds her crouched on the floor, fingers sifting glass. She looks up with fear in her eyes. "There's a message."

She points to a rock wrapped in burlap. He steps closer, careful not to crush glass into her wood floor. Peering down, he scans crooked black pen slashes.

SELL OR ELSE.

HE LOOKS AT JEN, struggling to make sense of it. "I'm guessing that's not a hint to hold a bake sale?"

The sound she makes is half laugh, half sob. "The property. Or the winery."

"Police."

"Sure, it could be them."

He blinks. "I meant we should call them." A suggestion he's stunned to be making. But her suggestion—"You think the police are behind this?"

Her jaw clenches as she gets to her feet. Squaring her shoulders, she stares him down with startling bravado. "Let's just say I'm suspicious of how my brother ended up behind bars."

Dante's not suspicious. He knows damn well how Matteo got there. Not details, not all of it. But a crooked cop put Teo behind bars. He's positive.

Proving it is another matter. Especially minus the evidence from the burned shed.

He's deciding what to say when Jen speaks again. "My brother's not a choirboy," she says. "But the crimes they locked him up for—that's not the brother I know."

"Okay." If he didn't know Teo, what would he say to that? "Um, what's he in prison for?"

"Cybercrime." She laughs. "Okay, *that* I'd believe. But doing it to steal money?" There's a wistful flare in her eyes as she shakes her head. "Not his style. My brother's good at making money. He doesn't need to steal to do it."

Matteo's good at lots more than money. Dante doesn't say so. He looks down and sees he's still holding the pistol. Should probably do something about that. "All right." He tucks the gun back in its holster.

Maybe they'll pretend that didn't happen.

Jen watches him stand, then waits for him to say something. He clears his throat. "What do you want to do?"

Again with the hybrid laugh-sob. "Gee, I was thinking maybe a nice game of Scrabble before we sit down for supper."

He can't help it. One edge of his mouth quirks, though he's fighting not to laugh. "I'm partial to Boggle."

"Fine. I've got that, too. You want an end piece or middle?"

"What?" This is not the conversation he expected.

"Meatloaf." She spins and yanks open the oven. "Looks done. Mashed potatoes are in the crockpot. You want gravy?"

"Um." He glances at the glass on the floor. "Got a broom?"

She sighs and grabs an oven mitt. "You don't need to sweep my floors."

"And you don't need to feed me." He yanks open a closet that turns out to be a pantry stuffed with canned food. Closes the door, then turns to the closet under the stairs. He finds a broom there, along with a dustpan. "The least I can do is help with cleanup."

Setting the meatloaf on the counter, she presses her lips together. "Thank you."

"No problem."

They work in silence, Jen slicing bread and tossing salad, Dante sweeping up glass. He's not surprised this is how she copes. The mundane tasks of plating food, pouring water in glasses. When he's processing something, he'll spend hours cleaning his weapons. They're alike in that way.

He handles the burlap rock with gloves in case she changes her mind about the cops. Not that they'd get prints off it, but it's worth being careful.

Spotting a hunk of cardboard next to her recycle bin, he picks it up. "Got duct tape?"

Jen snorts. "I'm a farm girl. There's a roll in every cupboard." Yanking open a kitchen drawer, she extracts a thick silver circle. "You don't have to—"

"Fix your window. I know."

But he does it anyway. By the time he's washing his hands in the powder room, Jen's setting the table. Two plates heaped with mashed potatoes and meatloaf and piles of fresh garden greens. Edible violas lace the edge of each salad, and Dante's heart twists at this tiny scrap of sweetness. Belly growling, he takes a seat and waits for her to do the same.

"Thank you." He picks up his fork but doesn't start. "You sure you're okay?"

"No. I'm not." She scoops a big forkful of mashed potatoes and takes her time savoring it. "But I've found that if I keep busy, I don't think about how fucked up things are."

"I get that." He's guilty of it himself. "I'm sorry that happened."

She looks up, fork poised over her salad. "Why, did you cause it?"

He tenses. Has she guessed why he's here? Who sent him or what he's really been thinking about—

"I'm pretty sure you didn't chuck a rock through my window," she continues. "So there's no need to apologize. But I'd like to figure out who did it."

"Same." She has no idea how badly he wants that. "You're positive you don't want to involve police?"

"Yep." She stabs her meatloaf with alarming force. "There are good cops out there. I'm not some anti-police activist. I just know how tough it is to tell good ones from bad ones. Until I've got that figured out, I'm not inviting any of them to my house."

"Fair enough." He takes a bite of meatloaf and almost moans. "This is incredible."

"Thanks. My brother's recipe."

His gut churns. He's sitting in his buddy's childhood home, eating the man's meatloaf and ogling his sister. What's wrong with him?

"So," Jen continues. "Nice piece you've got there."

He glances down at his plate, but she waves a hand in front of him. "Not the meatloaf. Your gun. A Sig, right?"

"Right." Okay, here they go.

"You're ex-military." A pause. "And you worked in palace security in Dovlano?"

He nods and picks up his water glass, grateful she's given him something besides wine. He needs his wits. "Correct."

She sighs and twirls her fork through the greens, threading the tines with ruffled arugula. "That explains the fancy clothes. Did you work a lot of royal balls and stuff like that?"

What?

He swallows more water, fumbling to find her angle. "I did. I led the team protecting the royal family. The Duke, Duchess Francesca, Lady Isabella—"

"You must have some crazy stories."

"Certainly." Few of them sharable at a dinner table. He hesitates. It's clear she needs distraction, and he's got that. "Once, Duchess Francesca was the target of a kidnapping plot."

"No kidding?"

He nods, not adding that Jen's own brother hacked the database to crack the case. Matteo's work for the Dovlanese government was confidential. The man took his secrets to prison.

"What happened?" Jen frowns. "Wait, didn't I see something about this on the news?"

"Perhaps." Rampant media coverage of the story is the only reason he's sharing. "We determined when the kidnappers planned to strike, then launched a counter-attack."

He's leaving out details, most bloody. The team of assailants was larger than expected. Dante took out six men, none of whom left the warehouse by their own power.

Clearing his throat, he takes another sip of water. "Duchess Francesca was unharmed, and the royal ball carried on as planned."

"I saw video on the news." Her eyes go dreamy. "That gown she wore—yellow, wasn't it?"

"Um." He could list the brand, model, and caliber of every weapon he took from the kidnappers. But the Duchess's gown? "Yellow sounds right."

"Tell me honestly." She sets down her fork, and he's braced for questions he can't answer. "Do they wear those butt poof things under royal gowns?"

"*What?*"

Blush stains her cheeks. "I don't know what they're called. The padding that makes women seem so curvy and perfect in those fancy dresses. Is it real or just foundation garments?"

"I—have no idea."

"Huh." She takes a sip of water, then picks up her fork again. "Do they take lessons on how to be royal? How to dress, how to act, how to use the right fork at dinner?"

"Yes." He looks at the fork in his hand. "The same was required of me."

"No kidding?" She stares at her own hand fisted around the shaft of her fork. Sighs and meets his eyes. "Are you silently judging my table manners?"

"Absolutely not."

"All right." Another sigh as she sets down her fork. "I'm calm now. I suppose I should make a list."

His brain ping-pongs from thwarted kidnappings to ball gowns to...groceries?

"A list?"

"Of who would throw a rock through my window." She picks up her fork and stabs the meatloaf. "There's this hotel chain. The Hart-Holden Group? They own a bunch of different hotels like the Spirata in Seattle."

"I've heard of them." Where is she going with this? "You're connected somehow."

"They want to build here in wine country." She flings a hand toward the cardboard-covered window. "They've approached several landowners, including me."

He frowns. "You think they'd throw rocks through your window so you sell?"

"Maybe." She scowls at her mashed potatoes. "At this point, I trust no one." She lifts a sheepish gaze. "No offense."

"None taken." He wouldn't trust him either. "Is there someone specific you'd suspect?"

If so, he'll cheerfully take them out.

Jen shakes her head. "Not really. They've mostly sent lawyers and PR people to talk to me. Lots of emails."

"The lawyer this morning—Rhett Strijker? You think he's connected?"

She sips her wine, considering. "I thought so at first, but no. I don't think so." Another sigh. "My brother said he'd send a lawyer. I guess that's him."

That sounds like Matteo. He almost says so, but catches himself. "What about your boyfriend?" His voice cracks oddly, and Jen gives him a look. "Ex-boyfriend," he adds.

She shrugs. "He's not really the violent type, but who knows?"

Dante drinks some water and says nothing. In his line of work, he's seen all kinds of people turn violent. Seen it more than he can count. The thought depresses him. Not what he's seen, because he's lived with that a long time. He's used to it.

It's the thought that if Jen knew who he was—*what* he was—she surely wouldn't share her meatloaf.

He sets down his glass. "The neighbor?"

"Gail and Harry Gibson are on the list." She shrugs and spears an edible flower. "Along with probably a hundred enemies my brother made over the years." With a grumble of frustration, she picks up her wineglass. "We'd have an easier time determining who *doesn't* want to screw with my family."

There's a sharp pain near his heart, and he wonders if it's sympathy. "I'm sorry."

"It's fine." She shrugs. "It is what it is."

Another American phrase he doesn't get. But he does grasp the need for a subject change. He surveys his plate in case the answer lies there. It holds one tight curl of parmesan. "Dinner was delicious."

"You want seconds?" She leaps from her chair and Dante gets to his feet.

"I'm good. Let me help with the dishes and I'll be on my way."

"But—dessert." She bites her lip. "No, I understand. It's your first day. You need to get settled."

She's taking it as a rejection. He sees it in her eyes, and he hates that he caused it.

He'll cause worse if he stays. This much he knows.

Her gaze shifts to the burlap-wrapped rock on the counter. He watches her shiver. "What a weird night."

Hell. He can't leave her like this, can he? "If you don't feel safe, I can stay." He instantly wants to kick himself. "On the porch. My night watch skills are solid."

She snorts and shakes her head. "Thanks, but no. I'm not afraid."

That makes one of them.

Because Dante's fucking terrified. The rock on the counter has nothing to do with it.

CHAPTER 6

*J*en gives Dan a wide berth the next day. It's not hard, since she's tasked him with barn repairs while she tidies the tasting room.

But the truth is she's embarrassed. Sitting on his lap, for God's sake. What was she thinking? It seemed practical at the time. She's short and he's tall and sitting like that made sense for hugging.

And maybe she didn't imagine the heat in his eyes. The mention of a kiss.

He's polite, that's all.

Knowing someone wants to harm her is hardly a turn-on. Not even for a man like Dan, burly and armed and brimming with protector instinct. She should apologize for the awkwardness and move on. Either that or pretend it didn't happen. That's simpler.

She's on her knees scrubbing the wine chiller when she hears gravel crunch outside.

Clambering to her feet, she peers through the window and sees a car—no, *two* cars— coming up the drive. A good sign when the tasting room's open. Not so much today.

Which means it might be friends of Matteo's. *Friends.* She scoffs at the word, recalling the cop who came looking for her brother. It happened the week Teo went missing. Months before they dragged him into custody.

Nondi met their badge-bearing guest with a shotgun. "This is private property." She spit on the ground. "You want my grandson, you'll have to get through me."

God, she misses her grandma. Her spirit, her toughness—why couldn't Jen have more of that? Or just have Nondi back. It's been over a year and the ache in her heart still brings Jen to her knees.

Fuck cancer.

Jen tries spitting on the ground, but barely misses the toe of her boot. Figures.

Shaking off sadness, she watches the cars crawl up the driveway. One red, one dark blue, about four hundred yards apart. Red's in the lead, so she focuses there.

Relief sweeps her as she recognizes her sister's station wagon. Nic bought a new Volvo last week. Running a daycare must be more lucrative than farming. Stepping outside, Jen wipes her hands on her jeans as Nicole comes up the walk.

"Hey there." Jen grabs her big sister in a hug as the other car parks beside Nic's station wagon. Dark blue sedan, tinted windows. No one's getting out.

Jen swallows unease. "What's up?"

Nic shoves a swath of blonde hair off her face. "Just bringing you that box of Grandma's things."

"You're sure it's stuff she wanted me to have?" Tendrils of grief twist in her chest. "It's not stuff for both of us?"

"Positive." Nic rolls her eyes. "The words 'for Jennifer' printed on the side of the box in Nondi's writing seemed pretty clear."

"Oh." Jen bites her lip. "What is it?"

"I didn't look closely. Family stuff, I think. Some of Mom's things are in there. Girly dress-up clothes, some perfume bottles.

Kinda frou-frou. Maybe not your style, but she wanted you to have some stuff from Mom."

"Right." Of course it's not her style. Jen is blue jeans and grubby nails, not silk scarves and eau de daffodil. She likes it that way, but still. "Anything else?"

"Some things I remember Nondi having when we were little. Must've ended up in storage somehow." Nic's expression softens. "I saw a couple photos and one of those old-fashioned candy dishes. I didn't want to pry, so I left it alone for you to look through."

"Oh. Thank you." She has no secrets from her sister, but that's sweet. "I can grab it now."

Nic's not listening. Not anymore. She's glaring at the dark blue sedan beside her car. "Who's that?"

"Beats me."

Nic's eyes narrow. "Want me to talk to them?"

"No." The last thing Jen needs is another guardian. "Probably someone tallying up a wine order."

"Huh." Nic doesn't sound convinced.

"Come on." Jen grabs her sister's arm. "You came for cobbler, right?"

Nic brightens. Pulls a can of whipped cream from her purse. "I brought this."

"You remembered!" Jen wipes her hands again and wishes she'd washed them. Wishes she knew who's sitting in that sedan. "I already packaged half for you. I'll go grab it."

She reaches for the can, but Nic snatches it back. "No way." Nic grins. "I think there's another reason you wanted this."

Jen sighs. "And what would that be?"

Her sister wiggles both brows and points at the barn. "Who's the shirtless hottie and how much of this can you lick off his abs?"

"Very funny." Jen swipes at the can again, but Nic's too fast.

"Seriously, that's your new farmhand? You definitely need a piece of that. Whipped cream optional."

"He's my employee." She makes another grab for the can. Nic gives up and hands it to her. "And you really think I need a relationship right now?"

"Who said anything about a relationship?"

The doors open on the sedan, and Nic whirls to face it. Her shoulders tense, and she shifts so she's shielding Jen.

Kid sister annoyance blooms in her chest, but Jen tamps it down. As she stares, a man and a woman get out and stroll toward them. Casually dressed, they wear jeans and blazers and fancy boots meant to look like farm wear. She's guessing they cost more than her tractor.

"Can I help you?" She tries to keep her voice cool, but it rattles at the end. "Tasting room's closed, but I'm doing bottle sales if you know what you need."

"We didn't come for wine, actually." The man looks around, nodding as he takes in her view of the valley. "Wow, it's nice up here. Great views."

"Thanks." Jen crosses her arms as the woman approaches.

"Sorry, where are our manners?" The woman extends a hand, and Jen unfolds to shake it. "Dawn Fitchkenyi, and this is Sean Kabisch. We're from The Hart-Holden Group."

Jen drops her hand. "I'm not interested."

Nicole swings from them to Jen and back again. "Wait." She frowns at Dawn and Sean, maybe wondering if the rhyming names are real. "You're the people tripping over your dicks to grab land that's been in our family for three generations?"

Jen tips her chin up. No sense clarifying that land ownership technically skipped their parents. "I'm running a business here," she says.

The man rocks back on his heels. "And with the money Hart-Holden Group is willing to pay, you could be running a more successful one." He lifts a well-groomed brow. "Someplace else, of course."

Nicole scoffs. "Winemaking is all about terroir and soil composition and elevation and sun exposure." She scowls at Sean. "Or something like that. I run a daycare. Jen's the land expert."

She rarely feels like much of an expert, but it's nice to have Nic's vote of confidence. "I've already seen the proposal," she says. "I'm not int—"

"There's a new proposal." Sean's vaguely smug. "One you'll find more to your liking."

"I doubt that." She just wants them to leave.

Dawn glances toward the Gibsons' farm. "It'd be a shame if we had to choose another building site. Something right up against your property line where you'd have traffic coming and going at all hours of the night."

Sean takes the bad cop ball and runs with it. "The outdoor pool can get noisy. And the playground with ziplines."

"And volleyball courts." Dawn shakes her head in a poor imitation of pity. "Balls flying everywhere, sometimes willy-nilly into grapevines or—"

"For fuck's sake." Jen huffs a breath. "I'm going to have to ask you to leave."

"Fine." Dawn presses her lips together. "The new proposal has been emailed. Take a look and let us know what you think."

She could tell them right now what she thinks, but Nondi taught her not to shout at strangers. Odd, since Grandma wasn't one to hold back. But she knew when to be a lady, which is more than Jen ever figured out.

"Bye." She points Sean and Dawn to their car. "Have a nice day."

"Or not," Nic adds, waving with her daycare teacher cheer. "It'd be a real shame if something popped your tire on the way back down."

Under her breath, Nic hisses something like *bullet*.

"Shh." Jen elbows her in the ribs.

"What? It's what Nondi would've said."

True. But Jen's not Nondi. She's not even as brave as her sister. "Leave. *Now*." She points at Sean and Dawn's car. "No means no."

"And 'fuck no' means get off our family land." Another smile from Nic. "Please."

"Fine." Sean sneers, then turns to follow Dawn to the car.

Nicole doesn't wait until they're out of earshot. "What assholes. You've told them no, right?"

"Repeatedly." She sighs as the car moves down the driveway. "I don't know…maybe I should consider it."

"Jen." Nic's eyes soften as they sweep her face. "This land means everything to you."

Not untrue. It's why Nondi left this place to her. Teo got the beach house, while Nic got the craftsman bungalow she transformed into Miss Gigglewink's Daycare.

Still… "Maybe I'm being too sentimental about dirt."

"No way." Nic snakes an arm around her and hugs hard enough to hurt. "You care about this place in ways Matty and I never did. If you want to hold on to it, you know we'll do what it takes to make that happen."

She forces a weak smile. "Please don't ask Matteo to get involved." God knows how her overbearing brother would handle it. "Still want to come in for cobbler? I've got leftover meatloaf, too."

"Actually, I've gotta run." Nic looks at her watch and makes a face. "Meeting with a new family."

Jen quirks a brow. "Interesting backstory?"

"Always." Nicole winks. "Can't talk about it, obviously."

"Of course." Pride swells her chest. Nic's daycare serves families with special needs. Not developmental delays, but witness protection. Her sister's soft spot is battered moms, and Jen loves her for it. "Let me grab your cobbler."

She starts toward the house, and Nic follows, frowning at the cardboard on her window. "What happened there?"

Shrugging, Jen pries open the fridge. "Someone's coming at four to replace it."

"Not an answer to the question." She leans against the counter. "Spill it. Wait—" Her brow furrows. "Mr. Tall, Hot, and Mysterious doesn't have something to do with that, does he?"

"What?" It dawns on her she's talking about Dan. "God, no. Dan was here when it happened. Just a rock thrown through the window. Nothing to fret about."

Nic's clearly fretting. "Are you serious? Jen—"

"I've got it handled."

Still frowning, Nicole searches her eyes. "I don't like this. Did you call the police?"

Jen gives her a look and doesn't say anything. Nic's shoulders slump. "Okay, yeah...no cops. Still, who do you think did it?"

"No idea." She shoves a plastic container of cobbler at her sister. "Probably kids pulling a prank."

They both know that's not true. Nic searches her eyes. "Please be careful."

"I'm always careful." Tries to be, anyway. "Besides, as you pointed out, I've got a burly beefcake living on site."

"That does ease my mind." Nic's forehead softens, but the furrow remains. "I don't like the look of those hotel people."

"You don't like the look of *anyone*." Her sister's the most mistrustful person she's ever met. Nic's got her reasons, but still.

Nicole checks her watch. "Dammit, I have to go."

"I'll walk you out." Jen pulls her hands from her pockets and shoves open the door.

They stroll together to the car, Jen kicking a pebble down the drive. It's unseasonably sunny, mud puddles flashing an echo of blue sky.

"Thanks for coming." Jen pulls her sister in for a hug. "Love you."

"I love you, too." Drawing back, Nicole frowns again. "You sure you're okay? Between the breakup and money stuff and missing Nondi, and now the rock through the window—"

"I'm fine." She pushes her mouth into a smile. "Promise."

"Okay." Nic gets in her car, clearly not believing it. As she shuts the door, she offers a small smile. "Next time, introduce me to your beefcake."

Jen rolls her eyes. "Get out of here."

Laughing, Nic yanks her door shut and pulls away. As she watches her go, Jen feels a funny clench in her gut. This is what Nondi wished for when she willed them each a property. This farm for her, the craftsman for Nic, the beach place bequeathed to Matteo. Gifts that should have set them up for a lifetime of security.

And Jen's gone and pissed hers away. Let Johnny get his hands on it, his mind wrapped around the idea that he's entitled to half. It's her own damn fault. She stares at Nic's taillights as they vanish down the highway.

Crap.

She forgot to grab the box from Nic.

Pulling out her phone, she fires off a text.

You forgot *to give me that box of Grandma's stuff.*

Nic's reply appears in seconds. Voice-to-text, probably.

Oops! *Distracted by your creepy guests, busted window, and shirtless farmhand.*

. . .

SMILING, she taps out a reply.

FUNNY. Lunch soon?

NIC RESPONDS with a smiley face and a date that works for her. Sighing, Jen tucks her phone in her pocket and gets back to work. The weather's too nice to be inside, so she sets out sweeping the front porch of the tasting room.

If she doesn't lose it all, this spot's perfect for events next summer. Maybe a wine bar over there with cozy little tables and fire pits. She should learn to weld, maybe watch YouTube videos on building some herself to save money.

Another crunch of gravel tugs her attention to the driveway. What the hell? A red Miata sends a sour gush through her gut.

"Dammit." She watches Johnny's car approach. "Not like I have to work or anything."

Penelope's perched in the passenger seat, sleek blonde hair held by a suede headband. A few pale wisps frame her face. If Jen tried that, she'd look like a dish brush. Leaning her broom on the porch rail, she steps forward to meet them. The last thing she needs is these two poking around her tasting room.

Johnny's already walking around the car to open Penelope's door. He glances up as Jen approaches. "Afternoon. Hope this is an okay time to grab those Claret bottles I left."

Jen grits her teeth. "You said you'd call first."

"I've been busy." He opens the passenger door, and Penelope steps out.

The woman waves, and Jen lifts a hand in spite of herself. Teeth grinding, she notes Johnny's hand on Penelope's back. For once, she feels nothing.

"Boxes are in the barn." Jen turns on her heel. "Come on." Might as well get this over with.

Johnny starts toward the barn like he owns the place, which makes Jen want to punch someone. Mostly him. She moves to follow, but Penelope touches her arm.

"Jennifer." The lilt of a British accent makes her name sound exotic. Jen reminds herself to hate her. "It's lovely to see you."

"Did you need something?"

Penelope bites her lip and glances toward Johnny's disappearing back. "This is bloody awkward. I want to address the elephant in the room and say I'm sorry. You must believe I had no idea he was taken."

She's tempted to say she doesn't have to believe a damn thing from either of them. "The fact that we lived together wasn't a clue?"

Penelope flinches. "A business arrangement. That's what I believed and what—well, what he let me believe." She glances toward Johnny and lowers her voice. "That doesn't excuse what happened, and I know Johnny bungled things terribly. But I hope someday we might be friends."

When hell freezes over is what Jen wants to say.

"Sure," she offers instead. She starts toward the barn, but Penelope heads her off again.

"I brought you something. A peace offering." She reaches into the car and pulls out a cardboard box. "I spotted it in a darling antique store and thought of you."

Curiosity tramples hostility and Jen takes the box. A wad of emotion wedges in her throat, and now she can't speak. She just stares at the box, wondering how the other woman knew.

Penelope fills the silence. "Johnny said you're half Italian, so I thought—"

"An antique pasta maker." She swallows hard and touches it. "It's exactly like one my grandma had."

"Really?"

It might even be the same one. The cast iron crank, the scars on the wood handle— "Where did you find this?"

58

"An antique store outside San Francisco. You like it?"

She loves it. She hates herself for loving it, which leaves her teary-eyed and hating herself more. "Thank you." With a deep breath, she sets the box on the tasting room deck. "I appreciate the gift."

"You're welcome." Penelope shares a small smile. "I know it doesn't make up for—well, everything." She hesitates, watching Jen's face. "You know, I worked in fashion before I got into wine. If you'd like sometime, we could do a girls' shopping trip to Portland. We could get facials, maybe makeovers and some pretty new clothes—"

"I think we should help Johnny." She's back to hating Penelope. Easier in the long run. "Come on."

She trudges to the barn, feeling mean and frumpy with the waiflike creature floating behind her. How can someone have Barbie doll curves and a lean, willowy frame all stacked together? It doesn't seem scientifically possible. Squaring her shoulders, Jen tries to walk with the same elegant grace. Trips on her boots and keeps going, blinking back the threat of tears as they reach the west barn.

"Ladies." Johnny smiles and hands Jen a box. "Could you be a love and give us a hand?"

She wants to hurl the box at his head, both for the faux British endearment and treating her like his pack mule.

But helping haul boxes will get them off her property faster. She carries it to the car while Penelope's laugh floats on the breeze. Jen cringes, annoyed that she cares if she's the butt of a joke.

"You're so strong." Penelope's puffing as she catches up carrying a box half the size of Jen's. "I remember seeing you carry a whole case of wine like it weighed nothing."

"Yep." She sets the box in the back of Johnny's car, probably more roughly than necessary. "Farm work builds muscle."

"I'm jealous." Penelope piles her box on top of Jen's, huffing as she hustles back to the barn. "You're so self-sufficient. I wish I could be more like that."

Johnny looks up and swipes a hand over his forehead. "Jen's used to doing everything on her own. Kinda intimidating for some men."

She's had enough. "Only for men insecure enough to be threatened by strong women."

The second she says it, she wants to shove the words back down her throat. They stare at her like she's peed on Penelope's shoe. Jen hates herself for letting them get to her.

She opens her mouth to apologize, but Penelope beats her to it.

"I'm sorry." She toys with a strap on her sundress. "I can see we've hurt you and I just want to apologize again for—"

"Please stop apologizing." She sighs, wondering what will get them gone quickly. What will make them stop looking at her like she's some wild, injured animal to be pitied. "I just want to move on."

Johnny nods knowingly and touches her hand. "You'll find someone, too—Jen. Someone who deserves you and appreciates you for the wonderful person you are."

The urge to gag wars with the need to bite her tongue, so she's probably making a weird face. She's still making it when a figure strolls from the far-off end of the east barn, humming as he peels down the top of his coveralls.

Dan's muscled arms gleam with sweat and sunlight as he ambles to the hose near the corral. He's still humming, a Dovlanese lullaby Matteo used to sing. He cranks the faucet, pecs rippling as he splashes cold water on his face. On his arms, on abs that could grace the cover of a men's magazine.

Jen doesn't know her mouth's hanging open until Penelope speaks.

"Who *is* that?"

Dan's far enough he doesn't seem to hear, though Jen swears she sees his shoulders tense. Can he hear them?

She hesitates. "My boyfriend." Regret rushes her, but Dan doesn't look up. She keeps going, her voice a low murmur. "We're...uh...seeing each other."

Johnny blinks. "You're dating." A glance at the corral "Dating a—um—"

"Yep!" She shouts it too loudly as Dan takes his time getting a drink. His throat moves as he swallows, and Jen's thirstier than she's ever been. Droplets of water trail down his chin, between his pecs, over his abs, into the dark path of fur pointing down to his—

"Yep, dating!" Why is she repeating it? But her mouth's off and running, and she can't seem to stop it. "Dating a while now. Pretty hot and heavy. Yep!"

He's far enough away, so surely he can't hear. If he could, he'd be here tendering his resignation. "So anyway, let's get these boxes loaded and—"

"Wait, hang on." Johnny smiles. "This is great. Seriously, babe. Congratulations. Is it serious?"

As serious as a punch in the crotch, which I'm about to give you if you don't—

"Oh, you know." She waves a hand and tries not to see Dan's biceps flex as he shifts the hose from one hand to the other. "We're...uh...bangin' it out on the regular."

Bangin' it out? Is that even a real phrase?

Johnny looks dubious, and she knows how this sounds. Guys like Dan don't date women like her; it's basic science.

But Johnny's smiling like he might actually believe it, and Jen holds her breath.

"Great." Johnny slings an arm around Penelope. "If you're happy, we're happy."

She hates them so hard. Almost as much as she hates herself. And she's terrified Dan will come over to say hello.

Please go back in the barn.

Please go back in the barn.

She's practically chanting it out loud. "Right, so the rest of the boxes—"

"I'd love to meet him." Penelope's smile is warm and genuine, with no hint of irony. "He looks very—competent."

Johnny barely hides his grimace. Turning to Dan, he calls Jen's bluff. "Hello there," he shouts. "Sir?"

Oh, Jesus.

Jen forces her face into a smile. "D—Dan," she stammers, heat rushing her face. "Sweetheart. Honey."

Crossing her fingers, she prays he'll play along. How much did he hear?

And how silly will she seem if he calls her out?

The man takes his time turning off the spigot and wiping his chin. Doesn't bother shrugging the coveralls back up. Just ambles up the barnyard like it's normal to nakedly greet gaping strangers.

"Babe." Jen clears her throat. "I'd like you to meet—"

That's all she gets out. Because Dan sweeps her into his arms and bows her back as he kisses her hard and deep and fierce. She clutches his shirt before remembering there isn't one. Just bare, sculpted chest and slick skin and *holy mother of God*, the man can kiss.

His tongue lashes hers, claiming her, possessing her, devouring her. She holds on for dear life, sure she'd topple without his hands on her ass, his hard body pushing her back against the barn as he slips one thick thigh between hers. Groaning at the friction, she anchors her nails in the broadest back she's ever touched.

When he draws back, he rests his forehead on hers. Icy eyes search hers as he cups her ass like he knows damn well her legs won't hold her anymore. There's no trace of a smile, but his eyes

—pale blue, ghostly—spark with mirth. Mirth, and something else.

Desire?

"Babe." He brushes hair from her face with a work-callused hand. "Need something?"

CHAPTER 7

*I*t's possible he overplayed his hand.

But the instant the fib slipped from Jen's lips, he had a duty to save her.

Duty. Who is he kidding? He's wanted to kiss her since the first time he saw her. Wants to kiss her still, if he's being honest.

Since she's staring in stunned awe, it's on him to fill the silence. Cuddling her close, he extends a hand to the smug bastard who brought this on. "Dan Goodman," he says. "You're Johnny?"

"Uh—" The idiot looks unsure. "Yes! Dan, good to meet you!" He clasps Dante's hand in a too-tight grip, an obvious power move. An excuse to squeeze harder, so Dante does.

Johnny pales and tries to pull his hand back. "I've heard so much about you."

A blatant untruth, but useful. Now he knows how the man looks lying through his teeth. "Same. I've heard plenty." He flicks a glance at the too-pale blonde, who squirms and glances away.

He looks back at Jen, since she's more interesting. "I was just coming to ask what I should make for dinner."

Chest heaving, she stares like he might be on the menu. "Um, well." She blushes. "Were you craving something special?"

"Yes." He lets the word hang there, throbbing with meaning.

"Right." She licks her lips again. "Well, um—pasta?"

The blonde perks up. "A chance to use your gift."

Her accent is moneyed Brit. He remembers they haven't been introduced. "Dan." He holds out a hand.

"Penelope." She folds her fingers into his palm, and it's like gripping a small dead bird. "Pleased to meet you."

"Likewise." He lets go and studies Jen. "Want me to make my special cream sauce?"

"I love your cream sauce." Her cheeks go redder, and it takes all his self-control not to kiss her again.

Since she set it up, he may as well run with it. "I know you do." He nuzzles her neck, blood warming as she melts in his arms and clutches his chest again.

He could get used to this.

"Well." Johnny clears his throat. "We won't take any more of your time." He backs up, bumping into the barn. "By the way. I had drinks with my financial advisor in Bend last night. He's urging me to move fast with separating our assets."

Jen slumps against him. Dante holds her tighter and focuses on Johnny. "You were in Bend last night?"

"I hosted a wine event there." He frowns. "Why?"

Dante shrugs. "Just wondering how the roads are."

Not true. He's wondering if the man has an alibi for the moment a rock crashed through Jen's window. He makes a mental note to put a tracker on the asshole's car. Surveillance isn't his specialty, but he knows a guy. Rumor has it Sebastian's in town.

"Been meaning to get back to Bend," Dante says to fill the silence. "I've got friends in Central Oregon."

"You don't say." Johnny turns back to Jen. "My attorney's

sending you several options for buying me out. We're operating on a pretty tight timeframe, so I'll need you to move quickly."

"Oh." Her voice sounds strained. "Uh, right."

He sees her face falling, so Dante kisses her again. A quick one this time, no tongue. It's still electric.

She comes up blinking at her ex. "I'll watch for that paperwork."

"Great." Pasting on a smile, Johnny holds a hand out to his girlfriend. "Ready?"

"Certainly." The blonde nods to them. "Lovely to see you again, Jennifer. Dan, a pleasure meeting you."

They scurry away, but Dante calls after them. "Don't forget your boxes."

"Right." Johnny scampers back and hoists two of them with effort. Wincing, Penelope picks up the last one, twiggy arms straining.

He should offer to help, but stops when Johnny calls, "Can't believe you still have that damn horse."

So Dante stays where he is, Jen tucked warm against his side. As soon as they're gone, she looks up with apology in her eyes. "I'm so, so, *so*—"

He kisses her again, savoring it this time. There's no audience now. Just the two of them, his tongue grazing hers, Jen moaning softly and clutching his shoulders. Her body curves with his, moving like they're built to fit together. She's softness and strength and so much heat he's dizzy.

When he draws back this time, she sucks in a breath. "They're gone." She blinks like she's spinning. "You didn't have to do that."

"I did."

She looks at him for a long moment. "Thank you."

"Thank *you*."

Closing her eyes, she lets out a long breath. "What am I going to do?"

He's stuck on the kiss, so he doesn't catch her meaning right away. "About the money." He releases her, recalling they meant to talk about this last night. "Guess it's more urgent than you thought."

She closes her eyes, shoulders slumping. "I don't know how to get that kind of cash."

"Your idea about naming the wine," he says. "That's a good one."

"I guess." She looks less certain. "Penelope—she's the one with the industry contacts. The ones we'd need to pull off something like that."

"Ah." He gets it now. "Kinda hard to trust someone who steals your soulmate."

"He wasn't my soulmate." She makes a face. "If I'm being honest, we were swirling the drain way before she showed up. I was thinking of calling off the wedding anyway."

"Huh." Hearing about her love life makes his chest hurt in strange places. So does the thought of an engagement that never made it to the altar.

Another thing they have in common.

Dante clears his throat. "Still no excuse."

"For swooping in and sweeping Johnny off his feet?" Shrugging, she drags the toe of her boot through the dirt. "She claims she didn't know."

"That he wasn't single?"

"We were acting more like siblings or business partners by then. We never had great chemistry, but I hoped—I assumed—" She stops and presses her lips together.

"What?"

Jen sighs. "I'm not exactly the sexy, sultry type. I figured I could work on that, but—"

"The fuck?" He looks at her. "What are you talking about?"

She stares. He's never sworn in front of her. He rarely swears at all, which means he's too rattled for conversation.

But there's no going back now. "Jen, you're the sexiest woman

I know. A guy who doesn't see that has his eyes stuck to his ballsack."

She bursts out laughing, grabbing his arm to stay steady. "That expression," she hoots, still laughing. "My brother used to say that."

Crap. Did he pick that up from Matteo?

"It's an old Dovlanese saying," he offers. "Might not translate very well."

"No, it's great. And thank you for saying so." She shakes her head, taking a few steps back. "And thank you for saving me. You didn't have to, but I'm grateful."

"No problem." Like he did it as a favor.

He kissed her because he's a selfish, stupid bastard who's thinking with his dick or his heart or other parts that shouldn't be running the show.

He needs to focus, so he takes a cue from her and moves back. "Better get to work."

"Mmm." Her eyes sweep his torso and she nods. "You do that."

She walks away, and it takes all his strength not to stare at her pert little butt. He turns away as a gust of wind kicks up. Grabbing the sleeve of his jumpsuit, he pulls it up over his shoulder.

D. Goodman flashes up at him, taunting. It was stitched on the uniform when he found it at a thrift store, so he made up the name to go with it.

But it's not real. None of it's real.

If he's a smart man, he'll remember that.

He trudges back to the barn, not feeling smart at all.

* * *

Matteo calls as Dante's cleaning his Barrett M82. His favorite sniper rifle. One he hasn't used in a while.

He answers on the first ring, impatient as the automated voice explains the source of the call.

This is a call from an inmate at an Oregon correctional facility...

"Good evening." He speaks in clipped Dovlanese, resting the firearm on the battered table. "Everything okay?"

"I'm in prison," Matteo mutters. "Everything's fucking great."

Dante flinches from the kick to his conscience. If he hadn't coaxed Matteo out of hiding for one last job—

"Don't."

Dante blinks. "What?"

"Don't start with the fucking apologies. It's not your fault I'm here, and do we really have to start every conversation like this?"

Probably. Today's guilt might have more to do with kissing Jen than Teo's arrest more than two years ago. "Thanks for the call."

"Yeah, well." Matteo clears his throat. "I got word you needed to be in touch."

God only knows how Matteo's communication channels work behind bars, but Dante's grateful. He rarely waits more than a few hours when he needs to hear from Teo.

"There's been a new development." Dante draws a deep breath. "Your sister's shed burned down."

There's a long pause. "When?"

"A month ago." He probed Jen for details, but she seemed sure it was an accident. Dante's not sure. "Some kind of electrical failure."

Teo's gone quiet. Too quiet. "I'm sorry," Dante says to fill the silence. "I know you hoped whatever was in there might—"

"Don't."

Right. It's not safe to talk about this on prison phone lines. Still, he needs to say something. "You don't belong behind bars. It's my fault you're there."

"Well, that's just fucking stupid."

"Matteo—"

"Dante, I'm done with this discussion. We'll find another way."

So. That's that. He's not sure what to say. He'd like to apologize again, but Teo cuts him off. "Tell me what's going on with Jen."

That, he can do. He catches Teo up on the rock through the window, the visit from the hotel people. The meeting with Johnny.

He leaves out the kiss, swallowing large lumps of guilt. "I checked Johnny's alibi," Dante adds. "He wasn't lying about the wine event."

"You sure?"

"Saw an Instagram shot of the prick pouring wine in Bend last night. Another one from brunch this morning."

He'd never been on Instagram. It took Dante an hour to learn how to poke around. Matteo could have hacked Johnny's account in two seconds while fast asleep.

"Huh." Matteo's thinking the same thing he is. It's a three-hour drive from here to Central Oregon. Odds aren't good the asshole drove home to hurl a rock through Jen's window and hustled back for eggs Benedict.

"Other suspects?" Matteo asks.

"I'm checking into it." He remembers Rhett the lawyer. "The attorney—you sent him?"

"Yes. He's shady."

"Good." He considers that. "He can be trusted to help her?"

"Yes." Matteo pauses. "So can you."

He hesitates, not sure if it's a question. The Dovlanese language tilts up at the end the same way a query would in English, but he still can't tell.

"I'll keep her safe." At least that's true. "I'll protect her with my life." Also true, though he winces at the feeling in his voice.

Matteo hears it, too. "You're not getting attached, are you?"

"I don't do attachments."

Silence follows. Dante's sure he noticed it's not a proper answer.

"She's vulnerable," Matteo says at last. "Nicole, she can take care of herself, but Jen—"

"Jen's tougher than you think."

The words surprise him. Teo, too, since he takes his time responding.

"You met days ago," he says slowly. "You know her better than I do?"

He needs to tread carefully. "I think losing you to prison and your grandma to—" He's actually not sure how Nondi died. "To the great beyond." He draws a breath and keeps going. "And losing her boyfriend to another woman—all of that required tremendous strength."

Matteo stays silent. Scary silent. The clock on the bunkhouse wall ticks ten seconds. Twenty.

"She saw our parents murdered."

Dante flinches. "How old?"

"Three. I wasn't there. Neither was Nicole, but Jen saw it all. Hid in a closet while thugs gunned them down."

Jesus. When he finds his voice, it cracks on the first try. "I can't imagine."

"She might seem tough, but she's been through a lot. Losing Nondi hit her harder than anyone. She doesn't need more trauma."

Dante hears the threat. Maybe not a threat. Could be his own guilty conscience. "I'll keep her safe," he says again.

"Do." Matteo pauses. "Thank you."

He closes his eyes again, reminding himself he hasn't gone too far. That he can step back and keep things professional with Jen.

"Any luck tracking down—"

"No." Matteo's voice sounds tight. "Not yet."

There's no need to say more. Teo's been tracking the cop who stuck him behind bars. Looking for justice or a way out. Dante does what he can to help, but it's not easy. Last he heard, Detec-

TAWNA FENSKE

tive Reggie Dowling left the Seattle police force. Transferred, or got out of cop life entirely? Dante's not sure.

"We'll figure it out." He hunts for something reassuring to say. "I heard Sebastian might be back on the West Coast. We could bring him in to help."

Matteo gives a low growl. "Forget about me. Keep your eyes on my sister."

"Of course." He squeezes his eyes shut. The opposite of what he's meant to do. "You can trust me."

His fingers brush the rifle as he hunts for something else to say.

Then a scream splits the night, and he bolts from his chair.

CHAPTER 8

*J*en stares at pools of sticky red, a lake of liquid lit by moonbeams.

Gone. Just…*gone*, forever.

The tasting room door slams open and Dan crashes through. There's a pistol in his hand and a fierceness in his eyes that steals her breath. He's shirtless again, because of course.

Jen steadies herself on the tasting room bar. "The Cabernet," she says. "Someone broke in and smashed all four barrels."

His eerie blue eyes sweep the ground, but he doesn't lower the pistol. The sight of it makes her shudder, makes her realize how lethal he is. How virile. If her last hope of financial freedom weren't swirling down the drain, she might appreciate it.

"Did you hear anything?" He prowls the room, stalking behind barrels, peering in corners. "Breaking glass, the sound of a car?"

"Nothing." Surveying the damage, she shudders again. "I only came out because I forgot to top the taster bottles with argon for preservation."

He frowns. "I don't want you walking around alone in the dark."

She shoves her hands in her armpits so he won't see them shaking. "You sound like my brother. I'm a big girl, Dan. I have a gun, too, you know."

He gives her a long look, probably guessing it's back in the house. She shivers and his eyes soften. "Are you okay?"

"Physically? Sure."

Emotionally, she's a wreck. What the hell will she do? "Maybe I should throw in the towel."

He nods, tucking the gun away as he surveys the damage. "Towels are good, but we'll need more than that to clean this up. A hose, maybe, or—"

"No, I mean quit." She studies the lake on the floor. "Doesn't it seem like signs are all pointing to this whole thing being a terrible idea? Like if I sold to the hotel group or Johnny, at least I'd walk away with cash. I could start over."

Dan stares at her for a long time. "Is that what you want?"

Of course it's not what she wants. But how is it practical hanging on to this land, this business, with every force of nature plotting against her?

Biting her lip, she pictures her grandma with a basket on her hip gathering greens from the same patch where Jen pulled radishes for dinner. Just north of there, Nic convinced Matteo to learn the Macarena, the two of them laughing and lurching through grapevines as Jen giggled in the grass.

She remembers the memorial, Nic in a red dress because Nondi loved color. Jen shivering beside her, a gauzy green dress billowing graceless around her knees. The smell of wet grass and spring onion and damp earth sucking their sandals. The shadow of rain clouds smothering the barn. Matteo mourning miles away behind bars, helpless to hold his sisters.

He'll never forgive himself for not being there, and that hurts Jen's heart most of all. She shuts her eyes tight, recalling the squeeze of her sister's hand that day.

"No," she murmurs now. "It's not what I want." When she

opens her eyes, he's watching her. "Not what my family would want, either."

He looks at her, *really* looks. So deep into her eyes that she swears he sees the back of her skull.

"Then we'll make it work." He gives a grim nod. "We'll find a way, okay?"

She nods, somehow believing him. "Okay."

"Hey." He takes a step closer, slipping an arm around her waist. "Don't cry."

She didn't realize she was, but yep, her cheeks feel wet. Not for the lost wine, but for her family. What this means for their legacy. Swiping a hand over her face, she takes a shaky breath.

"You know what my grandma used to say?"

"What?"

"Feel the sadness, then stomp the shit out of it." She laughs. "Probably an Italian saying that got lost in translation."

"Dovlanese, actually." He shrugs. "They're neighboring countries. There's lots of crossover."

"Huh." She swipes her eyes again. "Anyway, she'd say that, and then she'd take me to Eve's English Tea Room, and we'd eat ridiculously small sandwiches and drink Earl Grey and pretend to be fancy until we laughed so hard we forgot what made us sad."

He's still watching her, eyes missing nothing. For a moment, she thinks he might kiss her again. She hates the deep hunger in her core.

Instead, he steps away. "Let's go."

"What?"

"The tea house—it's still there?"

She blinks. "Sure, but it's after ten."

"We'll go tomorrow." He pauses. "Unless you'd rather go alone or with your sister or—"

"I want you." She winces. "I didn't mean it like that."

But she did, and they both know it. She can tell by the way he steps back, making space so it can't happen. Not tonight. "We should call the police."

She closes her eyes. Deep breath in, then out. "Please, no."

"Jen." His voice is so soft she looks up.

His eyes are soft, too. "Your brother. You said he's in prison."

The lump in her throat keeps her from speaking, so she nods instead.

"That has something to do with why you don't like the police?"

She nods again, finding her voice. "He was framed."

Dan's expression goes dubious, and she knows how it sounds. "It's true," she insists. "I could never prove it, but I did some digging." She might not be tough like Nic and Teo, but Jen's a scrappy snoop. "The cop—a guy named Reggie Dowling. He transferred someplace else, but I'm sure he's behind what happened to Teo and…"

As Dan's face darkens, she trails off. It sounds crazy, she knows that.

"It doesn't matter." She forces a tight laugh. "He doesn't even work in this precinct, so it's not like he'd show up here if I called 911."

Dan doesn't answer right away. "This Dowling guy—you know for sure he's still in law enforcement?"

She shrugs and tries to think of how to end this line of discussion. "I don't know for sure." A pause as she decides how much to share. "I drove to Southern Oregon last week to buy barrels at a vineyard down there. Could have sworn I saw him at a stoplight. He was definitely driving a cop car."

"Really." His voice is flat and impossible to read.

"It's probably nothing. I didn't even tell my brother because he gets all weird about this stuff. It's nothing, I'm positive." If she says "it's nothing" one more time, he'll know she's nuts. "Really, it's not a big deal."

He's quiet a long time. "If you feel strongly about something, it's a big deal."

"No, it's fine." She wipes her eyes and takes a deep breath. "You're right, we should call police."

She'd rather not, but there's not much choice. This is an attack on her business. If she wants to be a businesswoman, she needs to protect it. Sighing, she slips her phone out of her pocket. "I'll call insurance, too."

He nods. "Let me help." Dan doesn't wait for instruction. Reaching out, he gently pries the mop from her hands. "I've got this."

Let me help.

I've got this.

If men only knew those words mean more than the ones most guys use to get into women's pants. Or heart. Or—all right, this isn't helping. It's not why Dan's doing it, either. As he sets to work swabbing her floors, he starts to hum. His bare chest flexes, and her breath catches in her throat.

"I'll...um...make those calls now." She backs away, head reeling with loss and longing, with heartache and hunger. Rivaling emotions that don't go together.

Just like her and Dan.

She needs to remember that before her heart gets carried away. Taking a breath, she turns with her phone, leaving the man mopping in moonlight.

It's an image burned in her brain forever.

* * *

JEN RAPS THE BUNKHOUSE DOOR, then checks her watch. "We don't have to do this today," she calls. "You were just being nice about the tearoom, but I totally understand if you don't want—"

Her voice falters as the door swings open. Her heartbeat trips and drops. There's surely a way to pick her jaw up off the floor, but she's not sure how to close her mouth. Or how to stop staring at the handsome, uniformed gentleman filling the doorway.

"Guh," she manages, and Dan smiles.

"I wasn't sure about the dress code." He smooths down the front of his uniform, a crisp navy number lined with brass buttons. "Kept some uniforms from my palace security days. I'll change if it's too much."

"No!" She practically shouts as she grabs his arm. "It's perfect. You look great! Amazing!"

Stop yelling, Jen.

Dan nods and eyes her up and down. "You look very nice."

"Thank you." She drops her hand and surveys the sundress she found at the back of her closet. She'd forgotten she owned it, and self-consciousness squiggles in her belly. "My grandma and I always dressed up for these dates. I'm a little out of practice."

His gaze trails over her again, lingering on her bare arms. "You're beautiful in yellow. Regal."

Heat rushes her face and chest, turning her into a tomato. Very fetching. "You ready?"

"Yes, ma'am." He locks the door, a reminder to Jen she should do the same. "Hang on, I'll be right back."

She scurries past the barn and to her front door to check. By the time she reaches the parking area, Dan's ambling around the tasting room with a frown. "Did the insurance adjuster make it out this morning about the wine mess?"

"He just left." She shrugs. "Not a lot to go on."

"Like the police."

"Right." She fights the urge to feel crestfallen. Last night's visit from local law enforcement didn't leave her brimming with confidence, either. "Maybe the fingerprints will pan out."

"Maybe."

She doubts it, but no sense sharing that with Dan. "Come on. I thought we'd take the Spider."

He stops walking and stares. "The Spider." He blinks a few times. "The—it's not an Alfa Romeo Spider, is it?"

"It's my brother's," she admits, wondering why he's rattled. "A 1973. He asked me to look after it, so I drive it sometimes."

"Wow." Dan starts walking again, falling into step beside her. "That's a classic."

"My brother's pride and joy." She sounds sadder than she means to, so she forces some pep into it. "We restored it together. Matteo, Nicole, me—even Grandma got in on the action."

"Family's everything." He mumbles the words somewhat cryptically, and Jen wants to ask about his. She doesn't know if he has brothers or sisters back in Dovlano.

But before she can ask, he's peering at the keypad that opens the garage. "Very high-tech."

"My brother installed it. He's sort of a security geek."

Dan doesn't react. Just inspects the keypad and frowns. "Who else has the code?"

"Johnny, I guess." She winces. "Probably some workers from past harvest seasons. I should change it."

"I'll do it when we get back." He hesitates. "If you want."

"I want. Thank you."

He walks around to the passenger side, and Jen conceals a smile. The few times she took Johnny in the Spider, he insisted on driving. A guy thing. She hesitates, then holds up the keys. "Did you want to drive?"

Dan frowns. "Are you not comfortable?"

"No, I just thought—" She pauses, unsure what she meant to say. "It's a fun car. Thought you might like to try."

He opens the passenger door. "And take away your fun?"

She's still standing there as he clambers in, adjusting the seat to accommodate long legs. He whistles low while surveying the dash. "Very well-maintained."

"Can you send my brother a letter saying so?" She laughs and slides behind the wheel. "I swear he's more worried about his car than his sisters."

"I doubt that." His voice sounds tight as he meets her eyes. "I doubt that very much."

Rattled, she shoves the key in the ignition. The engine roars on the first try, and she lets it warm up for a minute. She's conscious of how close he's sitting, how she could reach out right now and touch his—

"I need to apologize," he says.

Jen blinks. "For what?"

"For kissing you. I got carried away."

She laughs and shakes her head. "I'm the one who lied to Johnny and Penelope. I left you no choice."

His eerie eyes hold hers. "There's always a choice."

"Right." She licks her lips and watches his eyes darken. "We should—um—go."

Or go back in the house and into the bedroom and—

"Jen." He hesitates, then touches her hand on the gearshift. "I want you to know I respect you."

Laughter spurts out of her. "Got it. Message received, don't worry." She's heard that her whole life.

I respect you.

I admire you.

You're such a hard worker.

Compliments, to be sure. She takes pride in her work ethic, so it shouldn't sting knowing she'll never hear those other compliments.

I want you.

I desire you.

I'm so fucking hot for you that I can't—

"Did I say something wrong?" Dan frowns. "I meant it as a compliment."

"I know that. Don't worry." She needs to get out of here.

Shoving the car in reverse, she backs up without looking. Flustered, she checks her mirrors with heat in her cheeks.

Dan's eyes follow her as she backs cautiously onto the gravel, then turns and aims down the driveway. She's a competent driver, a savvy businesswoman, a hard worker.

She doesn't need to be the object of anyone's lust.

As she hits the road with Dan's gaze searing her, she reminds herself this can't go anywhere with Dan. Shouldn't go anywhere.

Keep telling yourself that.

She will. She absolutely will.

CHAPTER 9

$\mathcal{H}$e's not sure what he said wrong in the garage, but he needs to be careful. He's riding in Matteo's car, wearing an ankle holster with a Sig P365 the man bought him for his birthday. The last thing Dante should do is lust after Teo's sister.

But that's exactly what's happening in his mind and his heart and other parts he'd rather not think about seated beside a lady. Fumbling for a safe subject, he grabs the first thought that flops on the floor of his brain.

"Tell me about your grandmother."

She flicks him a leery glance. "What do you want to know?"

"You said she's Italian. Maternal grandma, yes?"

"Yes." She presses her lips together and guides the car around a curve in the road. "My father came from Dovlano. My parents met in Rome but settled near the Dovlanese capital."

He wonders if they crossed paths at some point. Maybe he rode his tricycle past her house.

Then he remembers he never had a tricycle, or anything like a normal childhood. "What brought your grandmother to America?"

Jen doesn't answer right away. Her fingers curl tight around the steering wheel, and he watches her weighing her words. "We have—*had*—ties to organized crime. My family, I mean. I was too young to understand. My grandma arrived here with a lot of money she invested right away in real estate. When my parents died—" Her voice cracks, and Dante looks over.

She tilts her chin up and keeps going. "When my parents died, Nondi invited us to come here."

"Was there a grandfather in the picture?"

She shakes her head, eyes on the road as she switches lanes. "He died before I was born."

That's a lot of death in one family. He files that away, wondering if crime ties explain what's happening at her vineyard. "Your siblings—"

"Tell me about you." She shoots him a shy glance, then darts her gaze back at the road. "I feel like I'm always talking about myself or my family. I want to know about you."

Dread curdles his guts. "Not much to tell. Parents died when I was a kid. Forged papers got me into the Dovlanese military at fifteen."

Admitting to forgery isn't his best idea, but it's the reason he's had such a colorful career for someone so young. Not that she knows his age. Or his career.

Jen's quiet beside him. "So you're an orphan, too."

"Yes."

"It changes you; don't you think?"

"Probably." His chest aches, and he wonders how growing up parentless made him a gruff, lethal savage, while Jen grew up sweet and kind and beautiful and tough as fucking nails.

He senses she wants him to say something, but he's not sure what. As silence yawns, he hears himself blurting, "I suppose I have trust issues."

Where did that come from? He sounds like a fucking self-help book, but Jen just nods. "I understand. You'd think I would, too,

83

and maybe I ought to. Shouldn't have trusted Johnny, anyway."
She gives a brittle laugh that breaks his heart. "But I like seeing
the good in people. Especially people who don't see it in
themselves."

His chest squeezes so tight he can't breathe. He's never felt
this urgent need to touch another person. Hold her hand, hold
her body against his. He hardly knows her. What's wrong
with him?

Dante clears his throat. "Never change."

"What?" She drags her gaze off the road and stares at him.
"What was that?"

"You." He swallows back another lump. "It's a rare gift, seeing
good things in people."

"Thanks." Her eyes seem brighter as they skip back to the
road. "Not sure it's served me well, but it's who I am."

He's deciding on a response when she hits her turn signal and
spins into a parking lot. "Here we are." She claims a spot near the
door of a towering Tudor cottage with white gingerbread trim.
"It's a little fussy, but the food's good."

"Fussy I can manage." He's not sure what fussy means, but
there's not much he can't manage. He grabs the door handle as
she grabs him. His arm, not other parts.

Her green eyes glitter as she grips his wrist and offers a small
smile. "Thanks for doing this. I'm sure taking your employer to a
tearoom isn't your idea of a fun time."

"Maybe it is." He's never tried it, but there's not much he
wouldn't love with Jen by his side. He'd happily use his dick as a
cleaning rod for a rocket launcher if she stood by with the
gun oil.

There's a message for a Valentine's card. Besides, she said
"employer." That's the message he should focus on.

She's reminding him this isn't a date. That the kiss in the
barnyard was just for show. That her hand on his wrist now
means nothing.

Slipping from her grip, he opens the car door and marches around to get hers, but she's too quick. Jen's out and striding for the door. He scans the parking lot, squinting at shrubs for hidden shooters. He's conscious of the weapon at his ankle as he angles his body to shield her. There's a throwing knife between his shoulder blades, and he calculates how quickly he could get it. Not that tearooms are hotbeds of crime, but that's the reason to be watchful.

As he follows Jen into the lobby, a plump woman in an apron steps from behind a counter. She wears a small blue hat frothing with white feathers and she smiles at Jen. Then blinks as she takes in Dante. He does his best to look small and unthreatening, even forcing a smile.

The woman blushes and regards Jen. "Florence Davies, madam. How may I help you?"

The English accent sounds real. Yorkshire, maybe.

Jen rests a hand on the counter. "I have a reservation for two. Jennifer Bello."

"Jennifer. Of course!" Florence laughs and scans Jen with her eyes. "Almost didn't recognize you, dear. It's not often I see you dressed up like this."

Jen's cheeks glow as she bites her lip. "Yes, well. It's a special occasion."

"I see, I see." Florence scans a satin-wrapped datebook and makes a note. "We've got a lovely table for you in the atrium. Right this way."

Jen hoists her purse and follows Florence down a hall. Dante follows, watching Jen's back. He's keeping her safe, not noticing how the sundress drapes low between her shoulder blades, skimming freckled skin he aches to kiss.

But he's not doing that. He's surveying a table ringed with small girls in princess dresses. Age six, maybe seven, judging by bright pink birthday balloons dotted with the digit. His gaze sweeps the table, taking in a dozen pigtailed heads, the sea of tiny tea sandwiches, the ripple of girl giggles. Not a threat, but he catalogues it all to be thorough. One girl looks up, cinnamon pigtails swaying under her tiara. She spots Dante and gasps.

"The prince!" She throws white-gloved hands to her chest. "Prince Harrington has come to slay the dragon."

Dante looks around for a dragon. Doesn't see one, and he's almost sure that's not a codeword. He tips his hat, prompting peals of laughter and a startled blink from one tiny blonde who stares at his scar.

He puts his hat back on fast. "Ladies."

That gets more giggles. A dark-skinned girl with pink beads on her braids sets down a half-eaten cookie. "Where's your horse?"

"In the barn." That's where he last saw Maple. "Where's your horse?"

The girl huffs an impatient sigh. "Only the *prince* has a white horse. I'm a princess."

"Huh." Not a rule he's heard before. "What kind of horse does a princess have?"

She shrugs as another girl sneaks the half-eaten cookie off her plate. "Dunno. I've only been a princess since today."

"You're a natural." He glances at Jen, who's stopped to watch. He directs his attention back to the young royal. "Seems like a princess should have any color horse she wants."

The girl considers this. "Purple?"

"Sure."

"Pink?"

"Okay."

"Rainbow stripes with—"

"Yes, absolutely."

The blonde who spotted his scar speaks up. "Do you need a necklace?"

Dante frowns. "A necklace?"

She points to a bowl piled with plastic beads. "They're real diamonds and rubies and emeralds."

"I see that." He pauses, not sure what etiquette calls for.

Florence steps in to save him. "Your table is this way." Smiling, she touches his elbow. "Your Highness."

He nods and follows her into the atrium, dragging a hand down the row of metal buttons on his uniform. More giggles flutter from the princess table behind him.

"That was very sweet," Jen whispers. "You do sort of look like a prince."

He's not sure what to say, so he settles for pulling out her chair. One of two chairs at the tiny corner table draped in white lace. Dusty rose placemats hold cups and saucers and the tiniest forks he's ever seen. In the center sits a three-tiered silver stand filled with teacakes and buttery slabs of shortbread.

Florence sweeps a hand over the spread. "Will this be all right?"

"Wonderful, thank you." Jen drapes a napkin on her lap and smiles. "I already know what I want, but Dan needs a menu."

"Of course." Florence sweeps one off a dark oak side table, along with a flowered teapot. "Here you are now. Do make yourselves cozy."

Dante takes the menu and a seat in the second chair, angling it so his back's to the wall. The Sig feels heavy at his ankle, and he checks to be sure it's not showing. It isn't, but he adjusts his pant leg anyway. The chair creaks beneath him, and when he straightens, his knee bangs the table. He bites back a Dovlanese curse as Jen giggles.

"I don't think these tables are built for guys your size." She leans close, treating him to the scent of honey and sweet hay. "Turn your teacup over so she can fill it."

"Oh. Right." He grabs the fragile white china and flips it in his palm, admiring a ring of painted roses on the saucer.

Florence tuts and lifts a matching teapot. "My my," she

murmurs as she fills his cup. "That cup is a wee thimble in your hand."

Dante watches Jen press her lips together as a flush moves up her neck. "The sandwich list is at the bottom of the menu," she says. "We each choose three. They're pretty small."

He nods and studies the tidy row of script. Cucumber and smoked salmon. Cheese and chutney. Egg salad and watercress. His stomach rumbles as he sets down the menu. "I'll have whatever you're having."

Jen smiles at Florence and hands her Dante's menu. "The first three are my favorite," she says. "Could we also get the crumpets with jam and clotted cream?"

"Right away, dear." Florence tucks the menu under her arm and floats away, leaving Dante alone with Jen.

Jen and her lovely, freckled shoulders with small bows securing her dress in place. He could die from all this sweetness. Instead, he grabs the tiny tongs from the sugar dish. "Need a cube?"

"Please." She nudges her teacup toward him and picks up a small pitcher. "Milk?"

"Sure." It's how they drank it in the court of Dovlano. Not that he normally took tea with the Duke, but he knew the etiquette. Knew to watch the teacups so no one could slip poison inside. He sometimes tested to be sure.

Stirring his tea with a spoon the size of his pinkie, he watches Jen's face. "Your grandma brought you here?"

Jen picks up her cup. "The first time we came, I was still pretty young." As she takes a sip, her face softens. "We'd just arrived from Dovlano. Our parents died before we moved, and I was this scared, orphaned girl in a strange country living with a grandma I didn't know at all."

"Sounds hard."

"It was." Her lashes flutter. "Matty and Nic settled right in. They were older, but I was small and scared of everything. One morning, Nondi showed me her closet of princess dresses and told me to pick one. That she was taking me someplace special."

He pictures the table full of tiny princesses in the next room and feels his heart squeeze. "Just the two of you?"

"Yes. It was my first time doing anything in America without my brother or sister." She laughs and brushes hair off her face. "I felt so grown up getting to order whatever I wanted. I'm sure I looked silly with my skinned knees and dirty fingernails and hair I'd tried to put up in this fancy bun. Grandma took a picture, and when I saw it later, it looked like someone stuck a cinnamon roll on my head. At the time, though—I felt like the prettiest girl in the world."

You're still the prettiest girl in the world.

It's true, but he can't say it. Can't cross that line with his boss. His best friend's sister. He clears his throat. "My grandfather taught me to shoot. Target practice," he adds in case she's picturing a six-year-old assassin. "Lined cans up along the pasture fence and clapped every time I got close to hitting one. I was a terrible shot, but the way he carried on about how great I was—I felt like an expert marksman."

Jen's green eyes search his. "Isn't that funny? How someone telling you you're pretty or gifted or great at something makes it all feel different?"

He nods and picks up his teacup, surprised to see his hands aren't steady. He covers it, but not before a dribble of Earl Grey splashes the saucer. "So." He sips his tea. "Fundraising."

Her eyes dim as she looks down at her teacup. "Right. I guess we can forget auctioning off the Cab."

Recalling the sticky lake of red on the tasting room floor, he frowns. "There must be something else we could try. Another way to earn a lot of money quick."

She picks a piece of shortbread off the tiered tray, setting it on her plate with a sigh. "There's not enough wine inventory to do a big tasting event. Not until after harvest. After Leslie has a chance to make more."

"Leslie?"

"My new winemaker. You'll meet her next week."

Dante makes a mental note to check out Leslie. Search records for criminal history, search her car for any rocks scrawled with practice notes. "Harvest happens in September or October?"

"Usually." She makes a face. "It's a crapshoot, honestly. You can do everything right and still end up having to scrap a hundred acres of grapes. It happened to a friend of mine—a vine-yard owner in Roseburg. She lost half her harvest to wildfire last week."

"They burned?"

"Not burned." She takes a small sip of tea. "She lives miles from the fire, but the smoke got to the grapes. They're not usable for wine. Not even for grape juice. She'll probably have to give them away as pig feed or something."

"That's unfortunate." He considers how fragile wine grapes must be.

Jen sets down her teacup. "Anyway, I guess my situation could be worse?"

The hopefulness in her voice makes him nod. "Could be."

Surely there's some way to help. He's not used to feeling this useless. "Maybe there's another sort of fundraiser you could try. Something quick and easy."

"You have ideas?"

He considers the question, combing his brain for options. "What about bare-knuckle boxing?"

Her brow furrows. "You want me to punch Johnny?"

Not a bad plan, but no. "We could hold a tournament and charge money. Or what about kickboxing? I could teach a class for—"

"Um, do you have any ideas that don't involve violence?" Her laugh holds a nervous edge. "No offense, but I don't think this is in line with vineyard branding."

"Yeah, I get it." He shrugs. "Just remembering what your grandma said about stomping the shit out of sadness."

Jen gasps. "That's it!" She smacks a palm on the table, making teacups bounce. "A grape stomp. Dan, you're *brilliant*."

He stares, not certain what he's said that's smart. "Grape stomp?"

"Yes, it's perfect." She's bouncing so much her napkin hits the floor. "I buy my friend's smoked-out grapes at a discount. She'd maybe even give them to me."

Dante frowns. "What would you make with them?"

"Nothing, that's not the point. We'd hold a grape stomp for the public. Make it an old-fashioned harvest festival and charge money for people who want to whip off their shoes and take a turn stomping grapes."

"With their feet?"

"Yes! The timing might even be right to send finalists to the National Grape Stomp Cooperative. We can charge an entry fee, plus have food booths and wine and even carnival games. But it all centers around the grape stomp."

He frowns, struggling to wrap his brain around this. "People pay money for this? Squishing grapes with their toes?"

"It's the novelty of it. People love that sort of thing."

"Novelty." He rolls the word around on his tongue, making a mental note to look it up later. "This could work."

"It could." She beams at him. "You're a genius, Dan."

"Me?" He scowls. "Don't do that."

Jen blinks. "Do what?"

"Sell yourself short. It was your idea. All you. Don't give me credit for your smart thinking."

She opens her mouth like she's ready to argue, then stops. "You're right. I do that. My grandma even said so." Her face twists as she studies her plate. "That I sell myself short."

"Then it's time to change that." He plucks a tea cake from the tower and wonders what's taking so long with the sandwiches. A crash from the kitchen shoots his hand to his ankle. As his fingers brush steel, Florence hustles around the corner. "I'm so sorry. It's a stell."

"What's a stell?" Dante looks at Jen, whose face holds more sympathy than fear. "Is it dangerous?"

Jen gives a limp laugh. "*Estelle*. An old woman with dementia. She's convinced she's an English countess."

Florence makes a fretful noise. "She got into the kitchen this time. Tossed an entire tray of sandwiches saying the watercress isn't fresh and did we use proper English pumpernickel? I called her son, but he's not picking up."

Jen chews her lip. "She's getting worse." She turns to him. "Estelle's harmless. Mostly. Reminds me a little of my grandma."

Before he can reply, a white-haired woman in a nightgown wobbles down the hall. Her gnarled hand grips a cane like a scepter, and her cardboard crown is askew. On her feet are a pair of tattered slippers with plastic gems glued to the toes.

"There you are." Estelle waves the cane, narrowly missing a wall sconce. "Fetch me my footman. I've a list ten kilometers long of each task we must accomplish before the royal ball."

When no one leaps, she jabs the cane again, making Florence gasp. "Don't just sit there! We have a mere fortnight to prepare."

Dante looks at Florence. She's tapping her phone, maybe messaging the son. The princesses in the next room have gone silent. Jen bites her lip, sympathy in her eyes.

He's on his feet in an instant. Maybe he doesn't know this woman or what it's like to have dementia.

But he knows nobility, so he sweeps off his hat and drops to one knee. "My lady." He bows deeply, catching her gnarled hand in his. "Daniel Wutheringshire Goodman, Esquire, at your service."

CHAPTER 10

*J*t's the moment Jen thinks she might love him.

Dan, or the footman he's impersonating as he kneels in his crisp uniform at the feet of the stooped old woman. Estelle watches in wonder. Jen's seen the old lady's outbursts before, but never a response like Dan's.

He's speaking again, and Jen sits straighter. Dan's still bowing, planting a reverent kiss across Estelle's knotted knuckles.

"How may I be of service, my lady?"

The woman's cloudy eyes glow with a mix of joy and bewilderment.

"Young man." She drums her cane on the ground, knocking the Burger King crown from her head. "On your feet at once. I need someone to fetch my hat."

Jen fumbles for the fallen crown, but Dan beats her to it. "Madam." He gets to his feet and whips his napkin off the table. Draping it over one arm, he lays the crown on the mauve linen in a regal display.

"Your headwear, my lady?"

Estelle nods in wonder. "Indeed, it is."

"Shall I place it for you?"

The old woman straightens. "You may."

Dan arranges the crown on Estelle's wild nest of white hair. His tenderness lodges a lump in Jen's throat. It takes three tries to swallow it back.

He bows again and addresses Estelle. "Your ladyship. May I assist you in donning your cape?"

There's no cape in sight, but the old woman nods majestically. "Do be hasty about it, young man."

Dan bows again, then pulls a folded tablecloth off the side table. "Allow me, madam."

Estelle pivots so Dan can drape the fabric on her shoulders. He whips a gold pin off his uniform, fastening it in place. Someone sniffs, and Jen glances over to see Florence dabbing her eyes with a lace hankie.

"Footman," Estelle barks as she turns to face him. "Fetch my pearls."

"Of course, Madam."

Dan doesn't falter. Just strides through the door to the atrium. Jen creeps after him, peering around the corner to see him consulting tiny princesses.

"Your royal highnesses." He bows to them, keeping his cap on. "A word if I may?"

A freckled child with pigtails nods. "Okay."

A girl scowls beside her. "I thought you were a prince. Not a— what's a footman?"

A frosting-smeared blonde pipes up. "It's his secret disguise."

That seems to satisfy them. The blonde nibbles a cookie and watches Dan with curious eyes.

"Most noble ladies," he continues. "Countess Estelle of Castle Watershire hath bid me to request a strand of your most precious gems as a token of peace between your two nations. Wilt thou assist her?"

The pigtailed birthday girl scrunches her nose, but the girl with pink-beaded braids grabs a bowl of plastic necklaces. They're the kind Jen's seen at Dollar General, and the girl holds them out. "Does the Countess like pink or purple?"

Estelle fluffs her hair. "I prefer pink."

Dan gives a solemn nod. "Then it shall be so."

The girl retrieves a string of pink plastic beads and hands them over. "Tell her they're magical beads," she whispers.

"I shall indeed." Dan bows again, then takes the necklace as he turns back to the atrium. "Lady Estelle, your gemstones?"

"Very good." She tilts her head to let him slip them around her scrawny neck. The crown slips off, and Jen grabs it.

"My lady." She stands and replaces the headwear. "Wilt thou join us for a bit of refreshment?"

As accents go, Jen's is terrible, but Estelle's eyes dance. "I certainly do enjoy a good watercress sandwich."

Florence backs away, scurrying to the kitchen. "I'll be just two shakes of a lamb's tail."

Dan returns to the princess table and negotiates the procurement of an empty chair. Jen scoots aside to make room as he settles Estelle at the head of the table. He's closer now as he takes the seat beside her, knee brushing Jen's.

"Tea, my lady?" He's pouring as Estelle nods. "Perhaps a short-bread biscuit?"

"Two, please." Estelle smiles her crooked smile, and Jen sees the woman she must have been. A woman like Nondi, feisty and fierce and full of life.

A surge of missing her grandma sucks the breath from her lungs. Maybe she gasps, or maybe Dan reads her mind because he touches her hand beneath the table. "Srontica," he murmurs.

Her brain whirs, then recalibrates. It's not English, it's Dovlanese. One of the only words she knows.

Srontica.

You're wonderful.

Jen blinks hard, hearing Nondi say those words to her.

Matteo, too, and now Dan. How did he know it's what she most needs to hear? With a shuddery breath, she lifts her hand to pile shortbread on Estelle's plate.

The old woman beams. "We must be certain the egg salad sandwiches are made with proper English pumpernickel. None of that American rye bread, you see."

"Certainly." Dan stands and bows. "I'll make haste to the kitchen at once to ensure proper preparation of the royal feast."

"Thank you, good chap." Estelle's smiling as she watches him go. Once he's out of earshot, she turns to Jen with blue eyes sparkling. "Such a man." There's no trace of accent as she shoves a hunk of shortbread in her mouth.

Jen blinks. "I beg your pardon…um, madam?"

"That one." She jabs a bony finger toward the kitchen, then grins with cookie crumbs in her teeth. "Hang onto him, honey. They don't make 'em like that anymore."

Jen swallows hard, certain they're the truest words she's ever heard.

* * *

"That was really nice, what you did for Estelle." They're driving back to the farm with raindrops spattering the windshield. "Making her feel special like that?"

Dan tips his head and looks at her. "She *is* special. Seems right to treat her that way."

"Not everyone thinks like that. Some people get annoyed by her." Not Jen, not ever, though she's never handled her like Dan did. "Hopefully, her son follows through on hiring some in-home help."

"He seemed open to the suggestion."

A lot more open once Dan doffed his hat and towered over him. "You should take better care of your mother."

"I—um, yes." The man's throat moved as he backed up and banged against the wall.

Dan took a step closer. "I'll take it as a personal affront if you don't."

"Right. Um, yes." The guy gulped again. "I'll call about in-home care when I get back to my place."

"Do it now," Dan said.

And the man did. Whipped his phone out right there, dialing a number Dan read from an internet search for senior services.

Jen smiles at the memory. "Anyway, thanks." She takes her eyes off the road long enough to look at him. To remind herself how well he fills out a uniform. "You're a good guy."

He grunts and looks pained. They're approaching the vineyard, and Jen takes it easy up the gravel drive. She babies Matteo's car, needing him to know she can take care of what matters to him. His car. His guns. Her own health and happiness.

As they crest the driveway, she spots a white Porsche SUV. Her heart sinks as Dan tenses beside her. "Who's that?"

She sighs. "Johnny."

"I thought he drove a red Miata."

"He has a zillion cars, each more expensive than the others."

His brow furrows. "And he needs your money *why*?"

She ignores that since she doesn't have an answer. Also because she's focused on pulling into the garage and trying not to clench her jaw.

As she climbs from the car, Dan's there with a helping hand. He hoists her to her feet, slipping an arm around her waist.

"I can walk."

"I know you can." He pulls her closer. "I'm your boyfriend, remember?"

"Right." She'd forgotten, which proves she's a lousy liar.

Leaning into him feels like part of the act, and also, it's nice. He's warm and solid and strong, and when they reach Johnny's car, she's at ease with her body touching his. A girl could get used to this.

Johnny's not at his car, but she spots him peering in a window of the tasting room. Penelope's beside him in a white dress, hands floating at her sides.

A few feet away stands a spotted pig in a polka-dot collar. One black ear, one pink, the rounded body splotched with mottled hues of pink and black. Its corkscrew tail twitches as Jen and Dan approach.

Jen scans the animal, wondering what Johnny's doing now. "Why did you bring me a pig?"

He turns from the window. "It was here when we showed up." He frowns at Dan's uniform. "What are you supposed to be?"

"Alone with my girlfriend."

Jen swallows a smile.

"No, I mean the costume." Johnny drags a hand through the air. "Are you going to some kind of dress-up party?"

Dan stares, not dignifying that with an answer. He doesn't move, but she feels his big, steady hand on her waist.

Her pulse picks up as she finds her voice. "*The pig.*" She points, and the animal cocks its head. The wiry hairs dusting its body seem silver in the sunlight. A sow, she's pretty sure. "You're saying someone dropped it off?"

"Not the first time someone's dumped livestock here. Look." Johnny strides over and nudges the pig with a toe. The creature wobbles and lifts her right front hoof. He nudges again and the sow squeals. "It's injured," he says. "If you want, I could put it out of its miser—"

"No." Dan slams him to the tasting room door before Jen sees him move. "You do not kick, poke, shove, or torment animals on this property. On *any* property. Clear?"

Penelope gasps as Johnny turns an interesting shade of purple. He says nothing, possibly because Dan's pressing a forearm to his throat. Dan drops his arm but grips Johnny's shoulder. "Do. You. Understand?"

Wheezing, Johnny gives a feeble nod. "You're fucking crazy."

Dan flings him aside like a rag doll. "True."

Johnny falls back looking more pissed than scared. Penelope catches his arm, murmuring in her faint British accent. "Let it go, sweetheart."

He glares and shakes her off. "Fucking Neanderthal." He takes some steps back. "Did you see that? I oughtta call the cops."

"About trespassing on my property?" Jen folds her arms. "Good idea. I'll wait here."

Penelope holds her palms up. "Please, let's settle down." She strokes Johnny's arm. "We're just here to grab the wineglasses and we'll get out of your hair."

"Wineglasses?" Dan glares. "What wineglasses?"

"Oh, dear." Penelope frowns at Johnny. "You forgot to call about borrowing stemware for the party?"

"Didn't forget." Johnny kicks a toe through the gravel and the sow skitters back. "Until she buys me out, I still own half the assets. Wineglasses included."

Jen swallows back panic. "I need the stemware. The tasting room's open tomorrow."

"That's my problem?" Johnny flicks a glance at Dan. "Should have thought of that, shouldn't you?"

Dan growls low and fierce. He's poised to lunge when the pig squeals.

Freezing, Dan drops to his knees. He's scratching the sow behind one spotted ear, murmuring in Dovlanese. Jen can't make out the words, but the pig relaxes.

Johnny snorts his disgust. "You should let me put it down. A pig roast would be perfect with an earthy Pinot—"

"You're leaving now." Rising to his feet, Dan makes it happen. With one meaty hand in a vise grip on Johnny's arm, he drags him to the SUV.

"But the glasses—"

"We'll rent." Penelope shoots Jen a guilty look. "I'm so sorry. I really thought he'd cleared it with you."

"It's fine."

"It's not fine. I truly am sorry." She touches Jen's arm, and Jen fights the urge to step back. "He had big dreams for this place. Letting it go has been hard."

Jen swallows a dozen snarky retorts. One about the ease with which Johnny let *her* go, or the audacity of thinking she should surrender her family land for his dreams.

Instead, she takes the high road. "Disappointment doesn't bring out anyone's best self."

"That's so true." Penelope glances back to the SUV where Dan's growling at Johnny. "It's hard seeing the man you love upset."

Jen kind of likes seeing Dan upset, at least when Johnny's the target. Not that she loves Dan.

She sighs. Her ex has a point. Until she pays him off, he does own half this stuff. She looks at Penelope. "How many do you need?"

Penelope pauses. "Four dozen would be lovely. It's just a small dinner party before the wedding rehearsal."

Jen does mental math and calculates how many glasses she can spare. "Would three dozen help?"

"Of course!" Penelope smiles. "We'll bring them back washed first thing the next morning."

"That's fine."

"Truly, we appreciate it." Penelope offers an uncertain smile. "You really should join us at the wedding. Let bygones be bygones and such."

"Thanks. I'm good."

Good as in she'd rather saw off her arm with a butter knife than endure Johnny's wedding. She forces a smile as the pig grunts and sniffs Jen's shoe.

Glancing down, Penelope smiles. "I have some Prada sandals that would be lovely with that dress. If you'd ever like to borrow something a bit dressier, I think we wear the same s—"

"I'm fine." Jen grits her teeth as the pig snuffles her toes. Her pale, pasty toes with uneven nails and chipped polish. "Thank you."

"Don't mention it." Penelope backs toward the tasting room. "Glasses are still in the storage room behind the bar?"

"Yep." Jen pulls the keys from her purse. She unlocks the door but can't bring herself to help load the glasses. This olive branch is enough. She won't walk her good Riedel stemware out the door.

"Thank you, Jennifer." Penelope emerges with a box in her arms. "I'm sorry I'm bungling this so badly. I truly hoped we could be friends."

Guilt pinches her heart and Jen sighs. It's not Penelope's fault she fell for an idiot. Jen's done it herself. "It's fine." While they won't be friends, she doesn't need to be a bitch. "Enjoy the party."

"Thank you."

As Penelope walks toward the SUV, Jen watches Dan with Johnny. Dan's got his arms crossed, biceps flexing as Johnny gets in the driver's seat. Whatever Dan says makes him pale, then pull the door closed quick. Dan drops to one knee and starts to tie his shoe. Glancing around, he slips a hand in his pocket and—

"Pardon me, so sorry." Penelope hustles back for the rest of the glasses, murmuring another batch of apologies as she breezes past.

Jen follows her to the car, watching as Dan scowls at the glassware in Penelope's arms.

"It's okay." Jen touches his arm. "I let them borrow a few for the event."

The scowl deepens. "Why are you doing them favors?"

"It's not a favor. He's probably right he still owns some of this stuff."

"Doesn't give him the right to show up and help himself."

She sighs. "I'm choosing my battles."

Dan lifts an eyebrow. "You get a limited number?"

Johnny backs out fast, spitting gravel at their feet. The pig squeals and tries to move, hoisting its injured leg. Jen crouches to inspect it. "Hey, sweet girl. Let me look okay?"

She's using her soothing voice, and the sow stops edging away. Jen skims her fingers up the animal's leg, relieved not to feel any fractures. Lifting the hoof, she inspects the underside. "Has no one ever trimmed your hooves? You've got the start of a nasty sole ulcer."

Dan drops beside her, shoulders so broad they block the sun. "This happens a lot?"

"Sole ulcers? They're common."

"No, animals just showing up like this."

"Yes." She gently releases the pig's leg. "More often than you'd think."

"What the hell for?"

She inspects the hooves one at a time, relieved they're in good shape. "With pigs, it's usually someone who gets in over their head. They adopt one as a baby and think it'll stay a tiny house pet forever."

"So they bring it *here*?"

She stands and dusts her hands on her dress. "It's a small town. Folks know I help injured animals. They're embarrassed, so they dump them when I'm gone."

His jaw clenches. "I don't like it."

"People abandoning animals?"

"That, yes." A muscle twitches at his temple. "Or strangers wandering the property when you're not home."

Jen sighs. She gets that it's a bad idea, but she won't stop helping creatures who need her. A neighbor down the road posted "no dumping animals" on his fence line, but Jen could never do that. "It's not great, but it's better than the alternative. What people could be doing instead of bringing them to me."

Dan stares. "A bullet between the eyes."

She shivers and nods. "At least someone cared enough to bring her here."

He scans the pig again, watching like he expects a trap door to swing open. A trojan pig. Jen stifles a smile.

His gaze swings back to hers. "How can I help?"

"I could use a hand holding her. If she'll let me trim that hoof back, I can treat it with copper naphthenate and keep her comfortable while it heals."

"Sure. Anything you need."

She shivers again, but for a different reason.

"Keeping it clean might be tricky." She scratches the pig's backside, earning a grunt of pleasure. "I guess we can clean out a stall in the—"

"She'll stay with me. In my bunk where it's clean."

Jen blinks. "You're inviting a strange pig to sleep with you?"

"You're doctoring a strange pig. It's the least I can do." He stoops beside her to rub the sow's ears. Jen does her best not to stare at his hands. Not to wonder what they'd feel like stroking her the way he's drawing a gentle palm down the sow's body.

"Always wanted a pet pig." His voice is low, like he's confessing something.

"She's yours, then."

"Yeah?" The joy on his face is like she's offered nachos and a blowjob.

"All yours." She's definitely not blushing about the blowjob.

"Thanks."

Getting to her feet, she surveys her dress. Dirty handprints smear the cotton, dark splotches marking where she knelt in the dirt. Her sandals look like she dragged them from a tractor, and crescents of chipped pink polish cap each toenail. It's been five months since Nicole treated her to a pedicure. Longer since she did a girly shopping spree.

She sighs and stops staring at her feet. Penelope's right. It's a joke to think she could pull off glamour. This dress, this makeup —it's like putting a pig in a gown. A little girl playing princess, pretending to date the prince.

It wasn't a date. Just lunch with your employee.

She starts toward the barn to grab the hoof nippers. Makes it two steps when Dan catches her arm. "Hey."

Her breath catches. "Hey what?"

"Thanks."

"For what?"

Steely eyes hold hers. "For taking me to the teahouse."

A laugh slips out. "Thanks for being my date." Crap, wrong word. "Not date. I didn't mean it like that."

"Like what?"

Her arm feels hot where he's touching it and the heat spreads to her face. "I wasn't implying anything. It was a professional lunch. A perfectly platonic—"

"Are you done?"

She nods and forgets what she meant to say.

"Good." He clears his throat. "I want to say you're beautiful. Even with dirt on your dress or your shoes or hell—maybe because of it. You're *real*. That makes you beautiful. Fucking majestic. You're so goddamn pretty it hurts my eyes, if you want the truth."

Jen doesn't respond. What can she say? It's the longest string of words he's ever uttered. Maybe the best compliment she's heard. She licks her lips, stalling for a response. For anything better than throwing herself at him and begging to kiss him again.

Johnny's long gone, so there's no need to pretend they're lovers. Kissing him would be unnecessary. Wrong. Foolish. She takes a step back.

"Thank you." She takes a breath and one more step. "That means a lot."

Dan nods. "Sure."

One more step to snap the magnetic pull. To break the urge to throw herself at him. "I'll just get the—" Where was she going again? "Hoof nippers. From the barn. Right now. I'm going."

She spins and runs for the barn, dirty dress swirling at her shins. He's watching her, and she feels it. Feels his gaze like he's touching her, skating a palm down her back.

It's the sexiest touch that never happened.

CHAPTER 11

*I*t's after dark when a knock thumps the bunkhouse door. Dante looks down, deciding how to stash the arsenal. He's cleaning his weapons at the dining table. While most folks have guns in farm country, the quantity and caliber would raise questions.

The pig perks up on the sofa. Her pink ear twitches as the door bangs again.

"Who is it?" He gets to his feet, one hand on his Ruger.

"It's me." A pause. "Jen. Jennifer. I can come back. Sorry, I didn't realize how late it was. I was googling hoof ulcers and realized I have a different salve that's great for—"

"Hi." He's got the door open before she's done talking.

Dressed in jeans and a white t-shirt, she wears her hair loose around her shoulders. No makeup, sneakers on her feet. She's even sexier than she was in a sundress.

Palms sweating, he angles his shoulders to hide the table. "I can put the salve on her."

"Oh. Right. Yes, sure." She holds up a jar and slips it into his hand. "She's doing okay? The pig, I mean."

"Zsa Zsa."

"Zsa Zsa?"

"Gabor. Well, Ga-*boar*." A pig pun like Maple Stirrup and Scape Goat. "I tried Eva and Magda, but she's more of a Zsa Zsa."

The pig squeals behind him but stays on the couch. Maybe her hoof hurts, or maybe life's better on a La-Z-Boy.

Jen backs away. "I'll just get back to—"

"Stay." He winces, pretty sure commanding her like a dog isn't great. "I made elk chili."

She stops moving. "That's what smells so good?"

He nods and flicks a glance over his shoulder. The guns are a problem. "Give me two minutes to clean up. Laundry." He clears his throat. "Underwear."

"Oh. Right, yes. Sorry." She steps back, and he closes the door like a dick. What asshole shuts the door in a woman's face?

An asshole with an arsenal and no business wanting his best friend's sister.

He takes a minute and forty-three seconds to sweep everything into the gun safe and lock it tight. Ten more seconds to trek back to the tiny kitchen and check the chili. He adds a dash more cocoa powder and circles back to the door.

Jen looks lovely in the porch light. She bites her lip as he beckons her inside. "I didn't mean to invite myself to dinner," she says.

"You didn't." He swings the door wider and gestures to his firearm-free table. "Want wine or soda or—"

"Zsa Zsa!" Jen drops beside the couch and rubs the sow's spotted belly. The pig grunts and rolls for better access. "You're settling in, aren't you?"

Zsa Zsa grunts agreement and snuffles Jen's hand. Laughing as hair drifts over her forehead, Jen scratches lower. "Such a sweet girl, aren't you? And so pretty."

A knife blade twists in Dante's belly. Thirst, he decides as he spins toward the kitchen to grab two colas. Maybe stick his head in the freezer.

She's here to tend your pig, not turn you on.

He sets the sodas on the coffee table with a fresh box of Cheez-Its. Jen's doctoring Zsa Zsa's hoof, rubbing the ointment in small, soft circles. When she's done, her fingers probe the rest of the speckled body. So gentle. So sure.

Dante closes his eyes. He was once the most skilled gunman in Dovlano. Now he's envying a pig. He parks himself stiffly on the far end of the couch and twists the cap off his soda.

Jen looks up and smiles. "Oooh, Cheez-Its. Let me wash my hands real fast."

She bolts for the bathroom and he holds his breath. Is there anything incriminating in there? Boxer briefs or a hand grenade?

He has no business inviting her here. No right to play the host or sit thinking about the white lace he saw down the front of her t-shirt when she bent to tend his pet. He's playing with fire. There are too many secrets poised to blow like that damn grenade he hopes he remembered to stash in the medicine cabinet.

As she walks back to the living room, he watches her face. No signs of alarm, and she's not running for the door. He scratches Zsa Zsa's ear. "Chili's ready in thirty minutes."

"Great. Wonderful." Pausing, she takes a seat on the other end of the sofa.

With Zsa Zsa between them like a royal chaperone, some tension slips from his shoulders. He opens the box of crackers and nudges it toward her. "How's your evening?"

"Good." She picks up her cola bottle and twists off the top. "I had a gift box on my front porch from the hotel people. The Hart-Holden Group?"

Nerves prickle the backs of his hands. "What was it?"

"A bouquet. Lilies and roses and daisies." She laughs and plucks a Cheez-It from the box. "First time in my life someone's sent me flowers."

Hot fingers squeeze his heart. "You searched it?"

Jen frowns. "For what?"

"Bugs." Do normal people not do that?

She shrugs and takes another cracker. "Insects don't bother me. I figure they were there first."

Jesus. He's not cut out for human conversation. "So, someone was on your property."

"I guess." She shrugs and takes another cracker. "It had a handwritten note. Seemed like maybe Dawn and Sean brought it personally."

"Dawn and Sean." He doesn't like the sound of that. Not one bit. "What did the note say?"

She makes a face. "They wrote up a new offer. One where I'd stay on the property."

"How would that work?"

"They'd build me some kind of residence on the northeast edge so I could, in their words, 'maintain a connection to the land.'" She rolls her eyes and rests the soda bottle on her knee. "Like a tiny apartment on the corner of Nondi's farm would do that."

He frowns and spins his own soda in a palm. "Why the persistence? There are plenty of other vineyards."

She shrugs and grabs more crackers. "None that fit the parameters, I guess. There's no hotel property in wine country like what they're planning. Apparently, my place is well-situated." Sighing, she taps a fingernail on her soda bottle. "I'm changing the subject now, okay?"

"All right." He scratches Zsa Zsa's ears and gets a satisfied grunt from the sow.

"I called my friend with the grapes. She's letting me have them for free."

"The smoky ones?"

"Yeah. I'm driving to Roseburg next week. We'll do the grape stomp that weekend."

"So soon?"

"I need money fast." She nibbles a cracker. "I've got a friend at the local paper. He's sending someone out to write a story about it. They'll give me ads for half price."

He's not surprised she's a savvy businesswoman. That people want to help her. *He* wants to help her. Wants much more than that. "What can I do?"

"You really don't have to." She bites her lip. "I only hired you to—"

"I'm helping." He should sound less gruff about it. "Please."

She studies him, then nods. "I'll send you my task list. Lots of small things like hosing out macro bins and setting up tables for the event. Maybe big things like running to Roseburg with me to get the grapes."

"When?"

She bites her lip. "Next Thursday. I know it's soon, but—"

"I'm in." He's never seen that part of Oregon, and the drive will do him good.

A drive with Jen. Spending six hours in the truck together is a chance to know her better. If he knows her better, he can protect her better. That's all.

He gets up to check the chili. He's gone three steps when his phone buzzes behind him. Spinning back, he spots it on the coffee table and freezes.

Oswald Penn.

The screen blazes bright as neon. He lunges, sure she'll decode his nickname for the Oregon State Penitentiary. It's Matteo; she'll know it. The phone buzzes again, vibrating to the table's edge. She grabs it before it falls.

"Got it."

He holds his breath, hoping she doesn't see the screen. It rings again.

"I had an uncle named Oswald." She holds it out. "Sorry, I didn't mean to snoop. Just didn't want it to hit the floor."

"Thanks." He hits the decline button and shoves it in his shirt pocket. Stomps to the kitchen as the phone buzzes again. He's fumbling for the off switch as Jen stands. "You can take the call. I don't mind. I'll set the table if you point me to the—"

"Sit." Goddammit. There he goes, commanding her like a pet again. "You don't need to do that."

"It's the least I can do if you're feeding me."

He slips out the phone and sends the call to voicemail. As he fumbles to power it off, it rings again. "Goddammit."

"Someone really wants you."

He draws a ragged breath and tries to focus. She's in the kitchen ripping paper towels off his roll, folding them into neat rectangles beside chipped bowls. The phone buzzes in his hand.

Oswald Penn.

Something's wrong. It's the only reason he'd be this relentless. Dante hesitates, finger on the off switch.

"I really don't mind if you take that." She's in his silverware drawer now, rummaging for spoons. "I can step outside if you—"

"Hello?" He strides across the room, thumb tapping the volume down.

Not quick enough.

This is a call from an inmate at an Oregon correctional facility...

Jen blinks and Dante holds his breath. Did she hear?

He can't stick around and ask. Sprinting for the bathroom, he covers one ear with his hand. "What?" He slams the bathroom door shut as Matteo grunts.

"Sebastian's back."

"Back where?"

"Back here," Matteo says. "In Oregon."

"Oregon?" He'd heard Seb might've hit the West Coast, but here? "He's been out of touch a long time."

"Yeah. That business with his dad—"

"Right." Add that to the list of things they don't discuss. Family trouble. Politics. Prison time. The usual. "He's still free-lancing?"

"Not sure."

An American-based operator, Sebastian works for The Union. Different from the Dovlanese government where Dante and Teo honed their skills.

"Why is he here?"

"Don't know," Matteo says. "You'll find out."

He considers that. Seb's charming as hell, but lethal. A deadly mix. *The Dentist.* That's his code name, but also his job. A real fucking dentist. Damn good one, too.

Matteo respects him. So does Dante. He's like a brother to them.

A brother they don't totally trust. But Seb's an excellent shot. A surveillance expert and former Special Ops man. His skills could be handy.

"He'll come looking for you," Matteo growls. "Sebastian. Maybe he could be useful."

"Yeah." He thinks of Jen's story about spotting Reggie Dowling. He's deciding whether to share when Teo speaks again.

"Keep him away from my sisters."

"Sebastian?"

"Yeah. That guy-next-door shit. Too suave for his own good."

"All right." He runs a hand over his head, considering. Is it a coincidence Seb's in town? Not like he'd mess with Jen's vineyard. The busted wine barrel or poisoned vines. It's not Seb's style, and what's the motive?

But no one lasts this long in the business without switching it up. He's never sure how Seb's brain operates. How his network operates. "I'll keep an eye out."

"Good." Another pause. "Heard another rumor."

No point asking how he gets his information. "And?"

"Reggie Dowling. *Detective* Dowling." The word slips out on a sneer. "He's been spotted back in Seattle."

That's a long way from Southern Oregon. Eight hours, nine with bad traffic. "That's where he's working?"

"No."

"He's still a cop?"

"Trying to confirm." There's an edge to Teo's voice that wasn't there before. "His record's fucking clean."

They both know it can't be. He wiped it, same way he kicked dirt on Matteo's.

"What else?" He can tell from Teo's silence there's more.

"Asshole has a brother doing five years for fraud. Minimum security. Eastern Oregon."

Not the first dirty cop to have a sibling behind bars. There's more to the story. "And?"

"Got some intel he's getting out." Matteo pauses. "A free man, three months into his sentence. Someone pulled strings."

He doesn't have to ask who *someone* is.

But if Dowling can pull strings to spring his brother from the clink— "I'll look into it. See if I can find what rathole the bastard's biding his time in."

"Good." Matteo grunts. "While you're at it, figure out who's after my sister."

"I'm trying." God, he's trying. Glancing at the door, he prays she can't hear him. "Planted a tracker on her ex's car."

He leaves out the part about the tracker malfunctioning. He hasn't been able to get a signal. Surveillance is Sebastian's skill set. Maybe Seb really will be useful.

"What else are you doing?" Matteo growls. "To guard Jen?"

"I'm staying close. Sticking to her like glue."

A long pause as Matteo thinks the worst. Dante knows how his mind works.

"Protecting her," Dante adds when the silence stretches too long. "Someone dropped off a pig."

"A pig?" Another long pause. "That's code for something?"

"No, a pig—Sus scrofa domesticus. An actual pig."

Matteo's quiet. "Some kind of trojan horse?"

"Doubt it." It crossed his mind. "I'll sweep her for bugs to be safe." He should have done it already. He's slipping.

"Good." Matteo pauses. "Tell me what else you're doing to keep Jen safe."

A plate clatters in the other room, and Jen calls out to Zsa Zsa. "Sorry, girl." Her voice echoes across the house. "Didn't mean to drop that."

Dante waits a beat too long to answer.

"Is that her?" Matteo's pissed. "Where are you? Not at her house?"

"No." It's his turn to pause. "She's here for dinner. *Uninvited,*" he adds before Matteo can assume. "I couldn't shove her out the door when she showed up with pig medicine."

"That's Jen for you." His voice is equal parts disgust and admiration. "Keep your wits sharp. I'm counting on you."

"Yeah." He scrubs a palm across his head again. "I have to go."

He hangs up with a wet wad of guilt in his throat. He never answered the question. Never said what he's doing to keep Jen safe, because the truth is, he's doing a shitty job. He's too distracted. Too close to the subject he's sworn to protect.

He knows better.

Shoving open the door, he spots her on the couch and feels his heart sink slowly in warm quicksand. She's scratching the sow, hair falling soft around her face. He shoves the phone in his pocket and takes a breath. When she looks up and smiles, his heart goes under for good.

"Old friend," he says before she asks.

"Okay." She stands and goes to the kitchen to wash her hands. "I hope you don't mind; I took her collar off."

"Collar?" He studies the pig. "Oh. Fine."

"It's not a breakaway collar, and that's dangerous with livestock. I'll throw it in the barn in case someone comes back for her." She shuts off the tap and grabs a paper towel. "Is your friend in prison?"

Fuck.

He holds a straight face. "Prison?" He forces a chuckle, moving around her to check the chili. "I wish sometimes. Ever have a friend who won't quit breathing down your neck?"

She cocks her head. "Can't say I have." She's watching him, uncertainty in her eyes. "I thought I heard the automated message I get when my brother calls. I wasn't trying to eavesdrop. Your volume was high."

"Huh." He's toeing the line between evasive and flat-out lying. He doesn't want to lie to her. Not if he can help it.

That's a bad sign. What kind of hitman can't fib?

He clears his throat. "How early are we grabbing the grapes next Thursday?"

"Early." She pauses, then follows the flow. "Maybe four a.m.? It takes three hours to get there, three more to get back. I want enough daylight to unload. You're sure you don't mind?"

"Positive." After that call, no way he's letting her out of his sight.

He jerks the lid off the crock pot and starts dishing up chili. He wishes he'd made a salad. That he had fancy bowls of condiments like cilantro and chopped onion. He didn't plan for company. Didn't plan any of this.

But Jen deserves a nice dinner. She deserves steak and candles and flowers every day from a guy who's not a goddamn criminal. His chest pinches as she claims a ladder-back chair at the battered table. He sets a bowl in front of her and drags out a chair at the far end of the table.

"Thanks." She smiles again and lays a paper towel across her lap. "I didn't realize I was so hungry."

"Dig on." One of his favorite American expressions. Or did he get that wrong? "Dig *in*."

She laughs and lifts a spoon. "Thanks." Her lips close around the spoon and her green eyes go wide. "Oh my God."

"Too hot?"

"It's incredible." She takes another bite, closing her eyes in bliss. "I'm going to need this recipe."

He tastes some, glad he got the right mix of meat and spices. If he gives her the recipe, he won't see her face crease with ecstasy when he makes it. "I'll write it down."

His lust-syruped brain replays Matteo's words.

"Keep your wits sharp. I'm counting on you."

They both fall silent, focused on the food. He's inhaling chili like it's been years since his last meal. It's better than staring at Jen, wondering what it would be like if she spent the night. If he touched her, tasted her—

"Urk." Choking on chili, he sputters and grabs his soda.

"Are you okay?"

"Fine." He's wheezing, acting like a damn moron. "Good."

Get it together.

Not Matteo's words, but that's the voice in Dante's head.

"You're sure?" Jen's jumps off her chair. "If you want, I could—"

"No!" He shouts much louder than he means to. "Don't come close."

She frowns and sits back down. Great. He's hurt her feelings.

"It's just—" He fumbles for a good excuse. "I haven't showered."

"Oh."

His voice sounds scratchy, not just from choking. "The Heimlich means touching. There shouldn't be touching."

"Okay."

She picks up her spoon again, silent as she finishes the meal. When she sets down her spoon, he shoves his chair back. "More?"

Shaking her head, she grabs her empty bowl. "I'll just get the dishes."

"Please, no." He stands up and takes the bowl from her. "You're my guest."

Her laugh floats like bubbles. "A guest who invites herself to dinner. Please, let me help."

"No." Too brusque. "Relax. Please."

She darts a glance at the clock on his microwave. "I should go."

But she doesn't move. Neither does he. "Brownies?"

Jen blinks. "You made brownies?"

"No. But I can make some."

Laughing, she grabs her sweater off the back of her chair. "I really should go. Early morning and all."

Of course. It's a farm. Every morning's early.

He hates to see her go. Can't bear the thought of her staying. Where does that leave him? "So, next week." He scuffs a toe on the floor. "We can take my truck to get the grapes."

"No need. There's an old stake bed truck in the storage shed."

"Really?" He hasn't seen it.

"The shed on the far edge east of the property. A '51 International with a lift and a thirteen-foot stake bed." Her eyes soften. "*Mine*. It belonged to my grandma, so Johnny can't touch it."

"Damn right." Her claim to the truck makes him love her more.

Love.

Jesus. What is wrong with him?

"It's been a while since I used it," she's saying, "but it should be in good shape. I had it tuned up right before...before..." She closes her eyes. "Before my brother went to prison."

Another reminder for him to keep his damn hands to himself.

"Okay." Such a stupid answer. "Right. So, tomorrow. Pruning vines?"

"Yes." She makes a face. "Actually, I'd love to deer-proof the garden. Everything I've tried doesn't work."

"You've tried peeing?"

She blinks. "What?"

117

"Around the perimeter. Helps to mark your territory."

God, make him stop. He may as well pee on her while he's at it. It's the only way to make this conversation worse.

"I…um." She smiles. "I'll consider it."

"I'll take care of it."

Now he's made it worse.

Jen laughs and takes a step toward the door. "I'd love to see that."

"What?"

She jumps like she's startled. "I didn't mean it like that. I don't want to watch you—um." Color fills her cheeks. "I'm going now. Thank you for dinner."

God, she's adorable. And gorgeous. And sexy. And— "No problem."

"Thanks for lunch, too." Her laugh has a nervous edge as she takes another step back. "And for being there when Johnny showed up. I'm sorry you have to keep pretending you're my boyfriend."

"I'm not."

She stops. "Not what?"

He moves closer, meaning to get the door. To usher her out and watch through the window so she gets home safely.

But something happens. She goes to hug him or he reaches for her or maybe gravity slips. She's suddenly in his arms, body pressed lush against his. With a soft moan, she tips her head back and meets his eyes.

"Oh." She breathes the word like a prayer, and his heart squeezes.

He's not sure what to say, so screw words. His mouth finds hers, and he's kissing her. Kissing her like he has the right to. He's got no right, none at all, but she's kissing him back as his hands glide to cup her backside.

Going up on her toes, Jen fists his shirt in both hands and sweeps his tongue with hers. It's his turn to groan, to back her against the door and kiss her like he's wanted to all day. All week.

Hell, maybe his whole life.

"Dan." She breaks the kiss, breathless, eyes searching his.

Dan.

It's all wrong. So wrong.

"Not Dan." He swallows. *"Dante."*

She blinks. "Dante?"

What is he thinking?

But there's no going back. No way he can keep kissing her without telling her his real name. He needs to hear her say it. Say it like it means something.

"Dan's short for Dante," he says. "Not Daniel. Not Danny. *Dante.*"

She looks at him a long time. "It suits you."

"Yeah?"

"Yes." A breathy laugh slips out. "I never thought you seemed like a Daniel. Or *Daniel Wutheringshire Goodman, Esquire.* That's not you."

"It's not." If only she knew who he really is. He's already said too much.

Dante clears his throat. "I don't tell that to many people."

"But you told me."

"Yes."

She nods like she understands. Maybe she'll clue him in because he sure doesn't. He knows a thousand reasons what he's just done is idiotic, but he can't name one right now. Blame the light in her eyes, the softness of her hair. He reaches to touch it, threading his fingers through the strands.

"You should go."

She holds his gaze. "You want me to go?"

"No." He takes a breath. "But you should."

Her grip loosens from his shirt, but she flattens her palms on his chest. "You're probably right."

He knows he is. That doesn't make it easier to take a step back. "Good night," he says. "Jen."

Holding his gaze, she nods. "Good night." A pause. "Dante."

She walks out the door, taking his idiot heart with her.

* * *

THE GUARD BUZZES HIM THROUGH. Dante strides to the table in the visitor area, heart hammering his eardrums.

What the hell is he doing in prison? On this side of the bars, no less.

Matteo takes a seat across from him. His green eyes match Jen's, and Dante draws a breath to get his bearings.

It's been days since the chili dinner. Days since he held Jen in his arms and kissed her. He still feels his lips burning. Wonders if Matteo can see it.

"I saw Sebastian." Dante clears his throat. "He's set up a dental office in town."

"I know."

Fuck. What else does he know?

"Says he's on the straight and narrow now." Dante will believe that when he sees it. "Settling down, looking for a nice suburban life."

Matteo snorts. "Right."

He lets his eyes scan the room, taking in the concrete floors and bars on the doors. It's his first time coming here. First time taking this sort of risk. He wouldn't have come if he didn't have to. Some messages are too sensitive to deliver on the phone.

He clears his throat again. "I checked into our friend."

Matteo flinches at the word *friend*. "And?"

They're being careful. It's different on the phone with Dovlanese nicknames masking real ones. But here, with guards pacing four feet away, he needs to tread carefully. "Your intel's correct. Happened Friday morning."

Reggie Dowling's brother walked out a free man. Record expunged, no harm, no foul. It curdles Dante's blood.

Matteo scans his face. "Who picked him up?"

"Not our guy." Dowling's too cagey to claim his own brother. "Sebastian staked it out."

Both brows lift. "You're working with Seb on this?"

"He's got connections we don't. Skills we don't." Dante pauses. "Besides. I've got this tooth I need checked for—"

"Jesus." Matteo sighs. "All right, yeah. That makes sense. The Dentist knows what he's doing."

With more than oral hygiene. "It's easier that way," Dante adds. "Keeping him close."

"Understood." Matteo stares in silence.

How much does he know?

Can he guess Dante's had lunch with Jen every day this week? That she left a flannel shirt at the bunkhouse when she came to share some lasagna. That he fell asleep with the shirt on his pillow like some lovesick kid. The shirt smells like hay and honey and *her,* and he woke up smiling like a goddamn fool.

There's so much he wants to say to Teo. To tell him Jen's the most amazing woman he's ever met. That sunlight in her hair is the exact same shade as the gold arching the palace doors in Dovlano. That when he sees her, his chest feels like someone filled it with warm pudding.

But he can't say any of that, so he closes his eyes. "I probably shouldn't be here."

"Nope."

He takes a breath. "Neither should you."

Matteo says nothing, and Dante opens his eyes. "I'll fix this, okay?"

As he gets up to leave, he's not sure which problem he means.

CHAPTER 12

"What do you think of this font?" Nicole spins her laptop to face Jen. "Too cutesy?"

They're sitting in red and blue chairs at a two-foot high table stacked with finger-paints. A pink plush bunny flops in a green chair beside her. A sign on the door welcomes her to Miss Gigglewink's Daycare.

"I'm flooded with cute at the moment." Jen squints at the screen. "Is that the same font from the daycare opening?"

"No, but it's close." Nic frowns and makes a tweak. "There, how's that? Better for a winery event?"

"Yeah." She'd get up and hug her sister if her butt wasn't wedged in this chair.

Nic sees her squirming and smiles. "Only you and your tiny little hiney could fit in that thing."

"Me and a five-year-old, you mean."

"Your butt is perfect just the way it is." Nic hits another keystroke. "Curves are overrated."

"Says the woman stacked like a supermodel."

Nic drags her gaze off the screen. "Since when are you down on your body?"

Since my boyfriend ran off with a British Disney princess.

Ignoring the thought, she shrugs instead. "Just stressed, I guess."

Her sister eyes her, knowing that's not it. She doesn't push, though. It's the best thing about Nicole. She knows when to probe and when to keep quiet. It's why she's good at protecting parents fleeing abuse. Families in tough situations who put their lives in her hands. Nic knows when to bite her tongue.

Jen guides them back to the flyer. "The Chamber of Commerce offered to post these all over town if they're done today. Thanks again for making them."

"Consider it my gift to the cause." Nic hits a few more keystrokes, then toggles to a website. "I'm sending this to the print shop on Main Street. You can pick them up by five."

"I owe you." Jen forces herself up. "I should get going. Tons to do for the event."

"Oh! I'll walk with you." Nic gets to her feet. "I've still got that box of stuff for you."

"Stuff?"

"Nondi's goodies. The stuff I meant to give you last week?"

Jen almost forgot. "It's still in your car?"

"Yeah, come on." Nic leads her to the door and out into the overcast parking lot. "You're going tomorrow to get the grapes?"

"Sasha said she'll have them ready first thing in the morning."

"Is Dan going with you?"

"D—oh, my farmhand?" She catches it before she says *Dante.*

It's been a week since the chili. A week since the kiss that made her toes curl.

But they've had no more kisses. No touching or longing looks or...okay, maybe some looks. It can't go further. They work well together and like each other's cooking. Platonic lunches, professional workdays. That's enough. They can't cross the line again.

Jen takes a breath. "Dan's good. He's coming with me to Roseburg."

Nic wags her eyebrows. "Six round trip hours in a car. Whatever will you do?"

Rolling her eyes, Jen opens her car door. "It's just business. I need an extra set of hands."

"And what magnificent hands they are." Nic flips her ponytail off her shoulder. "I don't know how you can live two hundred yards from that scrumptious hunk of man meat and not want to jump him."

"I didn't say I don't want to jump him. I'm human."

"Glad to hear it."

She sighs and glances back toward the daycare. "I just don't need the mess of getting romantically involved with a guy I work with. You saw how things went with Johnny."

"True, but Johnny's a douche." Nic tugs her cable-knit cardigan around her, pausing in a patch of breezy sun. "Jury's still out on your farmhand."

"Hmm." She's deciding whether to say something about the kiss. It's not like her to keep things from her sister.

But this connection with Dante, it's so new. There's something fragile about it, delicate. She wants to guard it with her life.

"Jen?" Nicole studies her face. "Everything okay?"

"Yeah. It's great."

Her sister watches her. "You know I can keep secrets, right? It's kinda what I do."

"I know." She smiles to show she's really okay. "It's fine. Just stressed about the vineyard stuff. Missing Matteo. Missing Nondi."

"I get it." She pulls her in for a hug, rocking back and forth. "Maybe the stuff she boxed up for you will help."

"Help me feel less like an idiot for losing her property?" Doubtful, but Jen will take anything at this point.

"You are *not* an idiot." Nic draws back and grabs her car door. Reaches inside to lift a cardboard box. "And you're also not going to lose the property. You've got this, girl. *Srontica*. You're wonderful, as Nondi would say."

She shoves the box into Jen's arms, and Jen hugs it like a safety blanket. "What is all this?" Her eyes search the jumbled contents. "A crystal candy dish?"

"You know how Nondi made a big deal about every woman needing one." Nic shrugs and closes the car door. "A generational thing, I guess."

Another reminder Jen's not the sort of dainty lady to keep candies in crystal dishes. Penelope probably has a dozen of the things in her living room, all with color-coordinated M&Ms.

"Oh." Jen's self-pity slips as she spots the tattered photo poking out of a corner. "That picture! I haven't seen it for years."

"Isn't it cute?" Nic plucks it from the box and holds it up. Jen's six-year-old face stares back, freckles fanned out under a lopsided chignon. "Nondi took you out for tea, right?"

"That's right." She studies the picture until her heart loosens its grip on the bars of her ribcage. "I was thinking about that picture when I took Dan to the teahouse."

Nic smiles and sets it back in the box. "You look like a badass."

"I was trying for glamorous and sophisticated."

"Wouldn't you rather be a badass?"

Jen stuffs the box in her backseat and closes the car door. "Probably not."

"I would." Nic frowns as a sleek black sports car swings into the parking lot. "Ugh. It's him."

"Him?" Jen squints at the car. "Him who?"

"The new guy renting the space across the way. A chiropractor or optometrist or something."

They watch the driver park and get out, dark sunglasses shielding his eyes. There's a spring in his step that leaves Jen jovial, so she doesn't get why Nic's getting bristly. "Did he pee in your flower beds or something?"

Her own words shoot heat to her cheeks. Two days ago, she

walked outside to see Dante doing his duty around her garden. She stood staring at his backside, wondering what he looked like from the front. She watched a lot longer than she should have, burning the image in her brain.

She hasn't had deer in the garden all week.

Jen scans the black BMW. "What's your problem with sports car guy?"

"Nothing," Nic mutters. "He just—*looks* wrong."

"Looks wrong?" From where Jen's standing, the guy looks pretty good. Broad shoulders, big smile he's flashing at a couple shuffling to the entrance of the sushi shop next door. He holds the door for them, glancing at the daycare.

"Don't stare." Nicole grabs Jen's hand and pretends to admire her manicure. "When's the last time you had your nails done?"

"Christmas?" Jen tugs her hand back and steals a sidelong glance at the new guy. "He's gone. And I think you're being overly suspicious."

"Someone has to."

"What's that supposed to mean?"

"Just that Matty's not here to watch out for you. It's my job now."

Jen throws her hands up in exasperation. "Did it ever occur to you guys that I'm a grown-ass woman who can take care of herself?"

"You're right, you're right." Nicole pulls her in for another too-tight hug. "Sorry, *Lentiggini.*"

Freckles. The family nickname squeezes her heart as tight as Nic's hug. She closes her eyes, breathing in her sister's warmth.

"No fucking way!"

So much for the warmth.

Nic lets go, and Jen sees her scanning the storefront where the sports car's parked. The optometrist/chiropractor stands in the doorway, but he's not alone now. "Isn't that Dan?"

Jen stares and feels her heart start to gallop. "Maybe he needs an eye appointment?"

"Come on." Nic grabs her arm and tugs her toward them. "This seems fishy to me."

"*Everything* seems fishy to you."

It's Nic's suspicious nature that makes her good at her job, but it also makes her a pain in the ass. "The man deserves some privacy."

"We're just saying hello." She lifts a hand and calls out a greeting. "Hey! Dan, right? Fancy seeing you here."

Jen cringes as her sister pulls her the final few steps. The man beside Dan has dark hair and a mega-watt smile he turns on Nic. "Miss Gigglewink, right?"

"Right." Nic ignores him to address Dante. "We haven't formally met yet. I'm her sister, Nicole."

Frowning, he holds out a hand. "Dan Goodman."

"Pleasure to meet you, Dan." Nic shifts her gaze to the other guy, who hasn't taken his eyes off her. "You're the new tenant?"

"Dr. Sebastian LaDouceur, DDS." He holds out a hand. "Pleasure to meet you."

Nic sniffs and shakes his hand. "So you're a dentist?"

The way she says it sounds like *tax collector* or *exterminator*. "Ignore her," Jen says, shaking the dentist's hand with a lot less suspicion. "Traumatic childhood experience with orthodontia."

Dr. LaDouceur's grin gets wider. "Good thing I don't do orthodontics, then. Just straight up dentistry. Can I give you my card?"

"I'm good, thanks." Nicole turns to Dante. "You're here for an appointment?"

"Jesus, Nic." Jen shakes her head. "None of your business."

One edge of Dante's mouth twitches. "Yes. Dentist appointment."

"Gonna pull all his teeth." Dr. LaDouceur grins. "That'll keep him from grinding them all the time."

Nicole's gaze bounces between them. "You two know each other?"

Dante glares at the other man. "Something like that."

The dentist is unfazed. "We go way back."

"Seb's my dentist from a while ago."

"Seb?" Nic lifts an eyebrow.

"Sebastian." The man grins. "Which you can call me. Or Seb's fine. Really, whatever you'd like to call me."

Jen squeezes Nic's hand so she won't spew four-letter words. She's not sure what's got her sister's hackles up, but Nic clearly doesn't like the dentist. To Jen, he seems like a perfectly nice man.

Not that she's the best judge of character.

Nic's smiling at Dante, pointedly ignoring the dentist. "Dan, you seem like the sort of guy who'd be a difficult patient."

Sebastian hoots with laughter. "Nailed it."

"Oh?" It's the first time Nic's seemed interested.

"Yep." Sebastian grins. "I tell him to open up, he gives me the dead-eyed death stare."

Jen knows that stare. She also knows Dante's not big on opening up. Maybe he'll unhinge his jaw for dentists, but definitely not for most mortals. Does it mean something he's done it with her? That she knows his real name?

Sebastian's still smiling, still watching Nicole. "It's kinda like that old dentist joke. The one that goes, 'What does a dentist give a bear with a toothache?'"

Jen responds, since no one else jumps to answer. "What does a dentist give a bear with a toothache?"

"Anything it wants." Sebastian elbows Dante. "That's you, buddy. You're the bear."

Dante looks pained. "Anything I want?"

"Within reason."

He watches Jen a long time. Long enough for her belly to coil in warm loops. "What I want…" He says the words slowly trailing off as she waits for the rest.

"What?" she breathes when he doesn't finish.

Dante closes his eyes. "What I want is to reschedule my appointment."

Sebastian nods. "You sure?"

"Positive." He opens his eyes and looks at Jen again. "Big day tomorrow. Driving to Roseburg."

Seb gives a low whistle. "Long drive. All right, I'll have my receptionist call you to reschedule."

"Fine." Dante nods to Jen. "Need a ride?"

Nic giggles, and Jen thinks about punching her. That was *not* an innuendo. "I've got my car, thanks."

"I'll follow." He jabs a thumb at his work truck. "We're headed the same way, right?"

"Right." The words feel laced with more meaning than they're meant to.

She hates that she feels it. Hates that she's falling for him.

Taking a breath, she turns away. "See you back home."

Nic grabs her hand and squeezes, then lets go with a knowing smile.

Is it that obvious? Does everyone know she's hot for her farmhand?

She gets in her car staring straight ahead, not daring to meet anyone's eye. Not looking to see if Dante's watching. She knows he is. She feels it.

She's still feeling it as she drives away.

CHAPTER 13

"*I*'m glad you came with me." Jen looks up from her iPad to adjust the heater on the dash. "There's no way I could have loaded all those grapes without you."

"No problem." Dante checks the rearview mirror, confirming the giant plastic crates are secure. "WiFi okay out here?"

"It's great. Thanks again for driving. I'm almost caught up."

"No problem." He's glad to do it so she can tackle her busy-work. Details for the event. Emails for the winery. "Everything okay?"

She returns to tapping the iPad. "Getting there. I'm almost done reading the legal stuff Rhett Strijker sent. My brother's lawyer?" She scrolls to another screen. "Maybe there's a way we'll pull this off."

We. Does she mean the two of them? Today's been a blur of teamwork, both of them working together to load grapes, to secure them in the truck. Working beside her feels different than their tea date. Closer, maybe. He wonders if she's noticed.

Resting the tablet on her knees, she lets her head drop back against the seat. "Have you ever been married?"

"What?" The question packs a punch.

"Married. Sorry, if it's too personal you don't have to—"

"No." He flicks her a glance, relieved she's closed her eyes. "Almost."

"What's almost married? Like—living together?"

He doesn't risk looking at her again. "Engaged."

"Oh." It's hard to know how to feel about that.

"She died."

"Oh, Dante." She sits up and touches his forearm, her fingers cool and soft. "I'm so sorry."

"It was a long time ago."

"Still."

He waits for her to ask. To probe for details.

She's going to ask, right?

"I was young." Why is he sharing this? "Twenty-two. Like someone that age has any business getting married."

"Was she pretty?"

It's such a strange question that he risks glancing at her again. Green eyes glitter with emotion and he takes a deep breath. "Yes." He's not sure it's the answer she wants, but it's true. "She was a viscountess."

"Wow. Real nobility." She tilts her head. "Is that how you wound up working for the Duke?"

"Not quite." He's ready to be done talking, but his brain doesn't get the message. "Her parents didn't approve. We planned to run away together, get married in Italy. She'd gone to her parents' house to get some things. Never saw the truck that ran the stop sign."

"Oh, God." The pain in her voice pinches his chest. "I really am sorry."

"Thank you."

Truth is, he's not sorry. He's sad about Clarissa. Feels for her family, even after all these years. He misses her sometimes, wondering what life would be like if she'd lived. If it was him behind the wheel, watchful for danger.

But likely they'd both be dead. He'd never have come to America or met Jen or earned this fresh start. The thought leaves a lump in his throat. He hits the blinker to change lanes. "How about you?"

"What about me?"

"Johnny." The name makes his tongue itch. "You were supposed to get married?"

"In December." She makes a sound like a strangled laugh. "I should have known it was a bad sign when he was dead set on timing it after harvest."

"Why's that?"

His peripheral vision catches her shrug. "Zero passion, a hundred percent practical. He wasn't picturing green fields or flowers or me in a flowy white sundress with daisies in my hair."

He imagines her in that dress. The sun on her bare shoulders with wisps of sheer fabric swirling around pale shins. Her feet are bare, too, her toes in springy grass as she makes her way to the top of the aisle where Dante waits.

"Asshole." He means himself, but Jen laughs.

"I'm not sad about Johnny. Not really. I see him with Penelope and they're a much better match. I just wish—" She stops, biting her lip.

"What do you wish?"

He's nearing a steep curve in the road and can't look over. He wants to watch her face. To see if what she's telling him is a half-truth or a whole one.

"Jen?"

He can't glance over. They're almost at the curve. He taps the brake, and nothing happens. Jams it with the sole of his boot, heart thudding as the pedal hits the floor.

"Dante?" She gasps. "Slow down, you're scaring me."

He slams the brake pedal and feels nothing but air. "Hang on."

As Jen yelps, he pumps the brake. One, two, three times, four.

Still nothing. They're whipping downhill, gaining speed as the truck hurtles through the first hairpin.

"Seatbelt," he barks. He watched her hook it when they got in, but did she unclick to touch his arm? He'd never forgive himself.

"It's on. Oh God, Dante—"

"Steady." Does he mean her or himself?

He yanks the e-brake, and nothing happens. A sick vise grips his gut as he holds the wheel with fists. Sweat swells on his upper lip as he fights for control. As he stomps the clutch, the cargo lurches. He can't risk letting go to grab the gearshift.

"Downshift," he orders. "Please."

"Oh, Christ." Jen grabs the stick, and he knows without looking her hand is shaking.

She yanks it down, finding fourth. The truck lurches but keeps flying.

"Again." He stomps the clutch, and she shoves the stick up.

The engine growls as they barrel through the next curve. Something slams the truck bed, and he darts a glance in the mirror. Shifting cargo, or are they hit?

"Don't worry about the grapes." She breathes the words softly. "Just save us."

He will. Goddammit, he has to.

The truck whines as smoke wafts from the hood. Using the engine to slow them isn't a good plan. Not on this hill. Adjusting his grip on the wheel, he guides them through another curve.

"Should I shift again?"

"No." He sees it before she does. A tractor lumbering in their lane, crawling half in the shoulder. The guy's doing fifteen, maybe twenty miles an hour. The truck screams along at sixty-five.

In the next lane, a dozen cars crawl behind a semi heading the other way. There's nowhere to go.

"Brace yourself."

He pounds the horn as Jen reaches for him. Not for him, for the hazard lights. He should have thought of that.

"Please move," he whispers to the tractor. "Please."

But he can't move because where the fuck could he go? There's no pullout, not on this hill. Dante doesn't blink. He needs his eyes on the road as a guardrail whips into view.

"Hang on." He breathes deep, steadying himself. "Sorry about the paint."

"What?" Jen gasps. "Oh—"

He steers into the guardrail, dragging it along their passenger side. Jen shouts, but he barely hears it over the scream of metal scraping metal. Sweat drips in his eyes, but he can't wipe it away. Can't unlock his fingers from the wheel.

They're slowing, but not fast enough. There's a gravel pullout, a sign that says "scenic overlook." Aiming for it would be a suicide mission, but if the tractor moves aside—

Honk! Honk honk hoooooooonk!

He hammers the horn again and again, but nothing.

"Look." Jen points to the tractor driver. "Headphones. That's why he can't hear us."

"Son of a bitch."

They're running out of guardrail. Running out of ways to slow down.

That's when he spots it. A gravel hill ahead with a sign reading "runaway truck route."

With a silent prayer, he adds this to the things he loves about America.

"You see it?" Jen whispers.

"Yep." He's never used one, but he has no choice.

Blinking sweat from his eyes, he takes a breath. The guardrail runs out and they plunge past, picking up speed. The runaway ramp is a few hundred feet away, then fifty, then they're barreling up and into gravel mush. Jen yelps as the truck gives a guttural wheeze. They lurch to a crawl, then a stop as tires sink in soft gravel.

"Fuck." His seatbelt slams him against the bench, but he doesn't let go of the wheel. Doesn't dare move.

And just like that, they're stopped.

"Holy shit." Jen looks at him as Dante registers the fact there's no airbag. The truck's too old.

He surveys Jen, scanning for damage. "You okay?"

She nods but doesn't speak. Her eyes are wide and shimmery, knuckles white fists in her lap. She opens her mouth, but no sound comes out.

"Breathe." He lets go of the wheel and takes her hands, gently uncurling her fingers. "In for four. Out for four. Hold at the top."

She obeys, blinking hard against the blinding sun and the reality of what just happened.

What did happen?

"Dante?"

"Yeah?"

"What was that?"

If he says the words, it makes them true.

But truth is one thing he owes her.

"I'm not positive." He takes a deep breath. "But I'm pretty sure your brakes were cut."

CHAPTER 14

*J*en sits blinking in the sunlight. Dante's still talking to police. She knows she should join him, but can't make her legs work.

"Stay here."

His order should have pissed her off, but it didn't. She was shaking too hard to get out of the truck.

As she watches through the windshield, he nods at the officer and takes a slip of paper. They can't be ticketing him. She rolls down her window and hears the cop say "...for your insurance."

"I just called," she says. "They're sending roadside assistance."

"Ma'am." The cop touches the brim of his cap. "You're sure you don't want medics?"

"Positive."

The cop flicks a glance from her to Dante. "Anyone who might want to hurt either of you?"

Jen lets out a breath. So, Dante was right about the brakes being cut. "Could it happen by accident?" she tries. "Driving over a rock or something? The truck's pretty old."

The cop tilts his head, noting she didn't answer the question.

"Can't say for sure. I'm no mechanic. But your boyfriend says someone threw a rock at your house?"

She studies Dante, heart hopscotching at the word *boyfriend*. "You think it's connected?"

"There's also the smashed wine," he reminds her. "Too many coincidences."

Which means they're not coincidences. She knows she needs to face facts, but oh, God…she hates these facts.

"I don't know who'd want to hurt me." That's the God's honest truth. "I mean, I have some suspicions."

The cop frowns. "Can I ask you to write 'em down?"

Jen nods and the cop claps Dante on the shoulder. "Let me grab some paperwork."

He retreats to his car as Dante watches her through the passenger window. Once the officer's out of earshot, he speaks. "You're sure you're okay?"

"Yes."

What if she'd been behind the wheel? She closes her eyes but opens them again fast. Her eyelids' movie screens replay too much vivid detail. "I'm glad you were driving," she says. "You handled that better than I would have."

"I doubt it."

She doesn't. "You drove like someone who's handled a car with cut brakes."

It sounds like an accusation. Not how she means it, but she doesn't correct herself.

Dante stares. "Who's on your list?"

"List?"

"The one you're writing for the cops."

"Oh." She already forgot. Her brain feels like a can of shaken soda. "I don't know."

"Jen." He says it gently, but there's steel in his eyes.

"I just don't think he'd cut my brakes." Maybe she's naïve. "Johnny. That's who you mean?"

He doesn't answer, but his eyes do.

She sighs. "I'm considering it, okay?"

"Okay." He clears his throat. "Awfully convenient, him coming by the house last week. The day he grabbed the glasses."

"I don't think—"

"He knows where the truck's kept?"

A pause. "Yes, but he knows I rarely drive it." She frowns. "The delivery. The flowers last week from the hotel people?"

"Write it down." He tugs a tiny notepad and pencil from his pocket and hands it to her. "We should find out who brought Zsa Zsa."

"Right." What a relief they didn't bring the pig on this trip. Jen considered it, wanting to monitor the healing hoof. "I'm glad she's safe at home."

Dante nods. "I'll be back."

He sounds so much like The Terminator she almost laughs. Holding it back swells something inside her and the next thing she knows, she's got tears streaming down her face. She swipes them away, scribbling words on the paper.

Hart-Golden Hotel Group.

Gail and Harry Gibson (neighbors)

That one hurts eking out of the end of her pencil. Where does she draw the line?

She doesn't honestly think any of them would cut her brakes, but who else would?

She pauses, pencil in hand.

Johnny.

She almost crosses it out. It seems wrong to accuse him, but she's being thorough.

By the time the officer raps on her window, she's got a good list going. "Here." She tears off the page and hands it to him. "I don't know if it'll help."

"It's a start." He scans the paper, then folds it into his pocket. "There's your roadside assistance."

A tow truck lumbers up beside them. Probably not big enough to haul the rig, much less the grapes. They've got a long afternoon ahead of them.

She looks at Dante, standing straight and solid and muscular on the shoulder of the road. He's scowling at the truck, his face a lethal mask.

Shivering, she shoves open the truck door and steps out on shaky legs.

* * *

"YOU SURE YOU'RE OKAY?" Nic's eyes scan her face. "You don't seem okay."

"I'm fine." Jen's lying, and they both know it, so she grabs her sister for a hug. "I'll be fine once this event's behind me, all right?"

"All right." Nic squeezes her hard. "I'm glad Dan was driving."

Annoyance flicks her brain, even though she had the same thought. Does everyone think she's incapable? "I'm glad he saved the grapes."

"I'm glad he saved my *sister*." Nicole draws back to study her. "Seriously, that could have been bad. The police really don't know who did it?"

"Not yet. Dante had to run to an appointment as soon as we got back. I haven't asked if he learned anything new."

"Dante?"

Crap. She didn't mean to say that. "Dan. It's—you know what? I'm just so tired."

"I understand." Nic doesn't push, doesn't ask what sort of appointment her farmhand has after dark.

To be honest, she wondered herself.

But it's nearly midnight, and Jen's exhausted beyond words. Her sister checks her phone, frowning at the screen.

"Trouble?" She scans Nic's face. "Is everything okay?"

"Yeah. Just this complicated case." She shrugs and pockets her phone. "Mom's nervous. Dad's in jail. The kid's cute beyond words."

"The usual." It's more than Nic usually shares about her daycare families. They must both be exhausted. "I have to go to bed."

"Same." Nic hugs her again. "Lock your doors, okay? Deadbolt, too. And where's your gun?"

"Good night, Nicole." She ushers her out the door, then watches her drive away as she throws the deadbolt.

Alone in her kitchen, she stares at the clock. Midnight. For some reason, she's not ready for sleep. Blame adrenaline. Blame knowing Dante's just across the pasture. She saw his truck pull in an hour ago. She could go to him now. Just crawl into bed beside him and—

A fist drums the door. She knows instantly it's him.

"Jen? Are you in there? I need to know you're o—" He stops as she throws open the door.

"—kay." Steely eyes darken as he clears his throat. "Okay."

"I am. Okay."

"I see that."

Jen licks her lips, and his gaze drops to her mouth. His pupils flare, and she feels her breath snag in her throat. Her nipples pebble under her thin white tank top. As Dante drags his gaze back to her face, she watches his fingers clench.

Snort.

Zsa Zsa grunts at their feet, snapping the tension like wire. Jen stoops down, conscious of her tank top riding up above pink plaid boxers. Conscious of Dante's eyes on the strip of skin at the small of her back.

"You're ready for bed." Dante clears his throat. "You've got your gun out?"

"Yes, just like you asked." It's on the coffee table, safety on. He refused to leave for his appointment until she showed him. Until she promised her sister would stay until he got back.

"What a day." She drops to her haunches and inspects Zsa Zsa's hoof. "At least this is looking better. You're healing up perfectly, girl."

Dante shifts his weight. "Did he call back?"

She doesn't need to ask who he means, but she does anyway. "Johnny? Not yet. I left a message." She straightens and looks him in the eye.

Tries to, anyway. His eyes lock a foot lower, skimming her breasts beneath the thin tank. She crosses her arms, then uncrosses them. Like the man's never seen breasts before. Hers aren't that impressive, which is why she didn't bother with a bra.

"Come in." She leads him past the kitchen to the living room. "I made brownies last night if you want one."

"I'm good." He drops a sleeping bag on her couch.

It's the first she's noticed it. "What are you doing?"

"Sleeping here." Zsa Zsa hops on the sofa and curls up on the sleeping bag, snorting happily. Dante takes his shoes off one at a time. "It's the only way I'll know you're safe."

She should argue. She's a strong, independent woman. But the truth—

"Thank you." She sighs and sits on the other end of the sofa. "I know I should take care of myself, but—"

"No. You shouldn't." He looks her over and shakes his head. "Everyone needs someone to watch out for them."

"Do you?"

He doesn't answer. Just studies her for a long, long time. Then gets up and goes to the window, scowling silently at the darkness.

She's first to break the silence. "Officer Huey called. From earlier? He seems pretty positive someone cut the brakes."

"Yeah." He doesn't sound surprised.

"After I hung up, though, I got to thinking. We've had mice in that shed. What if they chewed through the brake lines?"

"Jen." That's all he says. As he turns to face her, his eyes say more.

141

You're grabbing at straws.

Probably true, but she's too tired to plead her case. Time for a subject change. "Did you make it to your appointment?"

"Yes." A muscle clenches in his jaw.

"Everything okay?"

"It's late."

He's making her nervous hovering over her like this, so she pats the sofa beside her. "Sit. Please."

Dante hesitates. Picks a spot at the other end, as far as he can sit and still be on the same sofa. Perching at the cushion's edge, he shoves his hands between his knees. After a long silence, he looks at her. "Any more ideas who'd have done it?"

She shakes her head, then stops.

Dante quirks a brow. "Thought of someone?"

"No." Jen bites her lip. "Not specifically. It's just—having a brother in prison."

God, she's really going there. Dante watches, not saying anything.

Jen takes a moment to center herself. "I know I told you he's not dangerous. Yes, he's in prison, but he's a good guy." She winces. "Mostly. But some of his associates..."

She trails off, hoping he'll fill in the blanks.

But the look he gives her is...well, *blank*. "You know many of your brother's...associates?"

"That's the thing; I don't." She flops back against the couch, forgetting she has no bra. There's some bouncing beneath her thin white tank, but Dante locks his eyes on her face. "There's no proof, but I always got the sense he tangled with some bad people. That's how he landed in prison—not through something he did, but someone he *knew*."

"I see." His voice sounds flat. Like it's an everyday thing conversing about criminals.

She sits up again, crossing her arms to keep from jiggling. Belatedly, she sees she's squashed her boobs up into the neckline of her top. Dropping her hands in her lap, she sighs. "I just have a hard time believing someone would try to hurt me. Who would do that?"

"I don't know." He looks pained, and Jen wonders if it's getting to him. Threats of violence and danger and—

"I feel bad dragging you into this," she says. "You just wanted a farmhand job and now you're wrapped up in this drama."

"I don't mind."

"But—"

"Jen." The word is almost a growl. "I mean it."

Releasing a breath, she lifts her arms to fix her ponytail. Wisps of hair tickle her cheeks, a reminder she's due for a trim. "For what it's worth, I'm glad you're here."

"Why?"

She drops her arms, regarding him curiously. "I feel safer having you here." Hesitating, she goes all in. "Also, I like you."

He winces like she's kicked him in the nuts. "I like you, too."

The man doesn't sound happy about that. Jen shifts to pull her legs up under her, to warm bare feet beneath her bony butt. She's not sure she should voice the words bubbling in her brain, but they tumble out anyway.

"After Matteo went away—" Her voice wobbles. She can't bear to say *prison*. "And after Johnny left—um, I questioned myself so much. Wondered if I even knew the difference between good guys and bad guys. But Dante, I'm sure about you."

He looks pained. "What about me?"

"You're one of the good ones."

She watches his chest rise as he takes a deep breath. He lets it out slowly, closing his eyes. "Jesus."

"What?"

He opens his eyes again, shaking his head. Stands up fast and makes a beeline for the sink. As Jen watches, he pulls a glass off the shelf above and fills it with tap water. She hurries in after him.

"Sorry, I should have offered."

"I can operate a sink."

"Still—"

"Jen?" He sets down the glass and grips the edge of the sink. "I need you to do one of two things." The tension in his voice prickles her arms.

"What's that?"

His throat moves as he swallows. He's not meeting her eyes. "I need you to go change into something else." His fingers grip the edge of the counter. "A sweater or a burlap sack or something. Maybe stay upstairs while you're at it."

Heat coils in her belly. "Was that one thing or both?"

His eyes open and his gaze glides over her. "One."

"And the other?"

He looks at her with an intensity that makes her toes curl. Stares long and hard and steady. Takes a deep breath. "I need you to tell me if you want me to stop."

"Stop wha—*oh*." And then she's in his arms.

He's kissing her like last week, but it's different this time. Hungrier, hotter, as he presses her back against the kitchen counter and plunders her mouth with his tongue. She clutches his shoulders, clawing at the fabric of his shirt. She wants it off, needs it off.

Needs him inside her as fast as possible.

Pushing back, she's breathless. With the heels of her hands on the counter, she boosts herself up. The boxers are so short and the tile cold against the backs of her thighs, but the chill doesn't last. Wrapping her legs around him, she pulls him to her core. He doesn't stumble, pressing hard denim to her center. Gasping, she tilts her hips to feel him.

His fingers thread her hair and she kisses him again, surprised by her own boldness. He's not fighting her, but there's tension in his shoulders as her fingers trace his back.

It's Dante who breaks the kiss this time. "It's adrenaline."

She blinks. "What?"

"Adrenaline. From earlier. That's what this is."

It seems like he needs her to agree, so she nods. "Okay."

She knows it's more than that. He knows, too. This cracking between them, this electric snap. It's been there from the start.

He closes his eyes and utters a curse. Opens them and claims her mouth again. Hot hands roll down her sides, lifting the edge of her top. Her boxers grow damp and she rubs against him through the flannel. She could kiss like this all night.

Dante jerks back like he heard her thoughts. Drags a hand over his mouth. "Not here."

Jen swallows. "What?"

"If we're doing this, it's in a bed. Not on a kitchen counter. You're too good for that."

Desire flares in her belly. "All right."

His eyes search hers, hands locked on her waist. "Was that consent?"

Damn right it was. "Yes. Yes, please."

"Jesus, you're sweet."

Before she can ask if that's enough to make him stop, he scoops her off the counter. Cradling her in his arms, against a chest of solid granite, his eyes search hers. "Bedroom?"

"Upstairs. I can walk."

He shakes his head and starts for the stairwell. "I've got you."

She shivers, feeling the words to her core as he carries her up the steps.

CHAPTER 15

*T*his isn't happening.

There's no way he's laying Jen back on her blue and green quilt so her hair spills down pale gray pillows. No way the slab of lemon-yellow lamplight illuminates a smile that's just for him.

"Dante." She smiles again, twining fingers behind his neck.

He knows he should say something but can't break the spell. He kisses her again, hips settling in the space between her thighs. Bracing on his forearms, he watches her in wonder.

So fucking beautiful.

Jen's thighs hug his hips as her feet hook his butt. The warmth between her thighs sends him spinning, and he fights back dizziness with deep breaths. She smells amazing, like sunshine and honey and wildflowers.

For something not happening, this feels awfully real.

Jen breaks the kiss and smiles. "She found her spot."

"What?"

"Zsa Zsa." She nods to the corner where the sow snuggles on a nest of throw pillows he tossed off the bed. "She climbs stairs. Good girl."

146

He's wrecked the mood by bringing a pig to the bedroom. "Is that okay?"

"Her being up here?"

"Lying on your pillows."

She laughs, hair slipping on the soft sheets. "You're about to be inside me. You think I care about throw pillows?"

The words land like kisses. He didn't want to assume. Like maybe she came here just to kiss. To show him a clog in her bathroom sink.

But her thighs hugging his hips, the heat in her eyes, the wet stroke of flannel where she grinds against him—they're big clues where this is headed.

"Dante." She stretches up to kiss his throat. Her lips, featherlight and soft, brush a path from his pulse to the space behind his left ear. Closing his eyes, he knows he's felt nothing like this before. His arms quiver from holding himself up. He's trying not to crush her, not to lose control.

But she traces his earlobe with the tip of her tongue and control flies off the table. He's gone, soul circling the sun in crazy rings at the feel of her beneath him.

Shifting his weight to one arm, he lifts her tank top. He tries to tease, to take the slow route up her ribs. Jen grabs his hand through the thin cotton top. "More." She pushes his palm to her bare breast, and he groans.

So soft. Soft and lush and so fucking perfect he can't breathe. Burying his face in her neck, he breathes in sunshine and softness as he traces one nipple with his thumb. She arches up, filling his hand with heat. He's held grenades and automatic weapons, and once, a machete pulled from a fire. None gave this kind of heat.

"You're so perfect." He chokes out the words without meaning to.

Her lashes flutter, and she laughs. "That's me. Miss Perfect."

She's joking, but he can't see why. "It's true."

"Okay." She breathes it on a sigh, curious fingers moving

between them. Wrapping them around his shaft, she squeezes stiff denim. "Dante, please. Don't make me wait."

It's the sweetest order he's ever heard, so he has to obey. Heart hammering, he rolls away and tugs off her shirt. Tries not to see his fingers trembling on the drawstring of her shorts. His hands bare fresh swaths of skin as Jen pulls his shirt off and drags her hands down his chest.

"I'm on the pill." Pink stains her cheeks as her lashes flutter. "But, um—we should probably still use condoms."

"Okay." Protecting her is key, though he knows he's healthy. "In my wallet."

He shucks his hip holster, setting the Glock G19X on the nightstand. A gift from Sebastian, along with a metric ton of surveillance supplies. He'll think about that later.

Right now, Jen's got the wallet from his pocket. He grabs it and prays there's nothing weird inside. Just his ID, which bears his real name. The one he shared already, so much more intimate than what they're poised to do.

Jen waves the foil packet and smiles. "Can I put it on you?"

He nods, afraid to speak. "Yeah."

How did he get this lucky? Stripping his pants off, his breath snags as she rolls on the condom. If her hand feels this good, he'll lose his damn mind being inside her.

Her eyes flicker like she heard him. "I'm kinda nervous." She bites her lip. "Are you?"

Dante hesitates. Admitting he's fallible isn't normal. "Yeah." He rolls so she's under him, emboldened by the heat in her eyes. "Tell me if you need me to stop."

"Don't stop." Her smile spreads slow and sure, heels shifting to his low back to press him inside. "Please."

The groan rips out as he sinks inside her. God, she's exquisite. Slick and tight and so hot he nearly loses his mind. He's never felt anything like this. Not with anyone.

"Oh, God." She arches up, fingernails stinging his shoulder blades. "Feels so good."

At least he's not imagining it. He starts to move, slow at first. The way sensation blasts through him, he doesn't trust he can hold on. She's so small beneath him, even as muscular thighs clench his hips. Her hold on his shoulders stuns him with her strength. Lashes like butterfly wings brush his lips. He's never met a woman so delicate and daring, so fragile and fierce. She squeezes around him and the breath leaves his lungs.

He won't last like this but can't stop. Breathing against her neck, he prays for strength. "Jen. Jen." It's the only word that comes to him, so he says it again. "Jen."

On the next thrust she gasps. "Dante. I'm close."

Sirens sound in his brain. He knows this is wrong. Knows he shouldn't be here. Why was that again? He's taking advantage, that's it.

But guilt glides behind him as pleasure slams him against the wall.

"*Yes!*"

She squeezes her eyes shut and screams as he fights to hold on. It's no use. He's going under, chasing her over the edge, pleasure blasting him like a rocket. Words spill from his lips and he's not sure if it's English or Dovlanese or some secret language he never knew before.

Gripping his shoulders, she comes down slowly. "Wow."

He nods because what is there to say?

She's boneless beneath him, lashes fluttering. "What a way to end the day."

He laughs but it sounds like a sob. What has he done?

Swallowing hard, he tries to make the lump go away. Then she smiles and it melts like butterscotch candy.

"That was—" He doesn't have the word. Not in English or Dovlanese or any language he knows.

"Yeah." Her smile widens. "It was."

He kisses her again, hoping that works for the words he can't find. Maybe this will be okay. Maybe it wasn't the biggest mistake of his life. Maybe—

She snuggles against him, and he forgets everything but the feel of her in his arms.

Burrowing beneath his arm, Jen sighs. He tries to think of something to say. He should check in with her, make sure she's okay. Or maybe she needs to talk about what happened, either in this bed or out on the highway. So much adrenaline. She's not used to that.

Stroking her back, he searches for words. That's when she snores. It's soft and shallow and the sweetest sound in the world. Her foot twitches and she kicks his shin. She's out. Probably wouldn't wake if he drove a truck through the wall. His palm circles her back and she sighs.

Jesus.

She's too sweet. There's no way he deserves this. Deserves her.

Her earlier words nail him like a punch in the throat.

I questioned myself so much. Wondered if I even knew the difference between good guys and bad guys. But Dante, I'm sure about you.

He pinches his eyes shut, but memory kicks down the door of his heart.

You're one of the good ones.

It's not true. He knows this in his bones. He's deceived her about who he is, betrayed her brother, betrayed his own moral code. What kind of man is he?

As breath makes her back rise and fall beneath his palm, one word springs to mind.

Lucky.

He's the luckiest son of a bitch who ever lived.

But if Dante's learned anything, it's that luck never lasts. Knowing that doesn't stop him from holding her tighter. From burying his nose in her hair as guilt grips his balls and twists.

* * *

THE NOISE BLASTS HIM AWAKE.

Tumbling from bed, he's got his gun in hand before he knows where he is.

Jens's bed. *Jesus.*

What was that sound?

Glancing at the bed, he sees her sound asleep. He's crouched on the carpet, naked and alert, and she's snuggling a feather pillow. Rosy lips part, and her breathing hitches on a snore.

So lovely.

His heart hurts, but he drags his gaze off her. The clock on her nightstand says 3:39 a.m. It's dark outside. Grunting from the corner jerks his attention to where Zsa Zsa sits like Cleopatra on her nest of pillows.

The pig squeals again and Dante lifts a hand in greeting. "Need out?"

The sow tilts her head, black ear flopping. He glances at Jen, who still isn't moving. Exhausted from yesterday, so it's best to let her sleep. Finding his pants, he drags them on, then bends to grab his shirt off the bed. Might as well kiss Jen while he's here, inhaling the scent of her hair one last time. She smells sweet like honey and hay and his heart nearly bursts as he draws back.

This can't happen again. He knows that, even though knowing it makes his bones ache.

Tearing away, he pulls on his shirt. Zsa Zsa's on her feet, easing off the pillow nest.

"Let's go." He keeps his voice low, footsteps soft as he holsters the gun. "Don't judge," he mumbles as he hoists the pig in his arms. She got herself upstairs, but he's not sure she'll make it down on those stubby legs.

Zsa Zsa oinks and snuffles his chin. He sees tags in her ears and kicks himself. *Goddammit.* He meant to sweep for bugs before now. What kind of idiot waits a week?

Setting her down, he opens the front door. A dark shape darts in front of them and he grabs for his gun. Squinting, he sees it's just an opossum. Zsa Zsa starts after it.

"No." He shakes his head. "Know your enemy."

She cocks her head.

"Your enemy's not a marsupial."

Jesus, he's losing it. One roll in the hay with a woman—a perfect, stunning, wonderful woman—and he's giving combat tips to pigs. God help him.

He moves soundlessly across the pasture and through the door of his bunkhouse. Zsa Zsa's right behind him. The bug sweeper's in his safe, along with the trackers Seb gave him last night.

Last night.

Yesterday was the longest of his life. After a day spent loading grapes and wrestling a runaway truck, he paid a visit to Reggie Dowling's hideout. Seb's the one who tracked him down, calling in a favor with a Special Forces pal from his black ops days.

"Don't ask," Seb said, and Dante didn't.

They kicked down the door together, moving in tandem to guard each other's six.

Detective Dowling gaped with a forkful of mashed potatoes halfway to his mouth. "Who the fuck are you?"

"Friends of Matteo Bello." Dante advanced, shotgun aimed at the dirty cop's chest.

"Matteo *who?*" Dowling played dumb but paled as Sebastian stepped forward with a pistol in each hand.

"We understand you have a brother." Seb's boy-next-door smile gleamed ghoulish and lethal.

Dante pumped the shotgun, a Remington 870 he brought mostly for effect. "Matteo's like a brother to us."

The cop dropped his fork and put his hands up, jaw hinging like a hooked fish. "I don't know what you're talking about."

"Just like you don't know where those stolen guns came

from?" Seb whipped out his phone and snapped a pic of the pile of weapons behind Dowling. "Smile pretty for the camera."

"I can explain." The cop tried to get up, but Dante cut him off.

"We're not interested." They'd dug up enough dirt on Dowling to ensure cooperation.

Seb pocketed his phone and pointed his pistol again. "What interests us is how you sprung your brother from the clink."

"And how you'll make it happen for Matteo." Dante redirected his aim at Reggie's head. "Do we have an understanding?"

It turned out they did.

They've still got details to work out. Dirty cops aren't known for being trustworthy.

But he walked away from Dowling's hidey-hole considerably more confident in Matteo's early release. Also with a truckload of stolen weapons and a promise from Dowling to retire from illegal gun running.

So. That's that. For now, anyway.

Dante's got more to do, starting with figuring out who might harm Jen. Starting with bug sweeping his pig. "Hold still."

He moves the device over Zsa Zsa, who holds patiently steady. He scans her head and body, moving slowest near her ears and tail. Nothing. Not one blip, even on the ear tags.

Relief is a cold comfort. At least this time, distraction didn't bite him in the ass. *This time.*

He should scan the rest of Jen's house while she's sleeping. Plant a tracker or two while he's at it. The one on Johnny's car still isn't working, but Seb's got some troubleshooting tricks. For now, Dante needs to do what he came for. He's here to protect Jen, not to fall into bed with her and—

Well. What's done is done.

He stomps across the gravel, Zsa Zsa on his heels as he slips through the front door. "Wait here."

The sow takes a seat on the carpet, tail twitching as Dante creeps silently up the stairs. He scans Jen's bedroom first, careful not to wake her. The sun's easing up behind the hills, leaking faint yellow light through the blinds. She'll wake soon, so he needs to move fast.

He pauses near the bed, chest aching as he watches her sleep. What if he crawled in with her? Slid his arms around her like a normal guy, nose buried in her hair.

No. There's no time. He's here to do a job. To do it fast and get out.

Scanning the house takes forty-two minutes. Zsa Zsa trots along supervising. He checks paintings and throw pillows, toilets and spatulas. No bugs, but he doesn't trust that. At the kitchen sink, he gets a faint blip on the bug scanner. Fishing his hand down the garbage disposal, he comes up with a piece of mangled wire. Probably nothing, but he pulls out his phone and takes a photo.

The pig noses a pillow off the couch and lies down to watch from beneath a fringe of sooty lashes.

"I'm doing my job," he tells her. "Stop looking at me like that."

Zsa Zsa grunts and bows her head. With a sigh, he tucks the twisted wire in his pocket. Walks to the couch and stoops to scratch her ears. "Good pig. I'm sorry."

To be safe, he scans her again. Nothing.

He walks to the window and stares out at the darkness. Something's not sitting right with him. He's pissed the tracker on Johnny's car didn't work. User error, so he's mad at himself more than anything. If he'd done his job right, they'd have proof by now. Proof Johnny cut the brake lines.

In the dim dawn light, he sees Jen's work truck hunkered in by the barn. Bins of grapes brim from the bed. There's a lot of work ahead of him. Unloading will take hours.

He doesn't move. Just stares at the truck while wheels turn in his head.

Jen told him herself she hadn't used it for months. Who else knew her plans to take it yesterday?

She needs another list. A list of people who knew about yesterday's errand. Someone at the feed store? Maybe her friend at the Roseburg vineyard posted photos somewhere? Hell, her sister knew. Nic seems straight, but there's something odd about her. Something Dante can't quite place.

Seb. Even he's a suspect. Sure, Dante's glad to have him back in the picture. Glad the man had his back with the dirty cop. That he's trying to get the damn tracker to work. Maybe Sebastian means it about going straight. Maybe Dante does. Anything's possible.

He considers what Seb suggested as they left Detective Dowling's hideout. "Check her phone. Maybe someone's tracking it. And if they aren't, *you* should be."

Thinking this makes him an asshole. *More* of an asshole.

He slept with her. Now he plans to stalk her?

What a prick.

He needs coffee.

Spotting a contraption on her counter, he identifies it as a coffeemaker. One with all the fancy features. A few minutes of taking it apart and reassembling it convinces him to give it a go. He finds grounds in the freezer, filters in the cupboard. Pictures Jen shuffling to the kitchen in her white tank top, hair tousled and lovely. Her face brightening when she smells fresh-brewed coffee.

He's pathetic.

Pouring water with more force than necessary, he spills some. As he grabs a paper towel, he spots her phone by the dispenser.

Fate? He doesn't believe in that, but picks it up and taps the screen to wake it. Password protected. Of course. Matteo would have it cracked in six seconds, but he's not Matteo, so he tries the bug sweeper. Nothing.

He does what Seb showed him, opening the back and planting a tiny tracker the size of a flat bean. Snaps some photos while he's at it, planning to show Matteo later.

Much later, when he won't have to explain why he's in her house, holding her phone, before the sun's up.

Texting Seb seems safe enough.

PLANTED THE TRACKER. *Now what?*

HE DOESN'T EXPECT A RESPONSE. It's barely 5 a.m. But bubbles appear right away.

NOW WE WAIT. *By the way, I might have found a way to get your fucked up tracker working.*

HE STARES AT THE SCREEN, hardly believing his luck.

THE ONE ON *Johnny's car?*

MORE BUBBLES. Fucking bubbles.

THAT'S THE ONE. *Stay tuned.*

HE DOESN'T WANT to stay tuned. He wants answers now.

The coffee's done percolating, so he pours a cup and leaves the rest warming for her. He's halfway to the door when he spots a notepad. He can't leave without a note. Grabbing a pen, he taps it against his teeth.

Why is it so hard to find words?

Thank you seems rude. *That was great* seems creepy. *I love you* feels premature. All of it's true, but he can't write that. Scowling at the blank page, he uncaps the pen.

Jen,
    You're amazing. I feel....happy.

THAT'S ABSURD, but he keeps going. She deserves his words, even the dumb ones.

I'M in the barn working. Coffee's all yours.

HE PAUSES, considering what he could write. What he wants to write.

COFFEE'S ALL YOURS. *So am I.*

IT'S SO silly he can't believe he thought it. Definitely can't write it down. Except he just did. Scowling some more, he scratches out those last words. Scrawls his name at the bottom, a single word not preceded by "sincerely" or "yours" or "love" or anything else. Just *Dante*, hopelessly inadequate.

He drops the pen in the basket, disgusted with himself. Propping the note on the counter beside her phone, he skews it sideways so she'll see it when she comes downstairs.

With a deep breath, he turns to the door. Heart heavy in his chest, he forces himself to walk out into the cool morning with Zsa Zsa trotting beside him. He needs to get his head in the game. To forget what happened with Jen and focus on the job. It's what he knows, how he's made it this far in life.

Work. Duty. Protection.

That's why he's here. The only reason, the thing he must remember.

Zsa Zsa looks up when he sighs.

"Don't ask," he mutters, certain he doesn't have answers.

For the pig. For Jen. For anyone at this point.

CHAPTER 16

*S*he wakes after dawn, decadent and a little guilty. Has she ever slept past six? Not that she can remember. Definitely not since she launched the vineyard.

It's the sex, she decides as she touches the pillow where Dante's head lay all night.

All night.

She's not even sad they didn't stay up all night humping like bunnies the way they do in romance novels. The sex was outstanding. Otherworldly. Phenomenal.

But a man who lets her sleep, dosing her with pheromones to keep her conked out past sunrise? That's Jen's kind of romance.

She fumbles on the nightstand for her phone and comes up empty. Must be downstairs. That's also where the coffee waits.

Coffee?

She smells it from here, which must be Dante's doing.

Humming as she pads to the bathroom, she takes her time showering. Normally, she wouldn't bother before chores, but a quick turn under the spray melts the kinks in her neck. With her hair in a bun to keep it dry, she soaps and shaves and breathes sweet-scented steam.

It's almost enough to rinse away thoughts of her near-death experience. Then her loofa skims a sore swath of skin. "Ow."

She looks down, and yep—a mark from the seatbelt. Pale reddish-purple. By tomorrow she'll see fireworks of deep blues and browns. Sighing, she turns off the spray and wraps up in a fluffy yellow towel. She's humming again as she dresses, forcing her brain not to dwell on who might want to hurt her. Maybe no one.

Coincidence.

It has to be, right?

Or her own damn fault for leaving the truck unattended in the barn where mice could get to it. Nondi found a nest of them in her engine compartment once. The furry demons chewed through the electrical system, and didn't she warn Jen to watch for that?

Maybe she'll get a barn cat. Two of them, to keep each other company.

Trudging to the kitchen, she spies a full pot of coffee warming on the counter. There's a note propped beside it, so she grabs that first.

JEN,
> *You're amazing. I feel....happy.*
> *I'm in the barn working. Coffee's all yours.*
> *Dante*

THERE'S something scratched out between the last line and his name. She flips the page to see if she can make it out among pen dents on blank paper, but it's just a web of lines.

Huh.

She flips back to his note and reads it again. Feels warmth sliding to her belly, which has nothing to do with coffee.

Coffee.

Has anyone ever made her coffee? Such a simple thing, but combined with his declaration of happiness, it starts her day on a cheerful note. She's happy, too. And lucky her mouse-chewed brake lines didn't cause them any real harm.

By the time she strides outside, coffee mug in hand, she's got a spring in her step. She heads for the east barn, following the sound of shoveling. Dante got an early start. As she slips through the door, she sees his back first. Bunched muscles flex as he flings fresh straw into Maple's stall.

"Thanks for the coffee."

He spins around, shovel cocked to strike. Jen jumps back and chokes on a laugh. "Hey. It's just me."

"Jen."

The blaze in his eyes is nothing she's seen before. She fights the urge to take another step back. "You okay?"

"Sorry." He's slow to drop the shovel, scanning her from head to toe. "Didn't hear you come in."

"I'm in sneakers." She tips her foot to show her battered Nikes. "Seemed better for the running around we're doing today."

His scowl doesn't soften. "Did you tiptoe or something?"

"Not really." She sets down her travel mug with what's left of the coffee. "Guess you're just lost in thought?"

"Guess so." He doesn't look happy about it, so she doesn't offer a penny for his thoughts. Would his thoughts include what happened last night? She should probably say something about it.

"So." She takes a breath. "Last night—"

"—shouldn't have happened." He frowns. "I'm sorry, I got carried away. It won't happen again."

"What?" She stares, waiting for the punchline. He must be joking. "You left me a note." She replays the words in her mind, wondering what she missed. "You said you were happy."

It sounds silly when she says it out loud. Did she read something into it that wasn't there?

Judging by his face, maybe so.

"Yeah, uh…" He drags a gloved hand over his scalp, leaving a streak of dirt on his forehead. "Look, I was irresponsible. You're the boss and also vulnerable and I took advantage and I'm sorry."

The words run together like he rehearsed them but failed to stick the landing. What's going on?

Jen squares her shoulders. She's done letting men tell her how it is. "That's bullshit."

Dante blinks. "What?"

"It was amazing, and you know it, and I'd do it again in a heartbeat." She crosses her arms so he can't see her hands shake. "So would you."

His frown suggests this is not how he heard this conversation in his head. "Look, I—you're right, okay? It was great, but it wasn't a good idea. I see that now, and I'm—"

"If you say you're sorry one more time, I'm beating you with that shovel."

He shuts his mouth. Pauses. Without a word, he hands her the shovel.

"Uh…" She wraps her hands around the shaft. "What's this for?"

"Go on. Get it over with." One edge of his mouth quirks. "Please."

The strain in his voice suggests he's not kidding. Jen's irritation ebbs, but she's not done. "Why did you say that?"

"Get it over with?"

"No. The stuff about it being a bad idea. It wasn't, and you know it, and I want to know why you said it."

He stares at her, then shakes his head slowly. "You are not at all what I expected."

It's not at all what she thought he'd say. "Thank you." She's not sure it's a compliment. "Still not an answer."

"I guess it seemed like the thing I'm supposed to say." He rubs his head again, searching for words. "You know when someone cooks you dinner and serves you a second helping of mashed potatoes, and you clean your plate?"

"Uh…" She loves mashed potatoes, but that's probably not his point.

"You clean your plate again, and the host asks if you want a *third* helping," he continues. "You're supposed to say 'no thank you,' right?"

Jen frowns. "Am I mashed potatoes here?"

He groans and stares at the ground. "No, I just meant there's always the thing you *want* to say and the thing you *need* to say. They're rarely the same thing."

She only kinda follows. "This seems like a uniquely American conundrum."

"No kidding."

"Give me another example."

He peels off his gloves, letting out a long breath. "You're at the Sportsman's Warehouse with a couple shirts at ten minutes 'til closing. Saleslady asks if you'd like a fitting room, you're supposed to say 'thanks, I'm good.' Even though you want to try them on. *Need* to try them on."

"I—don't know what to do with that." This is the weirdest post-coital conversation she's ever had.

Weird, but…endearing?

"Or the waiter brings you chili when you asked for clam chowder," he continues, "but it turns out it's really great chili, and you end up eating it." He searches her eyes, willing her to understand. "When he stops by and asks, 'how's the chowder,' you say 'great, thank you' instead of 'it wasn't chowder' so you don't make it awkward. It's the same idea."

She gives up trying to figure out who's the chili and who's chowder. Strange as this is, this makes sense. "I might get it." She hesitates. "You get a scarf for your birthday. Handmade, from a friend you haven't seen for years. She says, 'I know you love blues and greens, and you said you always wanted a handmade scarf.'

And you love it to death, but you're positive you never said any of that, and also you only wear purples and reds. But you're so nuts about the scarf that you just—"

"Exactly."

She shakes her head, wishing she'd recorded this conversation. It's strange and heartfelt and confusing and touching and above all, completely unique.

It's Dante in a nutshell.

"I'm still not sure I get it," she says. "But I think it comes down to you saying what you think you're supposed to say in some twisted attempt to shield me or protect me or—"

"Yes." His face sags with relief. "That's it."

"Dante."

"Yeah?"

"Just say what you mean." She hesitates, then reaches out to touch his arm. "Even if it's awkward. Even if it seems like it's not the right thing. If it's the truth, it's always right."

His throat moves as he swallows. Eyes search hers, scanning to see if she means it. "It really was a bad idea."

"I disagree."

He nods and doesn't argue. Steely eyes search hers again. "I like you. A lot." He shakes his head like this isn't a good thing. "So fucking much. I haven't cared about anyone this much since— well. A long time. I'm falling for you, *hard*, and it scares the hell out of me."

She blinks. "Wow." The wheeze makes her choke, which turns into laughter. She's fighting for air but waving him off as he steps up to save her. "Oh my God, no—I'm not laughing at you. I just— wasn't expecting that."

Holy shit. That's more than she pictured in her fantasy when she rolled out of bed this morning.

From the look on his face, he's just as surprised. "Yeah." He clears his throat. "So, I just made this awkward. I'll get back to—"

"Dante, wait." She grabs his arm. "I care about you, too. Way more than I expected to." It's on the tip of her tongue to say she loves him. She might, but she knows better than to spring it on a guy the morning after sleeping with him the first time. "I like you so much it's insane."

He stops. "Yeah?"

"Yeah. Definitely." She keeps hold of him, though there's tension in the coiled muscle of his bicep. "I know the rules or etiquette books probably say it's too soon for us to go wearing our hearts on our sleeves. That we hardly know each other, but that's not true. I *know* you, Dante. You're a good guy, the best guy I know, and I've been falling for you since the first day we met."

Pain bends his brow, and she's not sure why. "I'm not that good a guy."

"You are in my book."

His lips twitch. "Your library's lacking."

She laughs and stretches to grab her work gloves off a shelf. "You kidding? I've got acres of books. The Dewy decimal system and everything. Now let's get to work."

He shakes his head like he can't believe they've had this conversation. She's a little confused herself, but in a good way.

He cares for her. Falling for her, even. That's unexpected.

Unexpected, but…nice.

They work in companionable silence for a stretch, Dante humming the Dovlanese lullaby she's heard before. When her phone rings in her hip pocket, she tugs off her gloves and fumbles to answer.

This is a call from an inmate at an Oregon correctional facility...

"Matteo," she says when he comes on the line.

Dante's head jerks up. Jen holds up a hand so he knows it's okay, but he doesn't go back to shoveling. She starts to take the call outside, but why? She has no secrets from Dante.

So she stays, tucking her hair behind her ear. "Hey, Matty."

"What the actual fuck?"

She tries not to flinch. "Who told you?"

TAWNA FENSKE

"Who told me my goddamn sister almost got killed when someone cut the brakes in the International?"

"We don't know for sure that—"

"Goddamn it, Jen. I saw the police report."

"How did you—" There's no point asking. "Never mind."

"There's no doubt now. Someone's after you."

"We don't know that for sure. It could be mice. Remember that time Nondi—"

"Where's your farmhand?" He huffs with exasperation. "Let me talk to him."

Jen frowns. Dante's watching her, expression unreadable. "Why?"

"He was driving?"

She's not surprised he knows. "He saved my life."

"I need to talk to him." Matteo huffs again. "To say thank you."

That sounds reasonable, so it's a red flag. "I won't let you do your scary asshole thing to him."

"Scary asshole thing?"

"He's a good guy, Matteo. If he hadn't been driving, I don't know what I'd have done. I won't let you be a jerk to someone I—"

"I've got it." Dante puts a hand out. "He wants to talk to me?"

She meets his eyes. "Yes, but you don't have to." She puts the phone to her chest. "My brother acts all scary and mean, but—"

"I can handle scary and mean."

She starts to argue, then recalls the moment she startled him. The steel in his eyes, the lethal grip on the shovel. With a sigh, she hands him the phone. "Just know he doesn't speak for me."

Dante nods and takes the phone. "Yeah?"

Her brother's voice goes mumbly, and she sees Dante thumbing down the volume. "Yeah." Dante clears his throat. "Police are checking into it."

The reply is so loud she hears it with the volume down. She loses count after half a dozen expletives.

166

"My goal is keeping your sister safe." A pause. "Sir."

Sir? Jen lifts a brow, but Dante's not watching her. He's focused on the call, spine ramrod straight. It's nice he's being respectful, but come on…

"I'll ask Jen to keep you apprised of updates." Another pause. "You have my word I'll do whatever it takes to keep your sister safe."

She shivers as Dante says a few more words and hands the phone back. Taking it, she covers the mouthpiece again. "Might want to tone down the 'whatever it takes' rhetoric to a guy in prison. You don't know my brother."

Dante doesn't blink. "I said what I said."

He turns and gets back to shoveling. She lifts the phone to her ear to address her brother again. "I hope you weren't a jerk to him."

Matteo grunts. "I'll see you Saturday?"

It's her usual day to visit, but she has the grape stomp. "I've got the event, and Nicole's got something after, so I might be late. It also might be just me this time."

A pause. "I might have news."

"News?"

"I'll see you Saturday."

He hangs up before she can press. She's still holding it when Dante looks up.

"Everything okay?"

"Yeah." She lowers the phone and shrugs. "He seemed sort of…weird."

"Weird?"

"He said he has news."

"Good news?"

"I don't know." She laughs and shoves the phone in her pocket. "You heard him. It's hard to tell with a guy like my brother. He could find out he won the lottery, and he'd still sound like someone ran over his cat."

Dante goes back to shoveling. "You're visiting him Saturday?"

"It's the day I normally go." She picks up a pitchfork. "I don't know what time the event will be over. Could be after visiting hours."

"I don't want you going anywhere alone."

She wants to argue, but what's the point? "I don't want me going anywhere alone, either."

Surprise flashes in his eyes. "Figured you'd fight me on that."

"I'm not an idiot."

"Never said you were."

Sighing, she grabs her pitchfork. "I'll figure something out."

For now, it's enough to be here in this barn, her animals snuffling around them, the man she's falling for working by her side. Tomorrow, she'll hold her wine event. Tomorrow, she'll know if she's come close to buying Johnny out. Reclaiming her land, her business, her career.

Her future with Dante?

She shivers and keeps shoveling.

CHAPTER 17

"*W*ow." Nicole scans the crowd with a low whistle. "I can't believe how many people came out for this."

Neither can Jen. "It's the front-page article in the paper."

"Maybe my magic flyers." Nic grins and bumps Jen with her hip. "Seriously, good job."

"We got lucky with the weather." Even luckier, no one's balking at the hundred-dollar entry fee. Even with part going to the National Grape Stomp Cooperative, it adds up with the day's food and beverage sales and what they're making on carnival games. The face-painting booth has a line miles long, and Dante's dart-throwing booth is a hit. "If people keep coming, we might actually pull this off."

"*You* might pull it off." Nic squeezes her hard, a surprising show of force from someone whose fitness routine involves Legos. "Proud of you, Jen. You made this happen."

Pride puffs her chest as she scans the crowd for Dante. The afternoon brought bright blue skies with just a dusting of cloud wisps. Grapevines trail proudly up their trellises, fat grapes bobbing in the breeze. In the corral, Maple, Scape, and Zsa Zsa munch grass like a scene from a farmland postcard.

Jen smiles, but she's still looking for Dante. She spots him by a row of split barrels where the stomping starts soon. He appears to be arguing with Sebastian the dentist. "That's a weird friendship."

"He's a weird guy." Nic frowns. "The dentist. Not your farm-hand. Is he packing heat?"

"Who?"

"Dan." Nic nods to the two men. "Either that's a gun in his pants, or he's real excited about his next dental cleaning."

Jen squints at the bulge beneath Dante's jacket and frowns. "Probably a pocketknife or pruning shears or something."

"If you say so." Nic turns to the parking lot and swears. "Fuck."

"What?"

"Look who's here." She points as Johnny's car slides up the driveway. The Miata this time. Her stomach churns as the car pauses at the "owner parking" sign. Johnny guns it into the spot and Jen grits her teeth so hard they squeak.

"Stay." Nicole puts a hand on her arm. "You focus on the event. I'll see what the asshole wants."

"Thank you."

"You'd do it for me."

She would if Nic dated. Someday, maybe Jen can return the favor.

Shoving Johnny from her mind, she strides across the grass to where Dante and Seb stand scowling at each other. Sebastian's speaking, hands moving as Dante stands with arms over his chest. "I'm telling you; a little sodium hydroxide and they'll break right down."

Dante growls. "We're not putting chemicals on fruit people touch with their bare feet."

"You've got a better plan?"

"A little C4. Small bottle bomb, maybe?" Dante glances up, and his eyes warm. "Hey, Jen."

"Is there a problem?" She considers touching his arm, but holds back. They're probably not at the PDA stage. They haven't even slept together again, though he rubbed her feet on the sofa last night after a day spent setting up the event.

Dante scrubs a hand over his chin. "Some of the grapes are too tough for stomping."

"The smaller ones." Sebastian digs in the barrel and pulls up a thick cluster. "Bare feet won't do the job right."

Dante grunts agreement. "Can't make wine if you can't crush the grapes." He flicks a thick-skinned grape and scowls. "We're discussing ways to soften them up."

She looks between the two, unsure if they're joking. "You know the goal's not really crushing the grapes, right?"

Sebastian cocks his head. "What's that?"

"The grape stomp." She swallows a laugh. "It's just for show. We're not really using the juice for anything."

"Huh?" Sebastian seems unable to wrap his head around this. "I don't get it."

"It's for fun," Jen offers. "To give people a chance to feel like they're taking part in an old vineyard ritual."

"I knew that." Dante glares at Seb. "Got wrapped up with problem-solving and forgot that part."

"It happens." Sebastian seems disappointed there's no chance for destruction. "Guess you're kinda distracted, huh?"

He's talking to Dante, who scowls in the direction of the parking lot. "Is that Johnny?"

"Yes, and Nicole has him handled."

Sebastian's watching Nic like he favors the thought of being handled. "Wonder if she needs help."

"No." Jen answers in sync with Dante, and they stare at each other.

"Take it from me," Dante says. "The Bello ladies don't need anyone's help unless they ask for it."

Sebastian nods and takes a few steps back. "Still, I'll keep an eye out."

They watch him go, an easy amble carrying him to where Nic's got a hand on Johnny's arm. Jen's blood pressure builds as she looks back at Dante. "You weren't really going to blow up the grapes, were you?"

"It crossed my mind."

She huffs out a breath. "You're such a *guy*."

"Is that a bad thing?"

"Not always." Not when he's naked and driving into her. Not when he's wrestling the steering wheel of a runaway truck. Jen shivers. "Guess I should go mingle with the guests."

"Need help?"

Shaking her head, she touches the bulge beneath his jacket. "If that's a gun, I'd prefer you keep it stashed. It's a family event."

He lifts the hem to show her a Leatherman multi-tool in a thick sheath. "Not a gun."

"Good." She's a jerk for suspecting, but she had to check. As she scans the field of guests, her gaze drifts to a casually dressed couple holding hands. "Why does that woman look familiar?"

Dante squints at where she's pointing. "That's Lady Isabella."

"The Duchess of Dovlano?" She gasps as the woman turns toward them and waves. "Oh my God, she's coming over here." Jen smooths her hair and wishes she'd worn something cuter. A ball gown, maybe. "Do I call her Your Highness or Your Excellency or—"

"Hi, Izzy." Dante puts out a hand, which the curly-haired brunette shoves away.

"Don't you dare handshake me, Dante." She throws slender arms around his middle and hugs hard. "After everything we've been through—"

"Hi, I'm Bradley." The man beside Izzy extends a hand, and Jen shakes it firmly. "Old friend of Dante's. We live over by Ponderosa Resort."

"A pleasure to meet you." Memory clicks into place. "You were on his reference list."

"Ah, you're the vineyard owner?" He releases her hand and slips an arm around his wife. "Beautiful place you have here."

"Thank you." She straightens as the Duchess turns to greet her. "It's a pleasure to meet you, Your um—Highness?" Crap, should she curtsy?

The woman smiles. "Just Izzy, please." She blows a dark curl off her forehead. "It's lovely to meet you, Jennifer."

"Just Jen." She's really having this conversation.

A breeze catches Izzy's curls, and she tucks some behind her ears. "Dante called yesterday to invite us," she says. "We've heard so much about you."

Dante invited freakin' royalty to her grape stomp? And told them about her? She scans his face but can't read anything. Not until he tucks an arm around her waist.

"Jen's the best." He looks down with one edge of his mouth quirking. "Coming here's been incredible."

"It's been great for me, too." Is this really happening? Heat floods her face as she tries to play it cool for Izzy and Bradley. "I can't believe you're here."

She can't believe *she's* here, rubbing shoulders with royalty as the hottest man she knows heaps praise on her. Whose life is this?

"We know you're busy, and we don't want to keep you." Izzy offers a hopeful smile. "We're in town for a few nights. Maybe we could have dinner together sometime?"

"I'd like that very much." Spotting a news crew across the pasture, Jen takes a step back. "Sorry, I need to grab that reporter before someone else does." Someone *else*, meaning Johnny. God only knows what he'd say to a camera.

As Izzy and Bradley stroll away, she turns back to Dante. "You think we'll be ready for the first round of stompers in twenty minutes?"

"Yep." He nods to the sign-up table. "Every slot's full, and there's a waiting list a hundred deep. Okay to use extra grapes to set up more rounds?"

"For sure. As many as we can."

"Done."

"Thank you." She aches to kiss him, but settles for patting his arm.

Arching an eyebrow, he flicks a glance at Johnny. "He's not watching."

"I know. I wasn't—"

"So if I kiss you, it's not for show. It's me wanting to kiss you because I want to fucking kiss you."

She swallows. "Is that your idea of requesting consent?"

"Is that your idea of saying yes?"

"Shut up and kiss me."

He snags an arm around her waist and pulls her to him. Lips claim hers, taking the kiss long and slow and languid as a pack of twenty-something guests applaud.

Jen's breathless by the time they pull apart. "Is that a promise of what's coming once the event's over?"

"Count on it."

As he strides away, her body buzzes in his wake. She covers a smile, tugging the sleeve of her flannel shirt as the hair on her neck prickles. Glancing behind her, she sees Johnny scowling from the edge of the corral. Penelope's nowhere in sight, and neither is Nicole.

Jen shivers, then heads for the sign-up table to get the event underway.

* * *

"LAST ROUND OF COMPETITION, FOLKS." Nicole holds the mike to catch the crowd's applause. "Who's it going to be—Team Johnson with Pete stomping and Katie swabbing? Or maybe Team Nielson-Krauss with Casey and Connor trading off this time?"

The crowd whoops as Nic keeps running down the roster. She's good at this, getting the crowd pumped. If Jen had Nic's charisma, maybe she'd have saved her farm a lot quicker. Certainly with much less heartache.

But if this works, she's cautiously optimistic. She scanned the sales numbers a minute ago, and while it won't cover everything, it's a big dent in what she owes her ex.

Speaking of Johnny, she hasn't seen him in a while.

Come to think of it, it's been a while since she saw Dante. He ran to the barn to find a sprinkler. Nic's plan to hold a kids' stomp called for fun cleanup, and wouldn't it be great to use the sprinkler they played in as kids? Jen smiles, recalling how they'd swoop through the spray, her and Nicole and Matteo and even Nondi in their swimsuits on a hot summer day.

The kids' stomp starts soon, so she really should find Dante.

She heads for the barn with crowd noise fading behind her. Penelope waves from her spot near the entry table, so Jen sighs and diverts.

"Jennifer, *hello*." Penelope smiles and blows a blonde wisp off her forehead. "Things are going brilliantly, yes?"

"Yes." She keeps her answer cautious, knowing it'll go right back to Johnny. "Tell your fiancé he should expect to hear from my attorney this week."

"Oh, of course." The upturned lilt in her British accent implies she hadn't even thought about the money. "I'll certainly let him know."

"Great." Jen starts to back away, but Penelope bites her lip.

"You haven't seen him, have you?"

"Johnny?" She shrugs. "I'm sure he's around somewhere."

"He's been gone a while." A breeze catches her skirt, and Penelope holds it down with one hand. "That's...odd."

"He'll turn up." She has no interest in helping hunt for him, but unease in the other woman's eyes halts her step back. "Everything okay?"

"Fine, fine." She bites her lip again. "Seems like he's been disappearing quite a little bit lately."

Jen sucks back a sigh. It'd be just like him to be banging the bartender in a back room. Jilting two women in two months— she wouldn't put it past him.

Or is she suggesting something else? Something more...sinister.

Jen shivers. "He's probably in the storage shed or something." She offers a smile she hopes seems sincere. "Maybe sniffing around for things he can take for the wedding."

Penelope brightens. "I'll make sure he returns anything he borrows. You can count on me." Guilt seeps into her gaze. "Even if you couldn't always count on Johnny."

She's not sure what to say to that. "It's fine. It all worked out in the end, didn't it?"

"It did." She lays a hand on Jen's arm. "You and that handsome farmhand are still dating?"

Dating. Is that the word for it? "Something like that." She backs away, aiming for the barn. "I have to go. I'm already late."

"Cheerio!"

The crowd fades behind her as she bypasses the west barn. She heads for the east barn where they've stashed extra grapes. Following a murmur of voices, she moves toward the back barn door.

Goosebumps ripple up her arms, and she's not sure why. As she slows her steps, the voices in the barn get louder.

"I've checked you out." It's Johnny, his tone low and sharp. "You didn't know that, did you?"

Jen slips forward, boots silent in the gravel. Is he talking to a woman?

"I know enough." *Dante*. His voice sounds deadly as Jen inches closer.

"Think so, huh?" Johnny's laugh holds no humor. "I'm willing to bet your girlfriend's not so informed."

Girlfriend? Jen's nails scrape her palms, but Dante speaks again.

"Leave Jen out of this."

Okay, that's…not so bad. Maybe good?

She risks another step forward. She's two feet from the barn door, still out of sight. If she can't see them, they can't see her. Is it wrong to eavesdrop? She did hear her name.

Johnny laughs again. "Leaving Jen out seems to be your strategy, isn't it?" A shuffling of shoes as someone moves. She holds her breath. "Since I know where you were last Monday morning."

Jen frowns. Monday? That's not ringing a bell.

"I'm gonna go out on a limb," Johnny continues, "and guess you haven't told her."

Told her what?

Dante stays silent. No sound at all, save the distant crowd. Jen's heart hammers in her ears. She needs to breathe, but she knows it'll come out a gasp. If she passes out, she'll miss his answer.

Uncurling her fingers, she risks small sips of air.

"Nothing?" Johnny snorts. "You've got nothing to say?"

A pause. "What are you driving at?"

Johnny hoots. "You know her brother. You visited the bastard in prison. That's a huge piece of information to withhold, don't you think?"

Wait. *What?*

Dante mutters a low curse. He doesn't deny it.

Jen shuts her eyes because *oh God*, it's true? He visited Matteo? Why would he—

"Take it from me," Johnny continues. "She's not a fan of men sneaking around behind her back."

"You know someone who is?"

"Just saying." Johnny snorts again. "I might've fucked up, but not on your scale."

Her heart pounds louder, and she wills Dante to correct him.

TAWNA FENSKE

To say he's mistaken. There's a misunderstanding. Anything to prove Johnny wrong.

To prove Dante's the good man she knows he is.

"Jen."

At his voice, her eyes flutter open. Does he know she's out here, or is it just a guess? She holds still, not breathing. Not moving a muscle.

"I know you're out there." His voice sounds tired. Resigned. "Come in. Please. I'll explain everything."

Her heart sinks. They're the same words Johnny said when she caught him in bed with Penelope.

I'll explain everything.

Like there's a reasonable explanation for cheating.

Like there's a reasonable explanation for Dante knowing her goddamn brother and not saying so. She combs her brain for something, *anything*, to make it make sense.

She grips the barn door, not daring to walk in. If she stays out here, it won't be true. Can't be true.

Johnny's voice pokes her in the ribs. "I'd love to hear you explain, *Dan.*" He snorts. "Please, tell us both what you were doing at the state penitentiary at 9:37 a.m. the Monday of last week. A couple days before your dental appointment, wasn't it?"

His words snatch Jen's last hope. She drops her hand from the barn door, balling hands into fists. Drawing a breath, stars blink behind her eyes.

It's true.

It's really true.

Releasing a breath, she takes a step. Then another. One more step, another breath.

In, out. Right, left. She uncurls her fists and feels her world start unraveling. As she steps through the barn door, her eyes lock with his.

The guilt in his gaze lands like a punch. She squares her shoulders and doesn't drop her gaze. "Tell me."

CHAPTER 18

*H*e knew better.

He knew and he did it anyway, and now he'll face the consequences. He's faced them before.

But he wasn't braced for the pain in Jen's eyes. He's taken bullets in the leg, one in an arm. A knife blade to the gut. None of it hurt like the searing betrayal he sees on her face.

"Jen." He lifts a hand, and she flinches.

Goddamn it.

His hand falls to his side, as useless as he is. He's lost the right to reach for her. Her lips press to a thin line as she holds his gaze without blinking. She's waiting for him to deny it, to explain somehow.

It's not possible.

A muscle ticks in her cheek as she unclenches her jaw. "It's true, isn't it?"

He owes an answer but can't make his voice work. A nod—he can manage that.

"Jesus." She closes her eyes and grabs the doorframe. Her knees wobble like she might drop.

Johnny steps toward her but Dante growls. "No."

The man halts. He might have the upper hand, but Dante's got fury on his side. Fury and a willingness to snap his neck if he lays a hand on Jen.

Besides, he knows Johnny's guilty. He can prove it, too. Seb got the tracker working. Archived data and everything, going back to the day Dante planted it on the SUV. There's no denying Johnny's stupid Porsche parked right next to the storage shed the night before Jen's brakes failed. He can prove it.

But first, Jen.

He takes a breath. "I can exp—"

"Answer the question." Her hands ball up tight. "You went to see my brother."

He hesitates. Nods once.

She flinches like he's hit her. "This wasn't some random visit to a guy you've never met. He sent you here, didn't he?"

A better operative would have an excuse ready.

A better man would've dodged this whole mess.

Dante just nods. "Yes."

Johnny—smug bastard—folds his arms. "My attorney's quite good. Subpoenaed records of your brother's visitors. You didn't know we could do that, did you?"

Jen doesn't react. Just keeps her eyes on Dante. On the lying, deceiving asshole who—

"Or maybe *you* sent him, Jen?" Johnny tilts his head at Jen. "Maybe that's it? You asked your farmhand—your *employee*—to see your jailbird brother for help hiding money?"

"What?" Jen frowns at Johnny. "What are you talking about?"

He shrugs like he hasn't lobbed a big, stinking crap bomb. "That was my theory. Instead of paying me like you're supposed to, you had Matteo stash funds in offshore accounts so they wouldn't show up when we reviewed—"

"Stop." She narrows her eyes. "That's absurd, and you know it."

"What?" His smile gets smugger. "Your brother has the brains to hide money. All I'm saying is—"

"Enough." Her voice slashes through the bullshit.

Dante scans her clenched fists and thinks how good it would feel to see her hit Johnny. Hit someone, *anyone*. Maybe him. They all deserve it. God knows he'd like to punch Johnny, then himself, in that order.

But none of that will make this better. Nothing will make this better.

Johnny tries another step toward her. "Jen. *Honey.*"

Dante moves quick, wedging his body between them. A fist forms at his side.

Johnny sneers. "You gonna hit me, big guy?"

A good idea, but no. "Do. Not. Touch. Her." He spits the words like bullets, daring the man to defy him.

"Fine." He puts up his hands and backs away. "Go ahead. Give it your best shot. Explain yourself, man."

With a deep breath, Dante looks at Jen. Her eyes are shuttered, but the pain's still there. Pain he caused.

But if he can take away some of it—

"Jen, he's guilty." Dante sounds like a third-grader tattling on a classmate, but he keeps going. "Johnny cut your brake line."

The man sputters. "I did no such thing!"

"Shut up, Johnny." Jen's bark silences him. "Just be quiet."

Johnny obeys. Smart man, for a guy not bright enough to scan for tracking devices before driving to his ex-girlfriend's house in the dead of night. A guy not bright enough to know a hundred better ways to hurt someone.

The fact that Dante *does* know isn't a point in his favor. "I can prove it," he tells Jen. "If you'll just let me—"

"No." Her eyes glitter, but she won't let tears fall. "You're not running this show. I'm still your boss."

He clamps his teeth together so he can't blurt the words. *I quit.*

That won't help. Nothing will help. Her eyes search his and come up empty.

"How could you?" Her voice trembles. "How could you do this?"

There's no good answer. Not one he can give her.

I'm a ruthless, no-good, spineless—

No. There's nothing he can say, so he keeps his mouth shut. Johnny's not as smart.

"Jen, honey." The man's not giving up. "Let me tell you what I know." He catches Jen's arm. "We'll go somewhere, and I'll expl—"

"That's it." Dante grabs his wrist and squeezes, so he drops to his knees. "I warned you."

Johnny turns a pale shade of purple and stays down. There's a crackle in his arm, but Dante doesn't let go. He could kill him right now, just snap his neck and—

"Stop."

Jen's voice breaks his grip. He lets go, leaving Johnny in a heap on the barn floor. As the man sags at Jen's feet, she jabs him with her toe. "Get out of here. *Now.*"

Johnny blinks. "But—"

"Now!"

He scrambles to his feet, loafers spinning straw as he beelines it for the barn door. Dante watches, glad Sebastian's outside. He won't let the man get far. Seb knows their evidence is rock-solid.

Alone with Jen, he turns to face her. She's staring with tears in her eyes. "Tell me. Everything. Right now."

His heart twists. A fine time to learn he has one. "I—"

I can't, he starts to say.

He swallows the words. Shoulders slumping, he drags a hand down his scalp. "What do you want to know?"

Blinking hard, she folds her arms. "Everything. I want to know how you met my brother. I want to know how you ended up at my farm." Her throat rolls as she swallows. "I want to know how you could touch me, kiss me, make love to me when—"

"Because I love you."

She chokes. He's said the wrong thing, but there's no going back, so he says it again. "I lo—"

"Don't." She squeaks the word like it's squeezed out of her by force. "You don't get to toss out those words and think they make anything okay."

He knows it'll never be okay. The vise on his heart tells him so. He takes another breath. "I won't betray Matteo's confidence. Some stories aren't mine to share."

"For fuck's sake—"

"But I'll tell you *my* story." What he can tell. Everything he's able to share without putting her in danger.

Jen blinks so hard her forehead creases. She's doing a damn fine job holding back tears. "So you'll betray me, but not my brother. Got it."

None of this is going how he'd hoped. Just five minutes ago, he knew he'd nailed her ex-fiancé. He'd solved the mystery to keep her safe. Hell, he's even close to getting her brother out of prison. How did it all go to hell?

But he owes her something. The truth, for starters.

Letting out a long breath, he turns to the door. Two strides and he's peering outside. No one's in earshot. Not Seb. Not Johnny. Not the crowd across the pasture. They're alone for the moment. Facing her again, he wishes he'd bug-swept the barn. So many ways he's failed her.

Her fists find their way beneath her crossed arms. "I'm waiting."

Dante takes a breath. Where to begin? "I told you about my job in Dovlano."

"Palace security?"

She spits the words like she knows they're false, and who can blame her?

"It's the truth," he says. "Palace security. But sometimes, that meant..." He searches for the right words. "My job required making people vanish."

That jolts her. "What people?"

"I only took out bad people. *Really* bad. Those who hurt others with no remorse or repercussion or—"

"Took out?" She rolls the words on her tongue. "You're a hitman."

He flinches. "I prefer 'bodyguard.'"

"And I prefer 'princess,' but I'm a goddamn farmer, okay?" Jen huffs a breath. "You're an assassin."

It's just semantics, and he knows he shouldn't argue, but— "Security professional."

She grits her teeth. "Hired gun. Thug. A fucking criminal."

That one hurts. "Keeper of the peace."

"For fuck's sake!" Jen stomps a boot. "We're splitting hairs over what to call a guy who kills people for money?"

It shouldn't matter, but he can't have the woman he loves thinking he's a heartless killer. "Everyone I've eliminated," he says softly, "*everyone*, no exceptions, harmed others first. Women, children, animals—"

"So you're a killer with a conscience?" She throws her hands in the air. "Great. The last guy I loved was a cheater. I go from that to an assassin."

His brain catches the words he knows aren't the point.

The last guy I loved...

She loves him? *Loved* him, past tense, but still. He fights the hope flaring in his chest. "It wasn't supposed to happen."

Jen frowns. "You'll have to be more specific. Killing people for a living?"

"No." He has no regrets there.

"Letting my brother send you to spy on me?"

"No."

"Then what, Dante? You're not sounding like a guy who'd undo anything here."

He chooses his words carefully. "It's true Matteo asked me to look after you. I agreed because I owe him my life. He's a good man, your brother."

She snorts. "Why am I not surprised your idea of a *good man* is someone doing hard time?"

He doesn't answer. Just waits for her to get there. She might hate him, but she knows what kind of man her brother is. The best guy they know. It's the one thing they agree on.

"Fine." It's all she says, but it's enough.

He draws another breath. "My goal was to keep you safe. I did that to the best of my ability."

"I never asked you to."

"Your brother did."

"Great." Her jaw tightens and he knows this is no point in his favor.

"Falling for you," he says softly. "That wasn't supposed to happen. Falling in love was never—"

"Stop saying that." She squeezes her eyes shut. "Do you even know what love is?"

He doesn't answer. Can't, because his throat feels like it's filled with rubber bands. His heart's pinching in on itself, while his stomach aches like he washed down a box of Cheez-Its with drain cleaner.

But none of that's love.

"Love is wanting what's best for you no matter what." His voice chokes with gravel, but he keeps going. "Wanting to protect you at all costs. Needing to see you, to be with you, to hear your laugh and see your smile and know I'm the lucky sonofabitch who gets to exist in your orbit."

She stares at him a long time. "Such pretty words, Dante. Too bad I can't trust any of them."

Stepping back, she moves to the barn door.

"Where are you going?"

"None of your business."

"Jen—"

"Don't talk to me." She whirls around, stalking toward the door. "You're a control freak criminal and I want you off my property."

Her words lodge like needles in his heart. She's almost to the door when he blurts the words. "Wait. Please. I'm begging you."

Jen stops but doesn't turn. "What?"

"He cut your brakes. Johnny? I can prove it."

She stiffens but doesn't turn around. She's wiping her cheek with the heel of her hand. "Prove it how?"

"Tracking device." He doesn't get credit, but he won't rat out Seb. "It showed Johnny's car here the night before we went to Roseburg."

She considers that, fingers gripping the barn door. "You've told police?"

"Not yet."

"You're planning to?"

"Eventually."

She snorts and looks over her shoulder. Her eyes are red and wet. "Wasn't it you insisting I bring them in?" A frown. "Which is weird, knowing you're a—"

"Don't."

She stares at him. "What is your plan here?"

He fights the urge to make fists. "I'd like to talk to him. Johnny."

"Is that code for—"

"No."

"Because I don't want him—"

"Understood." He doesn't want Johnny dead, either. Just very, very sorry. "I won't let anyone hurt you."

She stares at him, eyes so sad his spleen aches. Slowly, she shakes her head. "Too late."

Then she slumps out the door, gone from his life for good.

* * *

Sebastian's waiting by the west barn. Dante doesn't break stride as his friend falls in beside him, silent but entirely too cheerful. As Dante seethes, Seb waves at a family standing by the sno-cone booth.

"Dr. LaDouceur, I got third place!" A gap-toothed boy hoists a hand-lettered ribbon.

"Good job, Ashton." Sebastian tips his ball cap to the parents. "That new toothpaste working out okay?"

The mother smiles and hands a drooling toddler to her husband. "Ashy loves it, don't you, sweetie?"

Ashy—*Ashton*—nods gravely. "Tastes like bubblegum."

"Hard to believe it's good for you, huh?" Sebastian ruffles the kid's hair. "I expect to see those choppers in solid shape at your next appointment."

Dante grits his teeth and waits for this to end. For the crowd to fall away as they leave the little family and head for the far side of the farmhouse. Out of earshot, Seb drops his dentist smile. "You told Jen about Johnny?"

"Yep."

"Didn't go well?"

"Nope."

A pause. "Cover's blown?"

Dante flinches but keeps walking. "Yep."

"Had a hunch when she stalked past muttering how all men should be castrated at birth."

He doesn't press for details. Probably doesn't want them. "I didn't give you up," he says. "But she knows about her brother."

"What does she know?"

"That we're acquainted." Dante pauses. "That I saw him last week."

Fucking Johnny.

But fucking Dante, too. He knew better than to visit the damn penitentiary. Phone calls are fine. Monitored, but fine. An in-person visit, though...

"Stop kicking your own ass." Sebastian elbows him hard. "We've got another ass to kick."

Dante growls. "No violence."

"Since when?"

"Since this case is on the cops' radar. Johnny ending up dead would be bad."

"Who said anything about dead?" Seb grins as they spot the bastard alone by the storage shed. "We're talking to him."

"We?"

"You're in no state to do this alone."

He should argue, but what's the point? Sebastian's right. The way he's feeling, he'd wring the asshole's neck. Johnny deserves it, but the last thing they need is a body to bury. He's pretty sure that's not the grand gesture that'll win Jen back.

Like anything could win her back. She hates him. *Hates* him. The opposite of love.

Johnny spots them and freezes. He's holding a box as his gaze swings from Seb to Dante and back again. "It's my stuff." He grips the box tighter. "My wine keys and extra bar rags and—"

"Let's talk." Dante doesn't give him time to argue. Just grabs him by the arm and drags him toward the shed.

Sebastian twists the doorknob, but it doesn't budge.

"It's locked." Johnny looks smug. "And if you think I'm giving you the key—"

"No need." Dante's lock pick slips in before the man stops talking. Shoving the door open, he drags Johnny inside.

The man blanches as Seb kicks the door shut. Jen's ex is doing his best to play it cool, but Dante sees his knees shaking. Sees his throat rolling as he swallows and darts his eyes to Dante's.

"What do you want?"

"I'll take that." Sebastian grabs the box and drops it by a battered wooden chair. "Have a seat."

Sweat beads on Johnny's brow. "I don't—"

"Sit." Dante shoves his shoulder and makes it happen. "We're chatting."

Johnny looks at Seb and swipes his forehead. "Who are you?"

"A friend." Sebastian gives his dentist smile. "Not yours."

The sharpness in his voice makes Johnny squirm. "Wait. Aren't you the dentist? I saw you on a billboard with—"

"Yep." Sebastian's still smiling. "That's me. *The Dentist.*"

It sounds more menacing than it does in Seb's TV commercial. Dante's struck by an urge to high-five him, which he's never done in his life. It's a gauche American habit he can't wrap his brain around, but he's glad to have his colleague here. Seb's not so bad.

"The Dentist?" Johnny gulps. "Is that some sort of mobster thing? A serial killer nickname or something?"

"Or something." Sebastian smiles. "Your left front incisor is a shade darker than the right. A little laser whitening could fix that."

Jesus Christ. Dante drags a hand over his head. "We know you were here last Wednesday night."

At Johnny's blank look, Sebastian steps in. "The night before Jen's brakes went out?"

Johnny's gaze swings back and forth and sways a bit. The confusion in his face is comical. "Someone cut Jen's brakes?"

"Not what I said, is it?" Dante brushes back his jacket. Enough to show the butt of the Ruger in his chest holster. Johnny pales again. "I said her brakes went out. Nice of you to add the cutting detail, though."

"Very helpful," Seb agrees.

"Whoa, that's not what I'm saying." Johnny's got his hands up, eyes darting fast between them. "I just assumed—"

"You know what they say about assuming?" Seb leans on the shed wall, hands tucked in his pockets.

Johnny frowns. "It makes an *ass* out of *u* and *me*?"

"It's a good way to lose a finger." Dante takes out his multi-tool and starts to trim an errant hangnail.

Johnny gulps again. "Look, man. I don't know what you think I did, but I promise I never tried to hurt Jen."

There's a nerve twitching at the corner of Johnny's eye. As Dante stares, the man shifts in his chair. Dante trims another nail, not taking his eyes off Johnny. "You want to explain what you were doing here Wednesday night?"

"The night before Jen's brakes failed," Seb adds helpfully. "In case you forgot."

"I didn't forget." Johnny scowls. "I mean, I didn't know until you told me. Wednesday night?"

"Yep." Another hangnail bites the dust. "Take your time, give it plenty of thought."

The man shifts again, chair creaking beneath him. "This was the twelfth?"

"Yep." Sebastian folds his arms.

"Wait." Johnny's face brightens. "Wednesday night I was in Ashland for a wine dinner."

"Bullshit." Dante stops trimming but doesn't drop the tool. He holds it so it gleams in a slice of sunlight from a cracked window. He slides a glance to Seb. "Show him."

"No, please!" Johnny covers his face with his hands. "Please don't pull my teeth. Please don't pull my—"

"Get it together, man." Sebastian slaps his hands aside. "Here. *Look*." He holds his phone to Johnny's face. "That's an image pinpointing the location of your car on this property at 11:39 p.m. on Wednesday the twelfth."

"The night Jen's brakes were cut," Dante adds in case of a corollary between loss of bladder control and loss of memory.

Johnny frowns as he peers at the screen. "That's impossible."

"Nope." Seb holds the phone closer. "The tracking system doesn't lie."

"Unlike Johnny here." Dante goes back to trimming his nails.

With a shuddery breath, Johnny shakes his head. "That can't be right." He shoots a pleading glance at Seb, pinpointing him as the good cop in this film. "May I get my phone?"

"No!" Both men answer, but Dante's the loudest.

"All right, fine." He turns to Dante. "Are you on Facebook?"

"Do I look like someone on Facebook?"

"I am." Seb drags his phone back. "What am I looking at?"

Jesus. Of course Seb's a criminal with social media accounts.

"Find the Ashland Wine and Cheese Fest." Johnny rubs his palms on his legs, sweat streaking dark denim. "Got it?"

"Hang on." Seb's trigger finger taps the screen. "All right, I'm on the event page."

"Go to pictures. It's the fourth, maybe fifth one in the lineup."

Sebastian's frowning as Dante peers over his shoulder. It's a party, all right, with everyone in tuxes and fancy ball gowns. If it weren't for the American flag behind the buffet, it could be a royal ball in Dovlano.

"There." Dante points to an image. "That's you?"

"Hey, watch it." Seb shoves his hand away. "You're smudging the screen."

Dante glares at Johnny. "Big deal. You had your photo taken so you had an alibi before you ducked back here to do your dirty work."

"No way." He nods at the phone. "The event was in Ashland. That's a five-hour drive. And it didn't start until eight."

Dante scans the event info at the top, confirming the asshole's not lying. Not about this, anyway. He stares at Johnny, willing him to break. To explain what's going on.

"Penelope!" Johnny gasps as his eyes go wide. "She had the Porsche that night."

"Your girlfriend?" Dante's not surprised he'd throw a woman under the bus.

"Fiancée." Johnny tries to stand, but Seb shoves him down. "I left her the keys to take her girlfriends out for brunch the next morning."

Sebastian snorts. "Very nice. You're pinning this on your girlfriend?"

"*Fiancée*. And I'm not pinning anything on her. I'm sure there's a perfectly reasonable explanation why—"

But Dante's not listening. He's hearing puzzle pieces click into place. *Penelope*. The saccharine personality. Her urge to get close to Jen. The way she seems not to care about the vineyard, which in his experience, means she cares quite a lot.

None of it seemed suspicious alone, but added together...

Seb's watching him. "What are you thinking?"

"Same thing you are."

Christ.

Dante drags a hand over his head, forcing himself to think.

"She was here," Sebastian adds. "I saw Jen talking to her."

Fuck. Dante looks at Johnny. "Where is she?"

"Who?"

"Your *fiancée*, you dolt." He grabs him by the shirt front and pulls him so they're face to face. "Where is Penelope?"

"Outside somewhere. Or, wait." Johnny tries to pull back, but Dante fists his shirt harder. "She said something about running an errand. Something to help Jen."

He says it so virtuously that Dante almost feels sorry for the guy. If Penelope's helping Jen, then Dante's a priest.

He lets go of the shirt and Johnny slumps back in the chair. Sebastian turns as Dante pushes past. "Where are you going?"

"Out." His hand's on the doorknob, but his mind's racing.

"You can't just leave me here." Johnny sputters. "With *the dentist?*"

"We'll just stay and have a little chat." Seb smiles at Johnny. "About oral hygiene."

Jesus. It sounds menacing, but Dante would bet his last royal paycheck Seb's planning a lecture on gingivitis. He'll make it creepy as hell, too.

Sebastian nods at him. "You've got this?"

"Of course."

"Wait." Johnny struggles to stand, but Seb shoves him back in the chair and watches Dante.

"Need reinforcements?"

"No time." Heart pounding, Dante shoves through the door.

The sun's too bright and the crowd's too cheerful and somewhere out there, the woman he loves is in trouble.

He takes off at a run, not even sure where he's going.

But he'll find out. He'll do it or die trying.

CHAPTER 19

*J*en grips the steering wheel, conscious of her knuckles aching. Too bad it's not from punching someone. There are plenty of people she'd like to punch, starting with her own damn self, because what kind of loser falls for a hitman?

Releasing her death-grip, she flicks a glance at the speedometer. She lets out a breath and eases off the gas. The last thing she needs is a speeding ticket.

How she'd love to slug Dante. And Johnny. Maybe Matteo, come to think of it. Any man who hid the truth from her. Any man who underestimated her or claimed to be something he's not and then convinced himself it's for her own good. She hates that so much she tastes rage on the back of her tongue. What does rage taste like? Curdled milk and burnt vines and those little Vienna sausages overcooked in barbecue sauce.

Fighting the urge to flip off a slow driver, she eases into the next lane. "Asshole."

Who is she even talking to? Herself, mostly.

He *loves* her.

Claims to love her, which she knows can't be true. Not even if her heart kicked to a canter when he said the words. It's only anger, the same kind bubbling in her veins as she takes the exit toward the penitentiary.

Matteo has some explaining to do. She considers how to question him, how to avoid saying something to land him with a longer sentence. He's a good guy, her brother. Much as she hates admitting it, she knows that in her bones. Even Dante knows it.

Dante.

God. Leave it to her to fall for an assassin. Her epic judgment went from bad to worse. By the time she hits thirty, she'll be married to a...to a...

What's worse than a killer for hire?

He's a killer with a conscience, *fine*. She believes that, at least. Even through red rage, she trusts what he said about offing people who deserve it.

Like he gets to decide.

She spins the wheel toward the side road she and Nic normally take. A shortcut they found last month. As she nears the turn, she spots a white Porsche SUV.

Johnny?

No...Penelope. The flowered skirt swirls at her ankles as she stoops to inspect the right rear tire. Jen slows, annoyed with herself for caring. She doesn't care. Not really.

But Johnny's new bride won't know a lug nut from a lollipop, so Jen slows again when she sees the flat tire. A gust catches Penelope's blonde hair, and she brushes it back with one slender hand. Jen sighs and eases to a stop.

Penelope looks up as Jen flings her door open. "Jennifer?" Her face wilts with relief. "I'm so glad to see you."

Gritting her teeth, Jen gets out. "Got a flat?"

"I don't know what happened." Frowning, Penelope plucks a nail from the rubber. "Perhaps this is it."

"Happens a lot on farm roads." Jen heads for her trunk with

Penelope on her heels. "Did you check to see if your spare's in good shape?"

"Spare?"

Good Lord. "It should be in the trunk."

"Could I perhaps borrow yours?"

"It won't fit your car."

"I see." The other woman bites her lip. "I was going to call roadside assistance."

"Out here?" Jen shakes her head and pops her trunk. "You'll pay an arm and a leg. Better to limp along to a service station. There's one about a mile up the road."

"You're so clever." Penelope peers from behind her. "What are you hunting for?"

"A jack." Finding her own is easier than explaining what it looks like. "Go grab your spare, okay?"

"I truly can't thank you enough."

"It's fine." Honestly, it's nice to be needed. She's so tired of men in her life treating her like some helpless damsel. She'll never be that. Even if she envies Penelope's flowered skirts and floaty hair, Jen can change her own damn tire.

As Penelope trots back to her car, Jen finds her tool chest. She'll need the lug wrench, maybe work gloves to protect her hands. At the sight of her chipped nails, she sighs. Protection's beside the point, but at least she'll stay clean.

Grabbing the gloves, she heads for the Porsche to see how Penelope's coming along with the spare. She's bent over the trunk, rounded backside in the air as she digs in back. Jen sighs again.

Penelope looks up with a weak smile. "I can't seem to find it."

"Did you check under the carpet?"

"Carpet?" She frowns and peels back the edge. "I don't think there's anything but dirt and grime and—"

"Scoot over." Jen bumps her with a hip. "There's probably a compartment under here."

"I can't believe I didn't think of that."

Jen swallows a snarky response as she peels back the carpet. No spare, no handle to lift the bottom of the trunk. She leans inside, probing for something to tug.

"Do you see it?" Penelope's fretful voice is right in her ear.

"Could you grab me a flashlight?" Never mind, she surely won't have one. "Your phone. Flip on the flashlight from your phone."

"Righty-oh."

Jen leans in further, spotting the pull to draw back the cover. "Never mind, I think I found it."

As her fingers grip the nylon loop, a hand clamps her shoulder. Jen shrugs it off. "It's okay, I've g—"

A palm clamps her mouth, shoving a damp rag past her teeth. She sputters and kicks, but sweetness makes her woozy. As her senses dull, she flails a fist. Connects with something, an arm? More muscle than expected, and a grip that's tight and sure.

"Penel—"

Chloroform.

She's never smelled it, but knows instantly that's what's on the rag.

It's her last thought before light blinks out behind her eyelids and everything goes dark.

* * *

Jen wakes in some sort of warehouse. It smells like motor oil and Styrofoam peanuts and the ground feels gritty under her cheek. There's an ache in her wrists, and when she tugs, she finds them bound behind her back.

Holy shit.

She struggles to recall what happened, but her head's stuffed with steel wool. She tries not to stir, surveying the space through slitted eyes. Someone's close. And something tells her it's in her best interest to feign sleep.

Penelope.

Memory comes in a muddy rush. The flat tire. The damp rag. The sweet British lilt turning sharp and bitter as she ordered Jen to stop fighting, to get in the damn trunk. Like she had a choice.

There's the Porsche in the corner, but she feels a tire behind her butt. Another vehicle? She risks craning her neck, and yep... that's her own car.

What's going on?

"Get up." A toe jabs her ribs. "I know you're pretending to be asleep, Jennifer. *Get up.* We have work to do."

She opens her eyes, faking more grogginess than she feels. "Where am I?"

Penelope sighs. "That's not important. No one's going to find you here, so stop looking for a rescue."

Rescue hadn't crossed her mind, though it's a nice thing to wish for. One of those overprotective men would be handy right now. She struggles to sit up, which isn't easy with her hands bound. "What happened?"

"What *happened* is that you tried to jilt my fiancé out of his livelihood. The vineyard he worked for his whole career. That's what happened, but we're going to fix it."

"We are?"

"*You* are." Penelope's voice drips with anger and glee. A troubling combination. "Want to know how?"

Jen's not sure she does. Still struggling to sit up, she finally manages. Winded, she leans back against her car. It's her first time getting a look at Penelope since they stood behind her Porsche on the dusty roadside. Good Lord, is this the same woman? Same floaty skirt, same blonde hair. But the ice in her eyes curdles Jen's blood.

She tries to remember the question she's been asked. "How am I going to fix it?"

"By signing over the property." She bends and wags a pen in Jen's face. "It's rightfully his. You know he invested much more in the business than you did, so it's only fair."

There's nothing fair about this, but Jen doesn't argue.

Think.

She tries to rub her head, forgetting her hands are bound. As she starts to topple, her head clears a bit. Righting herself, she blinks a few times. "Signing over the property." Repeating the words doesn't make them any less absurd. "Why would I do that?"

"Because you don't have a choice."

As answers go, it's concise.

Jen fishes again. "Won't people be suspicious about my sudden change of heart?"

"People? What people?" She shrugs. "Your brother's in prison. Your sister's a dimwit daycare worker. Your boyfriend's not really your boyfriend, is he?"

Jen can't bring herself to answer. A lump lodges in her throat and she makes no move to swallow it back. Pain brings clarity, and right now, she needs more of that. She stays silent, sitting with the ache of knowing Dante's not her boyfriend. Not even close.

It shouldn't hurt knowing this. He's a damn hitman, for crying out loud.

"That's what I thought." Penelope laughs. "Dan or whoever he is? He's just an employee who does a fine job faking you're in a relationship to make Johnny jealous. But it didn't work, you know."

"Okay." The more Penelope says, the crazier she sounds. Jen can't say if that's a good thing, but she needs to keep her talking. It buys her more time to think. "Won't Johnny be suspicious I'm suddenly signing away my family's property?"

"Please." The look she gives her brims with good-time girl

talk vibes. Jen fights a shiver. "We both know Johnny's not one to ask a lot of questions."

"Good point."

"Besides, he'll be so thrilled with the wedding gift that he won't question it."

Jen finally gulps back the lump in her throat. "Why are you doing this?"

She doesn't expect an answer, so she jumps when Penelope barks out a laugh.

"People always underestimate me."

"No shit."

She's relating for real, but Penelope cocks her head. "Are you mocking me?"

"I'm not." After dating a hitman, bonding with her kidnapper doesn't seem far-fetched. "I know what you mean."

Penelope nods. "The truth of it is that I get what I want. And what I *want* is to start my married life free and clear of you with a vineyard all our own."

Clouds thin in Jen's mind, but she concentrates on looking bleary-eyed. She throws in a sway to make it convincing. Before she topples, she grips the tire with bound hands. It's a chance to test the restraints, to figure out what's binding her. Handcuffs? Must be. Metal, cold and hard, bites into her bones.

Is this how she dies?

She doesn't want the answer to that. Not yet. She tries another question. "Is Johnny in on this?"

"Of course not." Penelope crouches for more cheerful girl chat. "Between you and me, the man's not a deep thinker. But he's a genius with wine, and together we'll make Devon Vineyards the best in the country. Maybe the world, who knows?"

What Jen knows is that she doesn't have a lot of options. She's shackled in a warehouse and no one knows where she is.

Dante.

Dating a hitman wasn't awesome, but some lethal skills would be handy. But Jen's on her own, and Penelope's reading her thoughts.

"No one knows you're here, Jennifer." Her voice is melodic, almost sweet. "I got both our cars off the road quickly. This warehouse might be ugly, but it's soundproof. No one knows I rented it. Not even Johnny."

Jen squeezes her eyes shut. "So, what—I'm supposed to sign something?"

"For starters."

She opens her eyes to see Penelope scanning her face. "What's to stop me from contesting it?"

She knows before the question leaves her lips. She's not leaving here alive. That's the plan, anyway.

A cold ball rolls in her stomach. Penelope stretches a hand out and tucks a shock of hair behind Jen's ear. "You're a smart girl. I can't let you go, but if you play nice, I'll let your sister live. That's a good tradeoff, yes?"

"Not particularly."

"Good." She pats her cheek. "It's almost a shame. I was beginning to like you."

"Huh." The feeling's not mutual, but Jen bites her tongue. "We should go for tea. I know a place a few miles from here. Excellent Earl Grey."

"Oh, Jennifer." Another cheek pat sends Jen's skin crawling. "You're a funny girl."

Jen grits her teeth against the urge to bite that damn hand. She tugs the cuffs again, testing the tension.

Penelope laughs. "They're military issue. A souvenir from my time with the Special Reconnaissance Regiment. You didn't know I'm ex-military, did you?"

"You were in the British Army?" Jen shakes her head, struggling to wrap her brain around this. "You never mentioned it."

"Because it pays to let people underestimate you." She smiles like she's giving good life advice. "I left the UK before they started letting women into SAS. I would have made it, though."

A chill snakes down her arms. This changes things. Penelope's not just crazy. She's dangerous. A trained killer, like Dante.

"It's also how I got the handy listening device," she says. "The one planted on the pig?"

Jen tries to make sense of this detail. "You brought Zsa Zsa?"

"*Zsa Zsa?*" She throws back her head and laughs. "Oh, that's precious. Of course I didn't have a pig in my car. What do I look like?"

She looks like a raving lunatic, but that's beside the point. "You bugged a pig?"

"The collar. It was easy, knowing you'd take the filthy thing into your home. Good thing, too, since you washed the pasta maker. A thousand dollars worth of surveillance devices down the drain, *literally*. God."

"I don't know what you're talking about."

She laughs, and it's a bitter sound. "Of course you don't. But *I* know what *you're* talking about. That's the whole point. I've been listening to your silly conversations for weeks."

More clouds clear, and Jen's almost got her wits back. But they won't do much good with her hands bound.

"I'd love to hear more about the Special Reconnaissance Regiment," Jen tries. "Sounds fascinating."

"Nice try." Penelope stands and sticks a hand in the pocket of her skirt.

A gun. She's going for a gun.

Jen's thoughts spin, twirling with thoughts of Dante. How he'd sing to Zsa Zsa in the barn. The comforting spice of elk chili. His sweet smile in the teahouse as he laid the crown on Estelle's head. His hands on a pitchfork, on the wheel of a runaway truck. Hands on her body as he—

"Whoopsie daisy." Penelope pulls out a pen and drops to her knees, catching Jen's shoulder as she sways again. She's not faking this time. Her brain's gone swishy. Penelope waves the pen in Jen's face. "That chloroform takes a bit to wear off. You're still dizzy?"

Jen nods and tries to clutch her head. Stupid handcuffs. "I don't feel so great."

She tries toppling again, really leaning into it this time. "Can't. Stay. Up—"

"This won't do." Penelope stands and hoists her to her feet. "Come on. You can sit in the car while you sign things."

Jen forces herself to go limp, to play the groggy, helpless captive. "Can I have a drink of water?"

"After." Yanking open the car door, she shoves Jen in the backseat. "Lean back against the headrest. Try not to soil yourself, all right? This will be messy enough to clean up."

It's tempting to pee just to spite her, but that won't help. Surviving's the goal, so Jen feigns another bout of dizziness. "I'm not sure I can even hold a pen right now."

Penelope smiles and Jen's skin crawls again. "Lucky for you, I sticky-tabbed all the paperwork."

"Lucky me."

"Just a few signatures and we'll be done."

And so will Jen.

Think.

"Can I at least—"

"No." Penelope twirls toward the Porsche. "Enough stalling. Let's get this over with."

Footsteps tap the concrete floor as Jen's heart races. Shit. She's going to die if she doesn't think of something.

Dante's face floats in her mind, but she pushes it back. She needs to save herself.

Flicking a glance at Penelope, she sees her back turned. Jen steels herself and scans the contents of her car. Pine air freshener. Road map in the seat pocket. Empty water bottle. Dante's work gloves.

Her heart squeezes, but she forces herself to focus. Beside her on the backseat sits Nondi's box of mementos. Family photos. Some lace doilies. Placemats she'll never use. The crystal candy dish.

Oh.

A thought takes shape.

"Stay conscious, Jennifer." Penelope's voice bounces from the other side of the warehouse. "Blimey! Why is it so hard to find a bloody pen that works?"

Jen draws a breath. It's a crazy plan, but all she's got.

Thanking genes for her boyish figure, Jen jams her heels against the headrest. Hoisting her butt off the seat, she whips her hands beneath her. *Ow, ow, ow, her shoulder… okay!* Done. Bound hands in front now, she snatches the base of the candy bowl.

"Ah! Here it is."

Jen looks up to see Penelope spinning toward her. She shoves the candy bowl between her knees, conscious of her hands shaking. She coughs to hide the sound of handcuffs clanging crystal.

"You're not sick, are you?" Penelope draws closer, twenty feet, fifteen. "I can't get sick before my wedding."

Jen coughs again, turning so the dome light doesn't glint off crystal. "I'm okay."

Act weak, she reminds herself, and coughs again.

"Ugh, I really can't be ill." Penelope stops walking, ten feet from the car. "Perhaps I can toss the—"

"No!" Jen straightens. "I'm fine, really. Just allergies."

Please, please, come closer…

She fights to keep a straight face, to keep a grip on the crystal bowl in palms slick with sweat. She'll have one shot to do this. Only one.

"All right." Penelope's walking again, five feet away. Four, three, two…

"Jennifer? What are you d—"

Jen leaps and swings, shrieking like a lion. Bound wrists

above her head, she slams the dish on Penelope's skull. There's a crack and a scream and *oh God*, Jen's not sure who's yelling. Crystal spears her palm, and there's blood and pain and *holy shit*...is she shot?

Penelope crumples to the floor like a rag doll, but she's not down yet. "You bitch!"

She swipes at Jen's ankle and Jen jumps back. The candy dish splintered on one side, but it's still intact. Still clutched in Jen's sticky palms as she swings it overhead. Another shriek swells out of her as she brings it down and lets go. The bowl strikes Penelope's head with another *crack* and rolls away, spinning pinwheels of color on the floor.

This time, the bitch stays down.

Jen's breathing hard as she takes a step back. "Penelope?" She doesn't dare poke her with a toe. She's seen how that plays in horror flicks.

Another step back as the candy dish rolls to her feet. Keeping her eyes on the slumped body, she stoops to grab the bloodied crystal.

Penelope's not moving.

Jen's not taking chances.

"Penelope?"

No response. Christ, did she kill her?

Dante's words come back to her.

I only took out bad people. Really bad. Those who hurt others with no remorse or repercussion or—

Maybe the man had a point. Heart pounding in her ears, she watches Penelope's back. Blinking back tears, she waits for the rise and fall of breath. For any sign of life.

There. It's subtle, but steady. The whoosh of air fanning blonde hair off her face. She's breathing, at least.

"Fuck." Jen breathes the word as she steps back. Where is her phone? Or car keys. She could drive right through the door, just jam the pedal to the floor and—

"Jen!" A door crashes open. Literally—blown to smithereens. She spins with the bowl in her hands as smoke clears and Dante thunders through the haze. There's fury in his eyes and a gun gripped in his hand.

She's never been gladder to see someone.

As his steely eyes sweep the room, they land on her and soften. He stares at her hands, her blood-sticky fingers clutching bright crystal.

His eyes don't drift to Penelope as he steps over her prone form. "Dead?"

He doesn't sound disturbed by that.

Jen shakes her head. "Still breathing."

Penelope gives a muffled snore. Jen steps back, needing more distance from the woman who planned to kill her. Needing less distance from Dante. "You came."

He lowers the firearm. "I'll always come for you."

Jen's shaking hands send the handcuffs rattling. "Even when I call you a control-freak criminal and tell you to get off my property."

An edge of his mouth quirks. "Even then."

The shaking in her hands gets worse and her grip slips off the crystal. It crashes to the floor but doesn't break. Just bounces against Penelope's foot and spins to a stop.

Dante watches, then meets her eyes. "Beautiful *and* strong."

"My grandmother's," she says, conscious of her voice shaking. "It's real crystal."

"I wasn't talking about the dish."

She blinks, eyes filling with tears. "I'm still mad at you."

"I know."

"How did you find me?"

"I'm a control-freak criminal."

"I know." She smiles and lifts cuffed hands to swipe at her eyes, which are suddenly spilling tears. She sniffs and laughs and chokes with relief.

"Here." He holsters the gun and tugs something from his pocket. She's expecting a weapon, but he pulls out a wet wipe. "Hold this and I'll get the cuffs off."

"How—*oh*." He's so quick she doesn't see the lockpick. Rolling her wrists for circulation, she offers a shaky smile. "I can't believe you found me."

"I can't believe you thought I wouldn't."

They both look at Penelope, who's snoring even louder.

"Special Reconnaissance Regiment, huh?"

Jen blinks at him. "How did you—never mind." She shakes her head, cleaning her fingers with the wet wipe. "Maybe I don't want to know."

"If you do, I'll tell you." The low gravel in his voice sends her heart thudding. "I'll tell you anything."

"Anything?"

He hesitates. "Yes."

She wonders what secrets he's hiding. How many hits or kills or whatever he's had. Where he met her brother and whether Sebastian's more than a dentist. Maybe she doesn't want to know.

There's something she needs to know though. "Do you really love me?"

"Yes." No hesitation.

"Really?"

"More than anything." He takes a step closer, arms opening to enfold her. "More than chili or Cheez-Its or my Ruger Mark IV Hunter."

"More than Cheez-Its?" She draws back and gives him a skeptical look. "Sounds serious."

"You have no idea." He draws her into his arms and squeezes so tight she squeaks.

That's when Jen's phone blares. Matteo's ringtone. Jen jerks back and shakes herself from a love daze. She's an hour late to see him, which means he's ready to call out the cavalry.

Is Dante part of the cavalry? She watches his eyes for her answer. "Are you here because he sent you?"

"No." He doesn't flinch as the phone rings again. "I'm here because I love you."

He's telling the truth. Maybe her instincts steered her wrong before, but she'd stake her life on this.

The phone rings and she follows the sound beneath the driver's seat. As she fumbles it out, she braces herself for yelling. Not from her brother, from her. He's not the only one pissed off. With a glance at Penelope, Jen opens her mouth to speak her mind.

"Listen, Mat—*dammit*."

This is a call from an inmate at an Oregon correctional facility...

There's enough of a delay for her to swallow some anger, but Matteo's voice brings it back again.

"Where the fuck are you?" It's panic, not anger in his words.

Still.

"I'm safe." She flicks a glance at Dante. "I'm here with a friend of yours."

There's a long pause.

She fills it so he won't think the worst. "Dan's turned out to be a highly skilled farmhand." A pause of her own before she goes all in. "Besides bucking hay and sorting grapes, he's damn good in bed."

Dante winces and closes his eyes.

Matteo's not so silent. "Are you fucking kidding me right n—"

"No, you listen to me. I appreciate you looking out for me, and I get that I'm the baby sister. That you got even more protective after Nondi died, which is saying a lot. But I'm a grown-ass woman, Matteo. I make my own choices, and you know what? I choose him."

Dante's eyes open and he stares at her. His mouth twitches in silent approval.

But Jen doesn't need approval. Not from him, and not from

her brother, who's gone eerily quiet. "Matteo? Are you still there?"

"I'm still here." He doesn't sound happy about it. "You're serious."

"Dead." With a grimace, she glances at Penelope. She should call an ambulance. "You know what, Matteo? I'm kinda busy right now."

"You swear you're safe."

"Yes." She hesitates. "More than that, I'm happy."

Even with an unconscious kidnapper at her feet and a hitman by her side. Maybe because of it. She waits as Matteo processes her words.

"Put him on."

"Who?" He means Dante, but he'll have to say it.

"My *friend*." He's speaking through gritted teeth. "I'd like to speak with him."

Jen looks at Dante. Her phone's volume is loud enough he surely hears every word. She holds the phone out to him. "My brother would like to speak with you."

Dante lays his palm flat. She stares at it, memorizing weathered lines, thick calluses. A hand that's touched her everywhere. A hand she'd like touching her again soon. She lays the phone in his palm.

He draws a breath and taps the screen. "You're on speakerphone. Anything you have to say to me, you can say in front of Jen."

She's braced for a string of curses, but Matteo's gone silent. Not even a crackle of static. The line must be dead. She starts to reach for it when her brother speaks.

"That so?" Matteo clears his throat. "She knows you, hmm?"

Dante holds her gaze. "Better than anyone."

Her breath catches as Matteo grumbles something in Dovlanese. He doesn't sound as angry as she thought he would, so she waits for the other shoe to drop.

Dante speaks again. "You should know I love her. If that's a problem for you—"

"It's not." Matteo sighs. "Jesus. I can't believe I'm saying this."

"Saying what?" Jen holds her breath. It can't be this easy. "What are you saying?"

"It's mutual?" Matteo's voice is one she's never heard. "He loves you, which is a given. You're a loveable kid."

"Woman," Dante interrupts before she can. His eyes hold hers as he smiles. "I believe the term was 'grown-ass woman.'"

"Jesus." Matteo's muttering again but pulls himself out of it. "If he loves you and you love him—"

"I do." Jen's the one interrupting now, and that makes Dante smile. He reaches for her hand, lacing thick fingers through hers still sticky with blood. "And I'm done letting you make the call on who I date."

Matteo sighs. "No need. You picked a good one this time."

"What?" She gapes at Dante, sure she's heard wrong. "You're giving your blessing?"

"You *need* my blessing?"

"No. I don't." It's true, but she wants it.

"You've got it anyway." Matteo heaves another sigh. "You sound busy, so I'll let you go."

"Wait. What was so urgent?"

"Huh?"

"You wanted me to visit. You said you had news."

"Ah, right. Well, I'm getting out early."

"*What?*" Her screech makes Penelope stir, and Dante stoops to inspect her. Jen turns away, letting him handle it. "You're serious?"

"Yep. Evidence emerged proving I didn't commit the crime."

There's a story there, but now's not the time to ask for it. "So you're innocent."

"Well—"

"Innocent of this particular crime." She needs to hang up

before one of them incriminates him. "I'm speechless. Ecstatic. Dumbfoun—"

You have two minutes remaining.

Jen grits her teeth until the automated voice shuts up. She takes those seconds to blink back tears. "I love you, Matteo. I'll see you soon?"

"Count on it." His voice goes gravelly. "Love you, too, k—*Jen.*"

He hangs up before she can respond. As her gaze swings to Dante's, he gives a crooked smile. "Guess that worked out okay."

"Okay?" She throws her arms around his neck, nearly tripping over Penelope's feet.

The woman snuffles as her eyelids flutter. Dante's hand goes to his gun, but Jen touches his wrist. "Go."

"What?"

"I'll handle it. There's already a police file on this. I'll call it in and keep you out of this."

His eyes soften as he shakes his head. "We're in this together."

"But—"

"Not because I don't trust you to handle things yourself." He holds her gaze a moment. "It's that we're stronger together."

"That's true." Tears cloud her eyes again, which isn't what she needs now. There's an unconscious kidnapper to deal with, not to mention a lot of logistics to figure out.

Dante reads her mind. "We'll figure it out together." He kisses her again, then steps back and gets to work.

CHAPTER 20

"One more." Dante feeds a Cheez-It to Zsa Zsa. She's dainty as she takes it, snuffling his fingers with her wrinkly snout.

"You're spoiling that pig." Jen cuddles against his chest, hair tickling his chin. They're snuggling. *Snuggling.* Whose life is this?

It's Dante's and he can't believe it. They're on Jen's sofa, which is also sort of *his* sofa. He lives here now, moving from the bunkhouse last month. It's like he's morphed from a barn swine to a domesticated pet, but he likes it. Likes it a lot.

The TV's flickering with the sound off. A reality show called *Fresh Start at Juniper Ridge.* He likes the idea, the thought of fresh starts. He's found his own.

"You know what's great?" Jen's eyes slide to his and Dante knows exactly what's great.

"Yeah," he says. "What else?"

She tilts her head. "Huh?"

"What's great?"

"Oh. How Matteo's leaving lock-up the same day Penelope goes in. I know it's not the same prison, but it feels like poetic justice."

"Sure does."

Justice. The word has another meaning than it did in his former career. He's a farmer now. Nothing more, nothing less. Matteo made sure of it, using his magic tech skills to tidy up traces of Dante's former life. Seb's, too, while he was at it.

Dante's still Dante. Still too grumpy and still fond of firearms. Still makes the best damn elk chili around, and still likes watercress tea sandwiches and animals with funny names.

But forget Dan; forget pretending. He's just a guy in love with the woman he hopes might marry him. He hasn't asked yet, but he will. *Soon.*

"What time is dinner?" Not the question he wants to ask, but vital info anyway.

"Nicole's running late." Jen looks at her watch. "Some sort of challenge with a client."

"Everything okay?"

"I think so." Jen shrugs. "Single mom in trouble. Jailbird dad who's not in the picture. She can't say much, as usual."

Something prickles Dante's neck. He couldn't say why, but tucks the thought in the back of his mind.

"Almost forgot." He goes for the subject change. "Doc Parker asked for your meatloaf recipe. He wants to make it for Izzy."

"Shoot me his email and I'll send it to him." She smiles and strokes a hand over his chest. "I can't believe I had a Duchess over for dinner."

"And a cop." That one was his doing. "Chief Dugan liked the meatloaf, too."

"That's wild. It's like a punchline for a weird joke—A Duchess, a doctor, a police chief, and a resort owner walk into a farmhouse."

And they all live happily ever after.

He doesn't say that out loud, but his love-dipped brain fills it in. Dante knows both couples from his Ponderosa Resort days. Played poker with Doc Parker and Chief Dugan. Watched the men settle into marriage and family and thought for sure he'd never have that for himself.

He's glad to be wrong.

Glad his new family spans beyond Jen and Nicole and Matteo. "Harry invited me skeet shooting again. Do we have plans Tuesday?"

"Pretty sure it's free." She laughs. "I love that you've bonded with the neighbors. I never got on great with the Gibsons until you came along."

"It helps having stuff in common." A surly disposition. A love of farm life and firearms and Jen's brownies. "He's a lot more cheerful since the hotel people figured out how to build on a hill."

Pocketing a few million puts a spring in the step of even the grumpiest bastard. He likes Harry and Gail Gibson. Likes that they got to keep a corner of their property. Likes neighbors who stop by for a cup of sugar instead of assistance burying a body.

Not that Dante wouldn't help in a pinch.

He shifts Jen's weight on his chest and reaches under the end table. "I got you something."

"Me?" Jen cranes her neck to look at him. "What for? It's not my birthday."

"No, but we're celebrating."

"Celebrating what?"

"The fact that you're alive." That she testified against Penelope, her back ramrod straight as she took the stand and looked the judge right in the eye. Dante's heart nearly burst from his chest. He was so proud.

"That's worth celebrating," Jen agrees.

"Also, that you own Bello Vineyards free and clear." That it's called *Bello*, no more *Devon*. He changed the sign himself. "Want your gift now?"

"Yes, please." She bounces away from him on the cushion, knees brushing his. That earns a grunt from Zsa Zsa. Jen strokes the pig's soft ears. "I feel bad I didn't get you anything."

"You've given me plenty." Love. Affection. Unconditional fondness despite his past.

God, he loves her. Probably doesn't tell her enough, but two hundred times a day is a good start.

He finds the brown-wrapped package and feels self-conscious. He should have bought real wrapping paper or a bright gift bag. Pink or maybe green to match her eyes. As he hands it to her, she gives a squeak of joy.

"Thank you." She's tearing the tape off one end to peer through the opening. "Is it a book? No." Another tug at the tape. "A picture?"

He smiles as his heart sighs. "You could just open it. No need to save the paper."

"I always save the paper." She tugs the seam carefully, preserving the grocery bag. "Nondi taught me well."

"She did." He wishes he could thank her grandma. Shake her hand and tell her she raised the best human on the planet. *Humans.* He's always liked Matteo, and Nic's growing on him fast.

Jen's still working on the gift wrap. As she pulls out the frame, she gasps. Eyes shifting to his, he sees tears glittering in hers. "Is this what I think it is?"

"Depends." He thinks of Seb's social media lesson, an American pastime he can do without. "If you're expecting a dick pic, no."

Jen's laughing as she slugs him in the arm. "That's *not* what I thought." She opens the frame slowly, prying it open at the hinge to show photos on both sides.

One side holds the image of Jen as a little girl. Dark hair twists in a lopsided bun and freckles dust her nose. The dress she's wearing is too big, but she carries herself like a queen. Dante's known royalty, and Jen's more regal than all of them combined. He sees it even in her six-year-old self.

"Wow." She traces a fingertip over her photo, then shifts to the other side. She gasps again and taps the second image. "Is this you?"

He nods and swallows back a lump. "Yeah." Clears his throat. "Same age as you in that picture."

"Oh my God." Her eyes go back to the photo and she studies his awkward stance. The too-short sleeves of his suit coat and the shaggy hair in need of a trim. "You were cute."

"Hmph." He's surprised by the tightness in his chest. "I was awkward."

"Adorable."

"Uncomfortable."

"Sweet," she argues, fingertip tracing his face. When she looks up again, there's moisture in her eyes. "Seriously, Dante—this is amazing. I'll put it with the rest of my treasures."

His gaze goes to the mantel where she set the cracked candy dish. On the other side is a photo of Matteo as a little boy, fists gripping a toy computer. Beside that, a picture of Nicole with a BB gun over one shoulder.

What a great family. Odd, sure, but strong as hell and determined. He likes to think he fits right in.

He loves them all, but especially Jen. Slipping the frame from her hands, he carries it to the fireplace and sets it beside the crystal dish. "Here?"

"Perfect." She smiles and scratches Zsa Zsa's ears. "Thank you, Dante."

Dante.

He'll never tire of how she says his name. How she saves him the last Cheez-Its in the box and doesn't mind that he built a bed in their room just for Zsa Zsa.

Dante returns to the couch. "So Nicole's coming when?"

"Maybe seven? She'll call if the meeting lasts longer."

He nods, not wanting to focus on her sister anymore. That's Seb's domain. The man could talk all day about Jen's sister.

Dante's heard him do it. She's clearly not interested, but The Dentist doesn't give up easily.

Glancing at his watch, he sees they've got an hour. A whole hour alone, just the two of them. His libido stirs. He swears he doesn't move, doesn't change expressions.

But Jen's smiling now, a salacious smile spreading over her sweet face. "Know what would feel amazing?"

"Yes."

He's scooping her into his arms as she squeals, her fingers twining behind his neck as he carries her up the stairs. When her eyes meet his, there's fire there. "How did you know what I was going to say?"

"Lucky guess."

Lucky man. He's the luckiest bastard on earth, and it's all because of her.

She's breathing hard as he eases her onto the bed. Pulling her down to him, her lips part. "Dante?"

"Yeah?"

"Have I told you lately that I love you?"

"Yep." His heart squeezes every time she says it. He'll never tire of those words. Never tire of undressing her, planting soft rows of kisses down her center. He stops when he gets to the waistband of her jeans, gazing up at her over the span of her belly. "Have I mentioned you're the best thing that ever happened to me?"

Her eyebrow quirk is flirty. "Better than a royal ball?"

"A thousand times."

"Better than guns?"

"A million times."

She pretends to think. "Better than elk chili with cocoa powder?"

"Undoubtedly." As he drags down her jeans, he sets out to prove it again.

***

Did you read the free series prequel for **Assassins in Love**? In case you missed it, I'm giving away the *Killer Looks* prequel novella for zero pennies when you subscribe to my newsletter. Here's where to nab that:

https://BookHip.com/XWJJVFH

And now that you've seen Dante find his happy ending, it's time to check in with Matteo. What happens after he gets out of prison? If you read the free prequel novella, *Killer Looks*, you already know there's a woman Teo never quite got over. Keep reading for an exclusive glimpse at the first chapter of *Killer Moves*, where Matteo gets the shock of his life...

YOUR EXCLUSIVE PEEK AT KILLER MOVES

*M*atteo always said his first stop after prison would be Saucy Buns for a burger. Extra pickles, no mayo.

Turns out ground beef can't compete with his sisters.

Tech World barely could.

He only stopped for computer gear. His offshore accounts have plenty for a new laptop, plus external hard drive and six burner phones because that's just good business sense. Out front, he gives a homeless guy hand warmers from aisle six. Cookies from checkout, plus two hundred in cash. "Stay safe." He gets in his car without looking back.

Now Matteo's on I-5 in his 1973 Alfa Romeo Spider, headed for Miss Gigglewink's Daycare. Not a normal post-prison stop for a felon, but Matteo's hardly normal. Besides, his conviction's overturned. He's a free man.

He's got the top down, windows open, though it's fifty degrees and drizzly. Thank God his sisters brought the car. They wanted to pick him up, but Teo needed the closure of watching those concrete walls fade in his rearview mirror.

Needs his sisters not to see him detour past the home of the shady cop who stuck him behind bars. Detective Reggie Dowling doesn't even own the brick rambler anymore, but Matteo needs to see. Needs to know where the bastard landed after Teo's pals twisted his arm. The twisting might've freed Matteo, but it also sent Dowling underground.

He shouldn't care. He's free, and that's what matters.

Errands complete, Matteo's killed enough time to be sure all the students are gone from Miss Gigglewink's. It's farm show-and-tell day, so his sisters should be there.

Hitting his signal, he turns onto the road he knows like security code for a Unix operating system. Two more blocks and he's on the leafy street where his grandma's craftsman bungalow sits in the swoop of a cul-de-sac. His chest gets tight as his brain brews a memory of sitting on that curb with a grape soda.

"Tenants left this behind." Grandma Nondi wheeled the bike from the garage. "Looks your size. Almost new."

He'd never had a bike. Never dreamed of riding one. All the way home, he cried fat, quiet tears, smearing his face with a sleeve so she wouldn't see. They took it to the farm where he taught himself to ride. Taught Nic and Jen, hovering when they wobbled.

Nic got the bungalow when Nondi passed, and Jen got the farm. Matteo got the beach house, and he's glad about that. Maybe he'll buy a bike. A red one with a black seat so he can pedal to the shore with the sun on his back and his grandma's memory perched on his shoulder.

He parks at the curb and scans the dental clinic across the way. Sebastian LaDouceur, DDS. *The Dentist* swears he's going straight. Just a dentist now, not the kind that makes bad guys go away for money. Matteo will believe it when he sees it.

At the front door of the daycare, he hesitates. They expect him at the farm by five, but that's three hours. He needs to hug his sisters sooner.

"Matty!" Nic flings the door open and throws herself at his chest. "You're here! I hoped you'd come early."

"Hey, kid." Hugging hard, he wonders how the girl with pigtails and a lisp became a business owner. Not just any business. A daycare for folks fleeing bad situations. Pride floods his chest as he hugs her harder.

Pride and concern. "Is it okay if I'm here?" He sets her on the steps. "I can leave if—"

"No, you're good." She grabs his hand and hauls him inside. "Students are long gone. We're just cleaning up so we can load the lambs."

"Matty!" Jen wipes her hands on dirty blue jeans. "I shouldn't hug you. I'm covered in lamb poop, but I really *want* to hug you and—"

"Then we hug." He squeezes the girl whose diapers he once changed. All grown up and living with his best friend. Jesus. How did that happen? "Missed you."

"I missed you, too." She pulls back and laughs. "I know we saw each other three days ago, but this feels different."

"Damn right it does." If she only knew. "How's Dante?"

"Good." She wipes her hands again. "He'll be at dinner tonight."

"He's *making* dinner tonight." Nicole slaps a hand to her heart. "If Jen doesn't hurry and marry him, I'll bang the man silly for his elk chili recipe."

"Jesus." The throbbing in his head is new. "Can we maybe not talk about banging?"

An eye roll from Nic. "You just got out of prison. I'd worry if you didn't have banging on the brain."

More throbbing, mostly in his temples. "Let's also not say the *P* word." He scans a shelf lined with kids' board books. "Not here."

"P word?" Nic's grinning as she moves through his periphery

221

to straighten a stuffed animal. "Penis? Prick? Piss? Pussy?" She's enjoying this too much. "Or did you mean pris—"

"That."

"You're like a mime with his tongue yanked out." Nicole looks at Jen. "Let's load the lambs and get out of here."

"Actually, we kinda need you." Jen sidles over with her sweet little sister smile. "Think you could help for a sec?"

His gun hand slips to his belt before he remembers he's not carrying. Also, helping at a daycare doesn't require weapons. "Sure."

Nic points at a pen of bleating lambs. "One of my sweet little angel students broke the latch."

Jen mutters something like "demon child," but she's smiling. "The second we open that gate, the lambs will run for it. We need someone to hold it shut."

"Only until we get the first ones in the truck." Nic's already walking to the pen. "With five lambs, Jen and I can each get one on the first run, and then with the three of us—"

"I follow the math." He's got dual degrees in mathematics and computer science. He can figure out how to count sheep. "So I'm on guard duty."

"Not with brute force." Nic lifts an eyebrow. "We just need your body to block them from darting out."

He's done worse with his body for a lot less payoff. "Let's do it."

They get into position. Jen's got a hand on the gate, while he squats beside Nic as a human blockade.

"Let 'er rip," Nic calls.

Jen swings the gate open, and three lambs bolt. Nic snags the first one, while Matteo grabs the second, spinning so his back shoves the gate shut.

"Got you!" Jen scoops up the third lamb.

Behind him in the pen, two lambs bleat in protest. The one in his arms is a wriggling wad of fleece, baah-ing in his ear. "No complaining." He shifts so his back's firmly at the gate. "You're well fed, I'm positive. My sister's the world's biggest softie."

"Hey." Jen pretends to glare. "Who kicked ass on a kidnapper when—"

"We're not talking about it." Picturing his kid sister in danger has his head throbbing again. "Hurry up."

"Come on." Nic starts for the door. "You sure you're okay holding down the fort?"

"Positive." His lamb squirms some more. He scratches its ears, and the animal relaxes.

"We'll be quick." Jen shoves the front door as her lamb bleats. "It might take a sec to get them situated."

"Got it handled."

"Thanks, bro." Nicole follows her out the door calling, "Glad you're back!"

"It's good to be back." He says it to empty air, maybe the lambs. Brown eyes plead for freedom.

"Sorry about the cage." He's a sucker for brown eyes. "If it helps, I relate."

The smallest lamb bleats and rears behind the bars. Adjusting his hold on the one in his arms, he scans the classroom. Miss Gigglewink's. The cuteness hurts his teeth.

Bright plastic chairs march miniature rows around the room. The wall above the whiteboard holds paper cutouts of numbers formed by cartoon animals. A caterpillar three, a spider eight. There's a bookshelf with titles like *The Wonky Donkey* and *Never Ever Tickle a Turkey.*

Through the window, he scans the playground. Can kids really fit down that plastic slide? It resembles the trunk of an elephant, with steps up the back. So damn adorable.

And so far from where he's been. God, this is weird.

Stroking the lamb, he kicks his legs out in front of him. "My sisters are great, huh?"

The lamb bleats and wiggles.

"Smart," he continues. "Tough as hell." His throat's tight all of a sudden. "For a fuckup, I've got great sisters."

Another bleat from his fleecy friend. He shouldn't swear at daycare.

"Whoa!"

A child's squeal swings his eyes to the doorway. Matteo stares as a boy in red sneakers rockets toward him like a missile in overalls. *"Lambie Lambie Lambie Lambie!"*

The kid's red shirt ripples as his sneakers squeak the vinyl. There's a gleam in his green eyes, and Matteo's not sure if it's joy or budding psychosis.

"Hey there." Matteo shields the lamb with his body. "Can I help you with something?"

The kid skids to a stop. *"Lambie!"*

"Yes." He looks down and confirms. "Correct."

Clasping his hands together, the boy grins. "My hold?"

"Um." What's the protocol here? "You can pet, I guess."

The kid drops to his knees and sighs with joy. Eyes wide, he strokes the lamb's neck. "Gentle." He looks at Matteo and smiles. *"Gentle."*

"That's right." Cute kid. Looks like Jen as a toddler with those ocean eyes and sandy hair and a dusting of freckles. One strap of his overalls looks twisted. Should he fix it?

Better not. "You like lambs, huh?"

The kid nods at the dumb question. That's the great thing about kids. No judgment. Kinda like Nic when he gave her a haircut. He was twelve, and she was six, and their parents were dead, and what the hell did he know about girls' hair? She wasn't even pissed about the bowl cut. "You did your best, Teo."

Like that's enough.

Anyway, this kid has hair like that. Tiny Tic-Tac teeth that gleam when he smiles.

"Soft." He watches Matteo with his fingers raking fleece. "Sooofffft."

"That's right."

Footsteps approach the door left creaking in the wind. Matteo looks up and feels his heart stagger.

Her.

"AJ!" Renee scans the boy, and for six breathless seconds, Matteo scans her. The lush curves he knows by heart. The dainty fingers, the gold-brown hair to match her eyes.

Eyes that'll turn cold in five, four, three, two...

"AJ, we've talked about you running off and—*oh God.*"

The color leaves her face. A face framed with curls shorter than last time he saw her. She gapes with a look that's half stunned, half horrified, and a hundred percent unhappy to see him.

"Renee?" His voice comes out rusty, so he tries again. "Renee Lorenson?"

Three years, two months, and nineteen days. That's how long it's been. The buzz in his brain says he's missing something. That he'd already know it if his heart wasn't sucking all the blood from his brain.

"Don't call me that!" She bolts with a hand outstretched.

For an instant, he thinks she's reaching for him. He'll give her anything she wants. A handshake? A kidney? The keys to his car?

She snags the kid's hand instead. "We're going home."

"But Mama." The boy swings sad eyes to Matteo. No, not him. The lamb in his arms. "*My hold.*"

He sounds so pitiful Matteo's ready to hand over both the lamb and his pin number. "Another time, kid."

"No." Renee's voice snaps like lightning. "*Not* another time. Not ever. Not—"

"Wait." The buzzing spreads to his ears. Numbers whirl, dates and memories and a jumble of history. His brain's firing now.

The kid senses something because he tugs Matteo's sleeve. "Who you?"

"AJ." Renee's voice sounds strained.

Matteo swallows. He needs to know. "How old are you, AJ?"

The kid lifts one sticky, starfish hand. "This many."

One finger, two, three.

Realization dawns like a kick to the head. He's dizzy and dumbfounded and above all, sure of one thing.

"Renee." He gulps and drags his eyes to her face. "Were you going to tell me?"

***

Want to keep reading? Hop to the link below and grab *Killer Moves* now!

https://books2read.com/b/31R5Rn

Did you read the free series prequel for **Assassins in Love**? In case you missed it, I'm giving away the *Killer Looks* prequel novella for zero pennies when you subscribe to my newsletter. Here's where to nab that:

https://BookHip.com/XWJJVFH

ACKNOWLEDGMENTS

So much love and gratitude to my street team, Fenske's Frisky Posse. Besides naming nearly every character in this series after members of the Posse, I've counted on you for cover feedback, manuscript error assassination, moral support, and way more cheerleading than any author could wish for. Big thanks especially to Regina, Erin, Jennifer, and Judy for your extra efforts trolling for typos. Love you all!

Thank you to all the readers who loved Dante as much as I did in *Dr. Hot Stuff*, and who begged for more of him. I'm honored you loved him as much as I did, and I hope you've enjoyed watching him find his happy ending.

Thank you to Susan Bischoff and Lauralynn Elliott for your editing expertise, and to Meah Cukrov for keeping my ducks in a row (*quack quack!*)

A million thanks to my awesome family, Dixie & David Fenske; Aaron & Carlie & Paxton Fenske; Cedar & Violet Zagurski. Your love and support means the world to me.

And huge hugs and butt pats to my own happy ending partner, Craig Zagurski. Thanks for not murdering me as I drove us both bonkers with the stress of rapid-releasing a new series. Love you!

DON'T MISS OUT!

Want access to exclusive excerpts, behind-the-scenes stories about my books, cover reveals, and prize giveaways? You'll get all that by subscribing to my newsletter, plus **FREE** bonus scenes featuring your favorite characters from my rom-coms and erotic romances. Want to see Aidan and Lyla get hitched after *Eye Candy*? Or read a swoony proposal featuring Sean and Amber from *Chef Sugarlips*? It's all right here and free for the taking:

   https://tawnafenske.com/bonus-content/

ABOUT THE AUTHOR

When Tawna Fenske finished her English lit degree at 22, she celebrated by filling a giant trash bag full of romance novels and dragging it everywhere until she'd read them all. Now she's a RITA Award finalist, *USA Today* bestselling author who writes humorous fiction, risqué romance, and heartwarming love stories with a quirky twist. *Publishers Weekly* has praised Tawna's offbeat romances with multiple starred reviews and noted, "There's something wonderfully relaxing about being immersed in a story filled with over-the-top characters in undeniably relatable situations. Heartache and humor go hand in hand."

Tawna lives in Bend, Oregon, with her husband, step-kids, and a menagerie of ill-behaved pets. She loves hiking, snowshoeing, standup paddleboarding, and inventing excuses to sip wine on her back porch. She can peel a banana with her toes and loses an average of twenty pairs of eyeglasses per year. To find out more about Tawna and her books, visit www.tawnafenske.com.

ALSO BY TAWNA FENSKE

The Sugar & Spice Erotic Romance Series

Eye Candy

Tough Cookie

Honey Do

The Ponderosa Resort Romantic Comedy Series

Studmuffin Santa

Chef Sugarlips

Sergeant Sexypants

Hottie Lumberjack

Stiff Suit

Mancandy Crush (novella)

Captain Dreamboat

Snowbound Squeeze (novella)

Dr. Hot Stuff

The Juniper Ridge Romantic Comedy Series

Show Time

Let It Show

Show Down

Show of Honor

Just for Show

Show Off (coming soon!)

The Assassins in Love Series

Killer Looks (prequel novella)

Killer Instincts

Killer Moves

Killer Smile

The Where There's Smoke Series

The Two-Date Rule

Just a Little Bet

The Best Kept Secret

Standalone Romantic Comedies

At the Heart of It

This Time Around

Now That It's You

Let it Breathe

About That Fling

Frisky Business

Believe It or Not

Making Waves

The Front and Center Series

Marine for Hire

Fiancée for Hire

Best Man for Hire

Protector for Hire

The First Impressions Series

The Fix Up

The Hang Up

The Hook Up

The List Series

The List

The Test

The Last

<u>Standalone novellas and other wacky stuff</u>

Going Up (novella)

Eat, Play, Lust (novella)

Made in United States
North Haven, CT
12 July 2024

54733511R00135